Whirlybird Island

Whirlybird Island

ERNEST HEBERT

PLAIDSWEDE PUBLISHING
Concord, New Hampshire

Designed and composed at Hobblebush Design (www.hobblebush.com)

Printed in the United States of America

ISBN: 978-1-7323648-6-8
Library of Congress Control Number: 2021951218

Cover illustration by Ernest Hebert

Published by:

PLAIDSWEDE PUBLISHING
P.O. Box 269 · Concord, New Hampshire 03302-0269
www.plaidswede.com

Whirlybird Island is dedicated to the memory of Elphege J. Hebert and the countless other traumatized veterans of war.

"In war everybody dies, or it ain't a war."
JOSEPH BLAISE

"The dead are not altogether powerless."
CHIEF SEATTLE

Contents

Author's Note

AT AGE 33, MY FATHER, Elphege J. Hebert, was drafted into World War II. I was a toddler. He returned, like so many veterans, messed up in the head. He was never abusive, but he was remote and uncommunicative. He would dress in a suit and tie, sit in a living room chair, and stare out the window all day. It was six months before he was able to go back to work as a weaver in a textile mill. My dad eventually worked his way out of his problems and was a good father and provider. I never really knew him until in his eighties when he moved in with my family after my mother died. He surrendered to fatalism and loss, but without any despair or self-pity—quite the opposite—he was serene right to the day he died at 88, and he entertained us with a sneaky sense of humor. He taught his oldest son how to grow old.

Around age 18 I realized that the fathers of several my best friends, had also been traumatized by war. In college, I theorized that some of the sixties rebellion by youth was a result of blowback from the behavior of their screwed up veteran fathers. My way of dealing with such an idea is to write a novel about it, because I see my creative process as a personal inquiry through metaphor into my own psychology and history. But I could not bring myself to do it as long as those old vets were still alive.

Decades later, I happened to reunite with my cousin Mary Baglione. We talked about family where I learned that her father, a veteran of the Battle of the Bulge and her mother, an Army nurse in World War II, bore long-term scars from that terrible war. It was at that moment that I realized that the old vets in my life had died. I felt liberated to write about the trauma of war and its effects on the next generation. The year was 2017 when I started writing the novel that eventually would be titled *Whirlybird Island*.

Whirlybird Island

The First Death

"IT'S ALL ABOUT THE HEART, ISN'T IT?" I popped awake with the sound of my wife's voice speaking my father's words from half a century ago. In that zone between sleep and wakefulness, I thought that she was with me. And then I heard the waters of Grace Pond breaking gently on the shore, which told me I was awake and alone on my narrow bed on the sleeping porch of my log cabin. My lone eye was shut, but I could tell by the sounds that last night's storm was over. It was going to be a nice June day. I lay there listening to the pond and thinking about my wife and our life together.

Lynn and I, and her twin daughters, lived an off-the-grid homesteader life on Grace Pond in Darby, New Hampshire, but without the drugs and extravagances of the Red Shift commune that my mom had leased the family property to back in the 1970s. Lynn was an organic foods pioneer who had a dream that she expressed with her motto: *Bread Dough Rises and Conquers the World*. Within a few years Lynn's Farm Stand promoting "food without poisons" was well-established.

During the growing season I pitched in helping Lynn establish her organic garden business. After we closed the farm stand in the fall, I cut firewood for the following year, made repairs on the property, and Lynn and I wrote the organic gardening books we're known for under the pen name of J.B. Nielson. She did most of the thinking; I did most of the writing.

Funny how good years rocket by. You hardly remember the details. It's the nasty stuff that occupies most of the rooms in the memory house.

When our publisher stopped accepting manuscripts typed on my standard, manual Underwood typewriter, I had to hire a typist to prepare the pages for the editor. Lynn and I could have installed electric power in our home on the pond with solar panels. What stopped us was our shared belief in living close to nature.

We liked our nights dimly lit with votive candles. We liked our pond water. We liked our food cooked over wood fires that also gave us plenty of heat. When the occasion demanded that we use the telephone, we drove to

3

the village store that featured a phone booth. When Priscilla Ancharsky, the grand dame of the store, decided to remove the phone booth we paid the store a yearly fee to keep it as our private line.

We lived frugally, and our income grew preposterously over the years, especially after twin daughters Piety and Desire entered the business, Piety with her degree in botany and Desire with her MBA. I splurged on a new pickup truck with a plow to keep our 4,000-foot-long driveway clear in the winter. Lynn bought a Mini Cooper.

But everything changed quite suddenly three years later. Lynn and I were invited to do a book signing at the Savannah Book Festival. I never attended book signings. Lynn was a much more appealing figure to represent our enterprise than this old one-eyed jack. In my stubbornness, I refused to wear a patch over my missing right eye, so I was not a pretty sight. I wouldn't have admitted it at the time, but the real reason was I was uncomfortable when I left Grace Pond. Lynn tried to warn me that I was developing a mental illness, but I ignored her.

Just before she left to drive to the airport that day, we had one of our few arguments. A brand-new cell phone tower had been built at the top of the highest hill on the conservancy land that bordered our property and most of the pond.

"The girls have been after me to get a smartphone," Lynn said.

"So what?" I said, defensive.

"So, it's time, Junie. We need better communications for our business."

"We're doing just fine."

"You've seen the Facebook pictures." I must have given her my signature what-me-worry look, because she added. "You know, when the girls visit?"

"Lynn, you do what pleases you, but keep me out of it. I don't want no stinking smartphone."

And that was that, Lynn was off in a huff in her Mini. I felt self-righteous for about thirty seconds after she left when I realized how stupid and stubborn I'd been. A familiar nettlesome voice spoke in my head: Just think, Junie, if you had a smartphone you could call her right now and apologize. But I didn't have a smartphone, so my last memory of my dear wife will always be of us bickering.

Lynn was sitting at a table under a tent signing books in Savannah,

Georgia, when a man entered and shot her five times. Then the man put the gun to his head and pulled the trigger. He was later identified as a recently paroled felon, one Siegfried Howell. It was a name I was familiar with.

I was also familiar with the pattern. Violence seemed to follow me ever since that first death when I was fourteen. There's something noble about grief. It reminds you of your humanity, and unless you're the vengeful type, grief makes you more empathetic in your encounters with your fellow earth creatures. It wasn't grief that was haunting me, it wasn't even the memory of the violence, it was the uncanny that was associated with the grief. I needed explanations, some understanding of the sources of the violence. Some people deal with haunting and the constant presence of the uncanny through religion or some belief system. But that wasn't available to me. I was looking for something, but I didn't know what it was.

≈

I tried to go about my normal life. I rowed my green and gold johnboat from Shinbone Shack to Whirlybird Island wondering whether the wind had damaged the grand sugar maple that predated my family's log cabin, the Revolutionary War, The Big Bang, perhaps even creation itself.

After the storm, the sun gold on the water and green on the land, I could tell from the new bare spots in the canopy of the maple that the tree was nearing death. Then again, it had been nearing death since my mother moved herself and me to Grace Pond after my mad escapade following the death of my father in a hunting accident in 1968. "Tree," I said aloud, "we should all die like you—in slow mo over the centuries."

I checked the little pagoda under the tree where Osgood Stone, the leader of Red Shift, the commune that leased most of our land back in the 1970s, went to meditate every day. There was some rot at the base of the pine posts. They'd have to be replaced one of these days. Maybe I should meditate in honor of "Uncle Oggie." But I didn't want to meditate. I didn't want to calm down. I wanted . . . I wanted . . . I didn't know what I wanted.

Like I always did, I walked around the island to see what had changed. Nothing ever the same from moment to moment is what I liked about nature. I wandered to the shore where Lizzy Rondoh had discovered the body of Pete Shaughnessy, one of my father's Army buddies. I stood in some pine needles where it was likely that Pete, drunk and stoned, had stood before he dove in, hit his head on a rock, and drowned. That was 1978, the end days of the Red Shift commune. I was thinking that Pete, like my father, was a difficult person.

I shut my eyes, and as best I could, conjured my father's spirit back in 1968 when I was fourteen, that day my father's three Korean War Army buddies—Pete, Harry, and Pass—showed up for their annual week-long, late-fall deer hunt at the Blaise family hunting camp that we called Shinbone Shack.

My father would always accompany his buddies on their hunt unarmed, because he would already have bagged his deer for the season.

"You think I get my deer before you bums, because I have the home field advantage," he would say. "There's more to it than that. I hunt year-around. I walk the woods and I pick out the buck I want to kill. I learn his habits and habitat, and I follow him through the seasons. It's not only my way of relaxing; it's my way of worship, and the woods are my church. Eventually I know where my buck will be every day at dawn. First hour of the first day of deer season I'm waiting for him, and I ambush him with one shot through the heart. Hunting, whether man or beast, it's all about the heart, isn't it?"

Except 1968 was different. He didn't kill his buck that year. I wasn't the most perceptive teenager, but I knew something was wrong.

It was that thought—something was wrong—that was in my head when I saw a gleam in the sand on the pond bottom. The storm had roiled up a lost object.

I stripped off my clothes and walked in, dunked my head, and picked up a U.S. Army dog tag, old style, with the notch in it.

Back in high school, I believed that if a soldier was found dead on the battlefield the notches on his dog tag would be fitted between his teeth, and he would be kicked in the jaw to secure the metal tag. So many things we believe—and that guide our lives—are not true.

I had to put my 2.75 resolution glasses on to read the dog tag with my lone eye. "Stanton, Gerard, S, blood type O, RA78598421, Tetanus shot 1951, religion P." In those days as far as the military was concerned you were P (Protestant), C (Catholic), or H (Hebrew).

Occasionally visitors to the conservancy that surrounded most of the pond launched kayaks from shore and visited the island. Or just swam the hundred yards or so. Maybe one was a veteran who lost a dog tag. Quite a coincidence that a Korean War era veteran would lose a personal article in the same spot where another Korean War era veteran drowned. Soldiers of that era were issued two dog tags that traditionally they wore around their neck. Where was the other one? Was Gerard Stanton on the island without the knowledge of the Red Shift communards that partied on the island the night Pete died, and did Gerard Stanton have an animus toward Pete?

I fought my agoraphobia and forced myself to drive to the village store to call my mother in New Orleans. I relaxed a little when I squeezed into the old-fashion phone booth. Now in old age and supposedly retired, my mom still went into her law office every day for a couple hours to work even though she didn't need the money. I told her about finding the dog tag at the site of Pete's demise and my feelings of unease.

"I'll tell you what else bothers me," I said.

"That the tetanus shot date places Stanton during the Korean War, Joseph's war." My mom always referred to her husband as "Joseph." Everybody else called him Joe, and if you knew him real well, G.I. Joe. My mother was a West Texas teenager when she married Joseph Blaise, a New England farm boy turned B.A.R. man for Uncle Sam. Her name was Sarah Boyd, but everyone in my part of the world called her Sadie.

"Right," I said. "I looked him up in the Britannica, but I couldn't find anything."

My mother laughed, "You used that old encyclopedia in this day and age of the Internet?"

"I don't own a computer, mom. You know that! Lynn and I didn't even use light bulbs, just like when you and I lived in Shinbone Shack."

"Junie, get with it! That was decades ago. Haven't you noticed the cell tower on the conservancy land?"

"How do you know about that in NOLA?" I asked.

"I keep in touch with my online subscription to Dot McCurtin's *Darby Gazette*," Sadie said. "Get yourself to the Darby town library. They'll be very helpful."

"Okay, mom, I will." There must have been something false in my tone, because my mother picked up on it.

"Tell me what's wrong, Junie," she said.

I just blurted it out, "Mom, I freak when I leave the pond."

"I knew something was amiss. The girls are worried about you. You haven't visited in over a year. Lynn's death brought you back to the old griefs."

"Yeah, but in a bizarre way. When Lynn died it hit me real hard, but there was no unfinished business between us. The contrast made me realize it was a different kind of grief than dad's."

"Unfinished business issues hang around longer," Sadie said.

"Dad's death back when I was fourteen, Pete's death, Wiley Brewster's death, Uncle Oggie's disappearance and probable death at the People's Temple in '78. Lynn's death. That dog tag is telling us that somehow, they're all connected. I can't let this go."

"Yes, your time has come to act, Junie. You need to team up with an experienced investigator who can work in the field, since you don't leave the pond and don't even own a phone."

"You're better at reading my mind than I am."

There was a long pause. My mother was not one to mull things over in the middle of a conversation, so I was a little unsettled that I sensed she wasn't sure whether to help me or not.

Finally, she said, "Do you remember Maurice Landrieu?"

"Of course, one of dad's Army buddies, along with Pete Shaughnessy and Harry Cromwell. The shy one, the one they called Pass. The artist."

"Yes, Landrieu has made a fortune, though not as an artist. He has a granddaughter, Trinity Landrieu, that Maurice and Olivia raised after their son was killed in Iraq. At least I think Trinity is a granddaughter. At times it's hard to tell, and they're evasive when the subject of gender comes up."

"You mean it's not clear whether Trinity is male or female?"

"That's exactly what I mean. I asked Maurice flat out if Trinity is a boy or a girl, and he just smiled at me as if I'd stepped in something. Junie, all you need to know right now is that even though she's young she has experience as an investigator, and she is very talented. I know because well . . ."

After a pause, I said, "What is it, what are you not telling me?"

"Back in juvenile court, I got her off from a hacking escapade."

"She's reformed now?"

Sadie didn't answer but she did laugh ruefully. "Look, as an adult she's done work for our firm, and I can tell that she has a knack with analytics. No doubt she'll be attracted to your project since Maurice and Pete were Army cohorts. Hold on, while I look up her LinkedIn profile."

A minute or so later, my mother was back. She read three sterling recommendations along with contact information and a very brief teaser. "Trinity Landrieu, Shape-Shifter and Consulting Inquirer. Coding skill-sets in Java, Java Script, Ruby, PHP, C, Object C, Swift, lipstick, and elan."

Shape-Shifter

I WARMED TO TRINITY LANDRIEU the moment I saw her from a window in Shinbone Shack as she got out of the pickup truck with the homemade camper body and bounded up the outside stairs, carrying a smartphone in her right hand. In that motion, she struck me as determined, daring, and resourceful while at the same time scared as a little kid ascending for the first time on a Ferris wheel. I didn't wait for her to knock, but opened the door. She sliced right by me, glanced at her smartphone, and said, "Hi, Junie," as if we'd known each other for eons.

I followed speechless as she headed to my sleeping porch where she sat in the center chair, put her feet up on the railing, and looked out at the pond. She was five-nine or ten, looked to be somewhere between twenty-five and thirty, wearing green Yoga pants with a gold blouse, the top unbuttoned to show just a hint of cleavage, hair with wave action and the color of charcoal briquettes. She wore perhaps a little too much eyeliner for 3 o'clock in the afternoon. She had her grandfather Landrieu's complexion and bone structure. Among the four Korean War veterans who met once a year for a week-long deer hunt, Maurice Landrieu was known as Pass Landrieu because his Army buddies insisted he could pass as any race. You could say the same about his grandchild.

I was a little unsettled by the realization that she was wearing my colors—green and gold.

"Nice view," Trinity said, looking out at the pond, Whirlybird Island a half mile away, the wooded hills beyond, and above it all a reigning blue sky.

"How did you know this is where I wanted to talk with you," I asked.

"Easy peasey." She held up her phone. "Your stepdaughters with the cool names . . ."

"Piety and Desire—they're twins, but not identical."

"Right. They and your grandkids have posted a zillion pics of this place on Facebook, and they write about how you sleep out here, daydream out there, and type notes on your Gutenberg-era typewriter. Would you rather I call you Junie, Mr. Blaise, or maybe J.B. Nielson?"

"That's the pen name I used on the organic gardening books I wrote with my wife."

"Which is the real you?"

"All of them," I said.

"I would find a real me a hindrance." She grabbed my hand and shook it.

Trinity's hand might have been considered big for a woman's, average for a man's, grip maybe a little too deliberately steely, perhaps betraying a touch of insecurity.

"I was intrigued by your LinkedIn ad," I said. "What do you mean by shape-shifter? Is that a professional term or something personal?"

Trinity ignored my question, and said, "You're interviewing me. That's good. If we're going to work together, we need to dispense with the niceties. I like that you don't go with a fake eye." She pointed to the zippered skin where I used to have an eye. "You lost it cutting firewood, right?"

"Now you're interviewing me," I said.

"Maybe. Mainly, I'm showing off my skill set. You were on leave after basic training in the Army, and after the accident the Army decided it didn't want any one-eyed soldiers, so they kicked you out for medical reasons, and you never went to war."

"That's correct. I never went to war."

"You lucked out, Mister Blaise. But your buddy that you signed up with was killed in Vietnam, fragged in a tent, one William Brewster but he had a nickname."

"Wiley Brewster." Voicing the name of my best friend seemed to trip me into that hole where the real me resided, so I talked on. "I relate to the Cyclops creature of legend. Instead of referring to me as Junie or Mister Blaise or J.B. Nielson, just call me Cyclops." I wasn't serious. Maybe I was trying to be dourly funny. I dunno.

"Cyclops doesn't sound right coming off my tongue, and I trust my tongue," Trinity said. "I think I'll go with Uncle Cyclops. It's more intimate."

My attempt at humor had backfired. "Perfect," I said, though I didn't mean it.

Trinity then put her index finger under her own apparently real green-marble swirl of right eye. Until it was blue. She turned her back to me, turned again toward me, and now the eye was brown. Again and back to green.

"Quite a trick," I said.

"Not a trick, which implies a starting point for reality."

"That brings me back to my shape-shifter question," I said.

She waved the topic away. "You are a widower, Uncle Cyclops, I'm sorry."

"Yes, I am widowed."

"Do you find a void in your life since your wife passed away?" Trinity asked. I could see that she was leading up to something, and I went along because there was a seriousness in her demeanor now.

"Yes, a major void, which is part of the reason I've taken on the project I wrote to you about."

"To fill the void."

"That's correct."

"When you think about the concept of a void in human affairs, think of me, Uncle Cyclops. I am the ultimate void that I fill with experiments in identity."

"Shape-shifter, one who experiments with identities—you answered my earlier question," I said. "Can I offer you a beer?"

"Geek Chorus Amber, brewed locally by Geek Chorus Software, developer of the hit video game, Darby Doomsday—right?"

"You know my secrets," I said.

"Only the ones posted on social media. You can learn a lot about a person by analyzing the extraneous artifacts in a photograph posted on Facebook," Trinity said, as I rose from my chair and headed for the propane fridge.

I poured two mugs, which presently I brought out to the porch. Trinity and I sat for a few minutes in silence looking out at the pond.

Finally, Trinity said, "This job you have in mind for us is a search for clarity, right?"

"Yes. Violence and uncertainty have haunted my life, beginning with my father's getting shot by a random bullet in a hunting accident. You should know. Your grandfather was with him when it happened."

"Yes, Grandfather Maurice is not a stranger to violence, and neither am I."

"After Wiley's death there was Pete Shaughnessy's death, like my dad's, another stupid accident."

"Yes, and only a couple months later the mysterious disappearance of Osgood Stone, the leader of the Red Shift commune."

"Yes, Uncle Oggie was a mentor to me. It was like losing another father. I thought I put all the violence behind me when I married Lynn. Then the shock when she was targeted by a crazy former lover."

"And you couldn't even seek vengeance, because her assailant shot himself dead."

"Yes, but it wasn't until I found that dog tag from a Korean war era that it struck me that some or all of these events are linked. I want to find out how, not just for myself, but for history."

"Histrionics trump history every time, but never mind. I ran your info by Grandfather Maurice. He's going to fund our enterprise."

"He wants clarity, too, I imagine."

"No," Trinity said. "It's something else, and finding what that something else is, is another motive for me to get involved in the mess that is your life. He thinks we should start our inquiries with Pete's death. While Pete was a heavy drinker he was never completely out of control. Right?"

"Right," I said.

"The idea that he would dive into water that he knew to be shallow doesn't ring true, even if he was drunk: that's grandpa's analysis."

"Okay, let's start with Pete," I said.

At that point something on the pond caught Trinity's attention."

"What is that bird skipping along the surface?" Trinity asked.

"A loon," I said.

Trinity tapped her smartphone, and read aloud from the screen, "'Any of several large, short-tailed, web-footed, fish-eating diving birds of the genus Gavia of the Northern Hemisphere.'"

"Do you really care, or are you just showing off the powers of your phone?" I asked.

"Of course I care and of course I'm showing off." She pointed to my encyclopedias stacked on the floor against the wall, "If I had a more assertive digestive tract I would dine on those antique volumes, because I'm an information-devouring omnivore."

I blinked and my jaw dropped ever so slightly. "My mom bought those books at great expense back in the day when it was just the two of us living here."

"So I understand. You used to live in an apartment in Keene, but after your father died your mother moved out here—no electricity, no conventional plumbing. Why would a single mother with a halfway decent secretarial job in a nice little community make such a move?"

"For years I thought it was because, like me, she wanted the experience of living close to nature."

"But now you know different, Uncle Cyclops. Now you know that she chose to live here, because she believed it was best for her troubled and only child."

"Did she tell you that?"

"No. I have my flaws but analyzing data is not one of them. What I don't know is the inciting episode that led to her decision."

"Let's say it's related to the colors you are wearing."

"I got the idea to wear green and gold from a pic on Facebook of your little green and gold johnboat."

Trinity was inviting me to explain, but I didn't say anything. I felt quite smug. I could tell that I had Trinity stumped.

"How coy of you," Trinity said, and she must have been reading my body language, because she dispensed with the topic. "Someday you'll tell me about it," she said, and she rose from her chair and walked over to the encyclopedias stacked on the floor and opened a volume. A 3-by-5 notecard fell out. She picked up the notecard and read from it out loud, "'More to know about Women's Suffrage'. The page covers the 19th Amendment to the Constitution giving women the right to vote. You didn't write this note."

I couldn't help but chuckle. "Supposedly, Sadie bought those books—at great expense, I might add—for my education, but she ended up using them more than I did."

"How curious. But your dad was not the intellectual type," Trinity said.

"True enough," I said. "G.I. Joe never held a real job. He wanted to carry on the family tradition and be a farmer, but after his dad died suddenly of a heart attack my grandmother Isabelle sold the farm and moved to Florida with her daughters."

"I think your grandmother was a member of the locally notorious Jordan clan," Trinity said.

"Maybe. She was at pains to pronounce the name the French way and to spell it j-o-u-r-d-a-n. When she left town, she gave dad Shinbone Shack."

"To assuage his hurt," Trinity said.

"Yes, it was just a log hunting camp in those days. When dad got out of the Army he had ambitions to turn the pond property into a dairy farm. He built a barn, but he never did farm. He ended up as a sometimes-firewood dealer."

"No doubt your mom produced more income than your father did with her job as a secretary for a law firm."

"She liked big words. I remember once that dad teased her because she used the word 'abomination' to describe the Vietnam War. Anyway, after he died, she moved us out of our apartment on Church Street in Keene, and we settled here at Shinbone Shack."

"And she leased the rest of the property to the Red Shift commune. It was a pretty good deal, too."

"Do you know everything about me?" I asked.

"How could I? I don't even know everything about myself," Trinity said. "But I do know a few random things. With the increase in revenue, Sadie could cut her hours at the law firm and enroll at the local state college. Right?"

"Yes, eventually, she got her law degree at Tulane University in New Orleans," I said.

"She chose Tulane at the recommendation of Grandpa Maurice," Trinity said. "She stayed in New Orleans and made a name for herself practicing family law."

Trinity returned the Britannica volume to its stack against the wall and took her seat in the chair overlooking the pond. I was thinking that while Trinity's voice, gestures, and body language were classically female, her diction and assertiveness seemed male. She embodied the social displays of both genders. Was she an authentic person or an act?

"Did you know Sadie has a reputation as a lawyer-healer among her clients?" Trinity said.

"No, I didn't know."

"They say it's in her touch," Trinity said.

That word "touch" was like a kick to my solar plexus. I sucked in as much air as my lungs could hold. Finally, I said, "I experienced that touch, but only once."

"These days you're probably neither ready for, nor worthy of, a repeat of that touch," Trinity laughed a little too loud and long at her cruel little joke.

I winced. It was my first exposure to Trinity Landrieu's mocking laugh. I eventually understood that it wasn't a laugh necessarily launched at the person she was talking to, but to that unseen dark matter that surrounds and confounds us all for reasons we cannot fathom. Some people worship this force and call it God; other people wage war against the force and call it the devil. Trinity Landrieu's mocking laughter scorned it as the shit luck of quantum entanglement.

She must have read an expression on my face that I was unaware of, because her own expression changed from self-amused to concerned. I thought she might apologize. Instead, she said in a casual voice, "You going to show me around?"

Shinbone Shack and Environs

WE STARTED WITH THE PORCH on Shinbone Shack, 8-by-16, open to the weather, but screened in to keep the bugs out. I'd been sleeping out there since I was a teenager. Cabin proper with main room, 16-by-16, that included a couch, book shelves, wood stove with deer leg bones mortared into the stone hearth that gave the cabin its name, and a drop-down table of wormy butternut wood, upon which sat the standard Underwood typewriter that I typed the organic book manuscripts that Lynn and I wrote back in the day.

"That typewriter predates even you, old man," Trinity said.

"Yes, Uncle Oggie gave it to me shortly before he left Red Shift and joined the Reverend Jim Jones cult."

"The Peoples Temple, kind of a mix of Christianity, Communism, and Idiotism. Did Osgood Stone drink the Kool Aid in the Jonestown massacre?" Trinity asked.

"Presumably."

"You mean his body was not recovered."

"That's right," I said. "There's no hard evidence that he went to South America, but he certainly planned to and there's been no trace of him since he surprised the Red Shift hippies and me by taking off without us. See, we were all supposed to join the Peoples Temple."

"You don't strike me as the religious type, Uncle Cyclops."

"At that age I trusted Uncle Oggie," I said. "If he wanted me to go to Jonestown, I believed I should go. Sometimes I think Uncle Oggie had a premonition, and that's why he went alone."

"Could be, but we don't have enough data to say for sure."

I showed Trinity the tiny bedroom in Shinbone Shack where Lynn slept and before that, Sadie.

"You and Lynn raised twin girls—where did they sleep?"

"When they were toddlers, in the main room. Soon as they were old enough, we moved them to one of the abandoned hippie cabins and eventually they chose their own separate cabins."

The kitchen/entry included hand-carved hardwood pegs to hang coats, a propane refrigerator, and a toilet behind a curtain. Wastewater drained into a septic tank and leach field that Red Shift built, but there was no electricity, no running water, not even a well.

"You have to lug water from the pond to flush the toilet?" Trinity said.

"Uh-huh. In the winter, I keep holes open in the ice which double as locales for my ice fishing tip ups."

"I don't see a shower," Trinity said.

"Back in the day, I'd shower at the high school and my mother at her law firm's office. Later, Red Shift put in a shower room in the barn. Solar panels keep the water bearable, most of the time."

"Who built this place?"

"My great-grandfather, Alcide Blaise, built it from white pine tree logs on a foundation of field stones just laying around the property. You're the curious type, Trinity—right?"

"Not exactly. I acquire data to help me evaluate and analyze the world, not necessarily to satisfy my curiosity, which is a separate issue."

We went outside. I showed Trinity what my mother referred to as the "summer kitchen," just four pine posts to hold up a crude Japanese-style hip roof. Underneath was the wood-fire cooking grill on a stone base, wires with hooks dangling from the rafters to hold pots and pans.

"This structure resembles the picture of a pagoda on the island that I've seen on Instagram," Trinity said.

"The summer kitchen came first," I said. "Uncle Oggie admitted he got the idea of the pagoda from Sadie's cook hut."

I took Trinity to the barn, which had been remodeled by Red Shift with a kitchen, toilets, and shower room on the first floor and dormitory crash pad on the top story, which at one time had been a hayloft that never actually held hay, since my dad never did establish his dream farm.

We walked past the five 10-by-10′ Red Shift cabins to the converted school bus that brought the Red Shift communards from California to Grace Pond and later served as Uncle Oggie's dwelling and office. One half of the vehicle was painted with psychedelic colors featuring anti-war and pro-drug slogans: *Make Love Not War, Power to the People, Drop Acid Not Bombs, Never Trust the Man, Man.* The other side of the school bus was painted black, dotted with white and blue stars. In big red letters were the words "RED SHIFT: Our Universe is Expanding. Yours?" Faded tie-dyed curtains covered the windows.

"Ah, just as I suspected, Red Shift has multiple meanings," Trinity said.

Uh-huh." We went inside. "I haven't disturbed anything since Red Shift shut down at the end of the 1970s, and I keep the place relatively clean and intact," I said.

"So, you're some kind of sentimental fool?" Trinity said, accompanied by her mocking laugh.

"I guess. Osgood Stone—Uncle Oggie—was a mentor to me after my father died. This place keeps his memory vivid in my mind."

All the bus seats had been removed, leaving a two-room environment. The windows were covered with fading tie-dyed curtains that could be closed or opened to let in natural light. Heavy drapery separated the bedroom from the office, which was dominated by a huge oak desk and metal file cabinets that presently Trinity opened.

"Empty," Trinity looked at me in a way that made me wonder if she was firing a flare at my good eye.

"Uncle Oggie cleared out the files before leaving," I said.

Behind the drapery was a double-bed size futon on a foot-high platform and a dresser that Trinity rummaged through.

"From the clothes I'd say he was a little over six feet, medium-large build, size eleven shoe, and a full beard of dyed blond hair."

"I can see how you derive his physique from his clothes, but how could you correctly guess the beard?"

"Elementary, Uncle Cyclops." Trinity handed me a Kodak snapshot she pulled out of a drawer, showing Uncle Oggie and me as a twenty-year-old with long dark hair and a what-me-worry look on my scarred face. Time had softened over my facial scars, but in the pic the scars were lurid enough to make me turn away from the photograph.

"I bet Osgood Stone was a handsome man without that beard," Trinity said.

"It was well known that he had sex with the communards he recruited, both male and female."

"But he never hit on you?"

"Yes, how could you tell?"

"Your body language. Your trauma belongs to a different order." Trinity pointed to the rear window covered with a piece of plywood on which was tacked a faded poster of the incredibly sultry Jane Russell with print that read: "Howard Hughes presents THE OUTLAW, The Story of Billy the Kid."

"Why would a commune organizer feature a poster like that in his domicile?" Trinity asked.

"The story among the communards was that Uncle Oggie had had an affair with Jane Russell back in California," I said.

"What did Uncle Oggie have to say about that?"

"He neither confirmed nor denied the story—he just smiled."

"There's something to be learned from that poster," Trinity said.

"What?"

"I don't know yet."

We went outside.

"I like those little cabins," Trinity said. "Why are they all the same size?"

"They're 10-by-10 because anything larger can be taxed by the town," I said. "The two log cabins are reserved for my daughters and their families."

"Piety and Desire—how I enjoy voicing those names," Trinity said.

"You can stake a claim for one or more of the three unused cabins."

"Great. I'll take all three—one plywood shack for stuff, the other plywood shack for wardrobe, and the stone one for where I pretend I'm a normal human being."

"Do I detect a whiff of self-pity?" I said.

"Boo-hoo."

We entered the tiny fieldstone cabin.

"You picked this cabin because of the beauty and permanence of the stone?" I said.

"No, the great big mirror on the wall that I could see through the window—I love it. I'll move my things in tomorrow."

We returned to Shinbone Shack. "Supper will be served at seven—fish stew," I said.

Trinity shook her head. "Thanks, but I'm going into town. Don't wait up for me. I'll be in real late tonight."

I gave her a quizzical look.

"I've got a date," she said.

"How can that be? You don't know anybody in this area." I looked at her, no doubt with bewilderment, because she gave me a burst of that mocking laugh. Then she whipped out her smartphone and held it before me.

"Hookups are not hard to find when you have access to the world."

"With a stranger, isn't that dangerous?" I said.

"I hope so—it's more fun that way."

Trinity reached into her backpack and spilled some electronic gear on my log cabin's drop-down table. "These goodies are for you, Uncle Cyclops: Tablet with keyboard, cables, vehicle battery-charger, and a smartphone."

She handed me the phone. "I've set it up for you. You have your own phone number and email address."

"This wouldn't be part of the simple life I've tried to live," I said.

"No, it wouldn't. These devices will tip you upside down and shake the change out of your pockets, but they are necessary if we're going to work together."

"I don't have any electricity," I said.

"Yes, you do, in your truck battery." She dangled a cable in front of my nose. "Just plug this in the cigarette lighter socket to charge your phone."

≈

First thing next morning I received my first text message on my phone. It said, "bkfst?"

I texted back, "Coffee will be served in 15 minutes." Trinity had taught me the etiquette of texting, but I couldn't bear writing abbreviated English.

I went right to work on breakfast, pot of coffee, homemade bread toasted on the outside grill, eggs over easy. With an endless supply of free firewood, I kept a fire going outside in warm seasons, inside when it was cold. Almost exactly fifteen minutes later, I watched as Trinity emerged from her camper, wearing snug blue jeans, green and gold track shoes, and a green and gold T-shirt over her small breasts. Her hair was pulled back in a braid. You had to look close to discover she was wearing makeup designed to appear that she wasn't wearing make-up.

"I like the green and gold theme," I said.

"Yes, in your honor," Trinity said. "How about another hint."

"They're the colors of our local frogs," I said.

"You identify with frogs?"

"Yes, they taught me an important life lesson."

"Don't tell me anymore," Trinity said.

"You want to figure me out for yourself," I said.

"Yes, one of my foibles."

"You have an uncanny ability to see into people."

"Yes, uncanny because the Uncanny, capital "U", is my domain."

"What else can you tell me about my mindset right now?" I asked.

"You want to know how my date went last night," she said, as I poured her a coffee in a cup I'd hollowed out of a maple tree burl back when I was a teenager.

"In deference to your privacy I hadn't intended to bring up the subject," I said.

"I prefer bluntness to politeness."

"Okay, how did your date go last night?"

That mocking laugh. She wasn't going to tell me anything.

Connections

OVER THE COURSE OF A WEEK, Trinity schooled me in the uses of the smartphone and the tablet, and she introduced me to techniques for searching the Internet. As Sadie would say: "It wasn't all that hard to learn." Just frustrating at times. No, frustrating lots of times. Together we devised a plan, even though neither one of us was quite sure just what we were looking for in our investigation of Pete Shaughnessy's death.

I would remain at Shinbone Shack and Trinity would, as she put it, "Roam the solar system all the way from moon to Uranus" in her high-tech RV. We would keep in touch through a variety of devices and techniques—phone, text messages, webcam viewing, and perhaps most interesting, to me anyway, mic-ed-up body and vehicle cams. I would be able to see and hear what Trinity was doing in real time on my phone and tablet.

So that was the technical part, but what was our purpose? That was the tougher question. We discussed it every night on the cabin porch as we watched the sun set over Grace Pond.

"The only thing those four vets had in common, and Grandfather Landrieu repeated this over and over, was that they were the most skilled marksmen in their battalion, beginning with your dad, the B.A.R. man. The guy with the Browning Automatic Rifle." Trinity said.

"Then there's the rules they made," I said.

"Oh, you know about those, "the Golden Rules of our camaraderie," Grandfather Landrieu is fond of saying, and he's fond of reciting them to me. 'Golden Rule 1: No discussions of contemporary issues.' Which seems odd to me."

"Not so odd when you consider the time period in the country that they held their annual deer hunts," I said. "I remember violent arguments when they were drinking, so they often broke Golden Rule 1."

"But they never broke Golden Rule 2: 'WST. We Stick Together,'" Trinity said. "I asked Grandpa Maurice about 'Golden Rule 3: 'Draw straws.' And he said, 'Because it made the things you have to do in war, God's fault and not your own.' It appears fragmented and random, Uncle Cyclops, but really, I believe it's all connected. If we can make one connection, the others will fall into place."

I nodded, and then fetched a magic marker. I wrote CONNECTIONS! on a blank sheet of typing paper and tacked it to the log wall in the main room of Shinbone Shack.

"Grandpa Maurice wants timely reports of our endeavors," Trinity said.

"You're the professional coder and I'm the writer," I said, "so the reports will be my job."

"Right. Pretend you're writing a book," Trinity said.

"Preposterous. When you were growing up did your grandfather talk about the war?" I asked.

"Yes and no. I mean he couldn't seem not to talk about it, couldn't seem to separate himself from it." Trinity said. "At the same time, I always got the impression he was leaving out the important parts. What tool do you plan to use for our notes and reports?"

"My Underwood typewriter, of course."

Trinity shook her head. "By continuing to use the typewriter, you're clinging to a quaint and outdated habit."

"Uh-uh. You sound like Sadie. My typewriter is a word processor that saves directly to the paper. Top that."

Trinity responded with a delicate, feminine—if low-pitched—chuckle. "You're a man in love with his tool."

"Look who's talking," I said.

"I'm going to inject technology into your arteries, Uncle Cyclops. The flow will burst your heart. That's the real meaning of that old saying: blood will tell."

Around midnight, after Trinity had left to keep a date with another stranger, I went through the handwritten notes of the journal I'd kept since I was a boy, and sat down in front of the Underwood to work. The machine was such a beast, weighed down with cast iron and memories of Uncle Oggie and his crazy commune.

I stared at the typewriter, but I didn't touch the keys.

Beside it was my usual setup for writing, a yellow legal notepad and half dozen Bic pens and Number 2 graphite pencils handy beside the typewriter. An image of Lynn came to mind, but it was not in realistic pictures. It was abstract, green and gold swirls, and accompanied by a memory of her voice rambling on about theories of organic gardening. Me, writing fast, trying to keep up. Later, compiling the notes and typing them out on the Underwood. Pencil-editing a page. Retyping it over and over until I could not make it any better. Lynn editing my pages, adding corrections and new observations. Me, again retyping the notes into chapters. Eventually, we would have an organic gardening book by J.B. Nielson.

I came out of my revery with the realization that Lynn was gone forever from my life and—from what I could gather after instruction by Trinity Landrieu—so was my outdated typewriter.

I put the tablet Trinity had given me on the stand, and I typed my thoughts on the full-sized, Bluetooth keyboard that came with it. Words jumped to the Cloud. The work went well. No doubt my crash course in technology would help Trinity and me in our quest to find out what really happened to Pete Shaughnessy. At the same time, I felt I had lost part of myself.

I wrote a report of the week for Maurice Landrieu and that task triggered a memory of the last time I saw my father alive, so I wrote about that memory and included it with my report.

The Second Death

IT WAS DECEMBER 1968. My father's three buddies arrived at our apartment in Keene for their annual week-long deer hunt. At the time I didn't know a lot about these men. They were just dad's friends and in my mother's parlance "Army cohorts."

The first that year was Pete Shaughnessy, a native of Lowell, Massachusetts, who had meandered to California after the war. He was quite a sight in the 1960s in our state of clean-cut, clean-shaven men, because he looked like he'd stepped out of a California anti-Vietnam War rally—skinny body, long neck, goatee, dirty-brown hair with streaks of gray that he kept in a ponytail, leather vest, bell-bottom pants, and cowboy boots that made him tower over his pal, G.I. Joe Blaise.

"Hi, Sadie, you going to give me a kiss?" Pete said to mom.

My mother pecked Pete on the cheek, then she pulled back, looked him over, and said, "You're a little elongated in the tooth to be a hippie."

Pete laughed.

"Pete ain't a hippie. The hippies are young kids, Pete's an old beatnik," my father said.

Pete was single, and like my father, had not held a steady job since his military discharge. He liked to think of himself as a poet and philosopher, but as far as I know he never wrote anything, and the profound ideas he espoused came from other people, in particular Jack Kerouac who, like Pete, was a Lowell native.

"I'm the original Dharma bum," Pete would say.

My father and Pete were born the same month, May, and the same year, 1930, and though they were close friends, they often broke Rule 1 and argued about politics. Nineteen-sixty-eight was no exception. I heard heated discussions regarding the shooting deaths of Martin Luther King Jr. and Robert Kennedy, the Vietnam War, the recent presidential election, riots on college campuses, police brutality, the direction the country should take.

"The 'U-S-of-A' is going to hell in a hand-basket," my father said.

Listening to them, I couldn't get a handle on the terrible real-world events and problems of 1968. Instead, I wondered why a handbasket was a conveyance to hell? Was there a hell? Probably not, I concluded, but there should be to punish the wicked. What did it mean to be wicked? Let's say you killed some people but had good intentions because you believed your victims were wicked. Did that mean you were not wicked? These were the kinds of questions I asked myself when I was fourteen. Now that I'm over sixty I'm still short on answers.

The arrival of Harry Cromwell in his 1959 DeSoto Firedome temporarily put an end to the political discussions, and the subject matter turned to the hunt.

Harry's roots were in the South, though his family bounced around the country. Family? Did I say family? Harry had lived sometimes with his mother and sometimes in foster homes when she was in various insane asylums back when there were such institutions. His father abandoned the family when Harry was eight.

One year Harry shocked me when I overheard him say that if in his travels he happened upon his father, "I'd shoot him in the throat and watch him gag on his own blood." Harry worked on the road as a salesman for a firearms company.

He had a completely different look from his buddies. His idol was actor Craig Stevens in his role as Peter Gunn in the television series, and when he arrived that December in 1968 he was wearing a suit, white shirt, and narrow tie. Though he dressed like Peter Gunn, Harry looked more like the Lieutenant Jacoby character. He had a powerful but lumpy body. His hair was already thin, and his somewhat out-sized nose on his somewhat misshapen face displayed black-head pimples that my young eyes could detect ten feet away and that reminded me of my own zits. He never changed clothes for the hunt until after the men left our apartment and arrived at Shinbone Shack.

Mom was cordial to Harry, but behind his back she referred to him as Potato Head Cromwell. I liked Harry, because of all of dad's friends he was the most personable toward me. Sometime during his visits he'd find a private moment between the two of us and slip me a ten-dollar bill. "Here you go, an Al Hamilton for your piggy bank," he'd say. "Mum's the word."

Harry announced that he was a "free man," which drew a laugh from his fellow hunters. I didn't know at the time that "free man" meant recently divorced.

Oddly, enough, Harry named me. Early on, my mother and most people called me Joseph, never Joe. The land of "Joe" was my father's domain. My Dad, sometimes affectionately and sometimes sarcastically, would refer to me as Little Joe, inspired no doubt by the character on the Bonanza TV show, but usually I was just Junior. Then on one of the vet reunions, Harry started calling me Junie. The name stuck.

≈

The fourth member of the hunting party arrived by taxi. Maurice "Pass" Landrieu was a New Orleans native and fine arts painter living in New York. They called him Pass, because he could pass as any race. It was a joke and not a joke. Pass claimed to be part white, black, Asian, and Chitimacha, but my mother told me actually he was adopted and didn't know anything about his origins. Unlike his three over-the-top buddies, he came across as shy and insecure. Harry would say that Pass could paint but couldn't sell a painting, because he couldn't sell himself.

The previous year the Army buddies had met in Trinidad for Pass's marriage to a designer and researcher of Mardi Gras masks. Olivia Johnston, like Pass, was mixed race. There was an odd local connection to Olivia. Her father was descended from the famous Johnston family of Keene, New Hampshire, and movie fame. (See *Lost Boundaries*, 1949 film). Olivia's mother was of East Indian, African, and European descent from various Caribbean islands.

Something had happened to Maurice Landrieu in Korea that my father said had "done a number on him," but he wouldn't reveal the details. Pass had gone to college with the help of the GI Bill and gotten a degree in studio art. He'd already tried his hand at political cartooning, abstract expressionism, and Cubism. In the late 1960s, he was working with traditional watercolor paints in the modernist style of John Marin. Of course, none of his buddies knew what he was talking about, and neither did I until years later during the Red Shift days. Uncle Oggie used to say, "Junie you can thank me and my communards for your 'college education.'"

The men sat around and yakked about hunting and guns. One thing they all had in common and were happy to proclaim—over and over again—was that they could all shoot straight.

I watched my father reach under the carpet for the key to the gun cabinet. He opened it. I could see the 12-gauge pump-action shotgun for bird hunting, the bolt-action Remington .22 that Grandfather Norman Blaise had given to my dad when he was a boy, and two lever-action Model 94 Winchester deer rifles that presently my father removed from the gun cabinet and handed to Pete and Pass.

I knew those weapons intimately, though I had never fired them, because my father wouldn't take me shooting. I had read about them in my magazines, and I had taken G.I. Joe's guns apart and put them back together. There's something about touching a long gun, the feel on the hands, the smell of the oil, the view through the iron sights, the beauty of polished wood in proximity to black metal, that stirred me.

Did Dad know I was playing with his guns when he and Mom were out on the town? He must have. He hid the key in such an obvious place, and I could never quite put the guns back in the exact position that I found them. Yet he never said a word.

Harry had a new rifle to show off. Presently, he removed it from a leather case. It was beautiful, with a scope. "Get a load of this," he said.

"A Mannlicher-Schoenauer, just like Hemingway wrote about in *The Short Happy Life of Francis Macomber*, right?" Maurice said.

"Yeah, and I got it at a bargain price on a lawn from a guy who didn't know what he had."

"*The Short Happy Life of Francis Macomber* is a great story," Maurice said.

"I wouldn't know," Harry said. "Reading Hemingway is a waste of fucking time."

"Watch your language in front of the boy," my mother said.

"My apologies," Harry said, looking first at Sadie then at me in a sincere kind of way that even at my young age I could tell was out of character for Harry.

"Nice gun," I said, attempting to join the conversation.

My father reminded me that a rifle was called a rifle because it had rifling in the barrel while a gun had a smooth bore, so a Mannlicher-Schoenauer was not a gun.

Harry reverted to his true self. He held his "man licker" with one hand, grabbed his crotch with the other, and said, "This is my rifle, this is my gun, with this I shoot, with this I have fun." The men laughed, and I laughed but without mirth, because I wasn't sure what the point of the joke was. My mother did not laugh.

The plan, as usual, was to spend Friday night at Shinbone Shack and head out into the woods the next day. I hung around the men, hoping that this might be the year I was invited to join them. It didn't happen. In fact, my father avoided eye contact with me, and the men left in somber moods without goodbyes. That night lying in bed I seethed with anger at being left out.

Next day my mother dropped me off at the Keene Public Library, while she shopped and caught up with some work in the office. She had packed me a peanut butter and banana sandwich and a C-ration can of peaches that my father had purchased by the case at the local Army & Navy store but that he claimed—and I believed for years—that he had brought back from Korea. Along with my Swiss Army knife that I kept very sharp (in case I ever had occasion to skin a fur-bearing animal), I carried a GI P38 can opener that I bought from the same Army & Navy store.

At the library I sped through my homework and read hunting and fishing magazines to supply imagery and stories to stoke my fantasies about living in the woods. In a cabin. By myself. No mother. No father. No friends. Just the way I liked it. In my imagination, anyway. After lunch I walked to Zimmerman's Sporting Goods Store and ogled the guns, rods, reels, and muskrat traps.

I walked home, arriving in the late afternoon. My mother had a disturbed look on her face that I couldn't decipher. My first thought was that she was divorcing dad and returning to West Texas. I could not imagine that the news could be worse than that, but it was. My father had been shot dead apparently by a stray bullet fired presumably by an unknown hunter who probably didn't even know he'd killed somebody. My first unedited emotional reaction was a demonic voice in my head that told me I should be glad that G.I. Joe was dead. After that, part of me shut down for almost a decade.

≈

I emailed my report, including the remembrance, to Trinity and to Maurice. Maurice did not respond, and Trinity did not bring up the subject over breakfast on the porch at Shinbone Shack. Instead, we discussed setting up interviews in Lowell with Pete's high school sweetheart and his brother. Then Trinity asked me to row her over to Whirlybird Island.

Whirlybird Island

IT WAS AN OVERCAST DAY, but there was little threat of rain. The pond was nearly calm. I could see bugs on the surface. It was the kind of day where I might expect to see immature smallmouth bass jump out of the water and gulp down immature May flies. I rowed and Trinity sat facing me in the stern seat of the little boat.

"Did you learn anything from the story I sent you about my father's death?" I asked.

"It was helpful, gives us background, exposes your biases and limitations," she said. "What did you mean by the men leaving 'in somber moods'?"

"I don't know," I said. "It was just something I noticed. Usually when they left for Shinbone Shack, they'd be all excited and full of jokes, not that day."

"Uncle Cyclops, you left something out of your story."

"Well, dad and I were not getting along."

"And? Details, details—I need details."

I think my lips moved, but I didn't say anything, because I felt a pang, an intrusion into a part of myself that I had sealed off.

"Okay, I get it—you're not ready," Trinity said. "It's not important right now. Let's stick to the Pete Shaughnessy plan and see what develops."

There was a brief silence, so that we heard but did not see a fish jump out of the water. I grabbed my fly rod and cast toward the center of the ripples. A second later, a pumpkinseed hit my dry fly, and I took that interruption of our conversation as a sign from heaven—or whatever was out there in charge of human fate—to take Trinity's advice and back off from that searing incident that occurred in the weeks before dad was shot.

I brought in the fat little fish and showed it to Trinity. I didn't touch it, just let it dangle from the hook. Trinity had fished in the ocean bays of Trinidad with drop lines, but never in fresh water with a fly rod.

"See, green and gold—it's a . . ." I start to speak.

"No, no. Allow me." Trinity photographed the fish on her smartphone, tapped away on the keyboard, and less than a minute later said, "a sunfish."

"Close enough," I forced a frown, "Are you and the Internet ever wrong?"

"Well, I won't speak for the Internet."

I flipped the little fish from the hook and it fell into the pond and zipped off while Trinity inspected the fly.

"What did you use to break the barb on the hook?" Trinity said.

"Pliers."

"To make it easier to release them."

"Yes, I catch more fish than I want to eat."

Trinity took a picture of the artificial fly, and searching on my phone, tried without success to find a name for it online. Finally, she pointed at the screen of her phone, "This one's pretty close."

It was the first time I'd heard any insecurity in her voice. "That's a Royal Coachman," I said, "a very famous fishing fly, but it's not this fly."

The truth dawned on her then, "You made this one yourself."

"Yes, I tie my own flies, mainly from found materials here in my domain— bird feathers, critter furs, fish line, junk around the cabin like aluminum foil. I name them after people in my life. Except there's no Sadie. I couldn't bring myself to name an imitation bug after my mother. This is the Lizzy Rondoh."

"You're a bit of a momma's boy, aren't you?" Trinity said.

"You're not the first person to notice that."

As I rowed the johnboat into the tiny cove on the leeward side of Whirlybird Island, Trinity pointed at the great maple that held sway over Grace Pond, and said, "That's quite a specimen."

"Whirlybird Island is named after that tree. In the fall when the whirly-bird seeds drop from the tree, the wind blows them onto the pond. They end up everywhere."

Once started, I couldn't seem to stop talking about my world. "Grace Pond began as an impoundment created by beavers that the early settlers trapped out and built their own dam where the falling waters powered a sawmill. In the late 19th century, the sawmill built by Abner Grace burned to the ground, and my great-grandfather bought up the property and later built the hunting cabin that my great-grandmother Ruth named Shinbone Shack. Their daughter married a Quebec Frenchman, and that's how I became a Blaise."

"When nobody was looking, the beavers came back." Trinity pointed to a beaver lodge close to the shore and about halfway between Shinbone Shack and the island.

"Uh-huh."

"It looks like a native American wigwam," Trinity said.

"Maybe the Native Americans got the idea for their domiciles from the beavers," I said.

"Or maybe the beavers got the idea from the natives," Trinity said.

"I looked up public records on the Internet. The island was part of the deal when your great-grandfather bought the Shinbone Shack property. He cut down all the trees and burned the stumps to create field-grass to graze sheep."

"Yes," I said. "He left the maple tree to provide shade in the summer for the sheep. The idea was to prevent attacks by wolves."

"But it didn't work," Trinity said. "The wolves just swam over and dined to their hearts content. Anyway, that's what it says in your town archives."

I pulled my little craft up on the ledge and we followed a narrow path that wound around the island. The interior of the island was dense with pine and hemlock trees that grew up in the last century. Where sunlight came through, blueberry bushes set up shop. The perimeter of the island was rocky with glacial erratics. Above it all was the lightning-scarred sugar maple.

Eventually, we reached one of the few spots along the shallows where, in this light, I could see a sandy bottom.

"There," I pointed, "that's where Pete supposedly dove in, hit his head, and drowned."

"Where were you when it happened?" Trinity asked.

I laughed a little, a nervous laugh, and shook my head. "It's a long, involved story," I said. "Do you want me to tell it to you?"

"No, I want you to type it up and email it to me and Maurice."

The Third Death

HERE'S MY REPORT TO TRINITY AND MAURICE.

In the months before Pete met his demise, problems for the commune, like communes everywhere in those days, had mounted. Most of the original members had left, and the replacements tended to be attracted to the sex part of Uncle Oggie's free-love theology, not the responsible or the philosophical part. Uncle Oggie screened the applicants with increased vigor, but that only had the effect of reducing the numbers in the commune. Members tended to stay only a few months.

In the end, so-called free love wasn't enough. What all these young people seemed to want was their own place in the country to share with a partner, modeled on the book *Living the Good Life* by Helen and Scott Nearing and in the back-to-land articles in the *Mother Earth News* that I occasionally wrote for in my capacity as Red Shift's scribe. In other words, what the young people in the commune really wanted was the opposite of communal living.

The roof on a yurt I helped build collapsed from the weight of a heavy snowfall followed by a hard rain. I wrote a piece about it for CCN (*The Counterculture News.*)

A personal problem cropped up. I started to feel vaguely anxious and panicky when I had to leave the pond, the early signs of what one day would be .44 magnum panic attacks.

Meanwhile, Sadie graduated from Keene State College on the President's Honors List and was accepted at Tulane University Law School in New Orleans. She had left in August of 1973 for the Gulf Coast, and in 1976 she passed the Louisiana bar exam and went to work for the law firm of Fulton, Chambers, Canal, and Spring.

After Sadie's departure from Grace Pond, I had Shinbone Shack to myself and was free to take over my mother's bedroom, but I still slept on the porch with the elements. In the days of my youth, I was chronically uncentered. Something wasn't quite right, but I had no idea what that something was. Kinda crazy but I cheered up during weather disasters. The worse the weather, the closer I came to normal human equilibrium. I had no girlfriend. My lovers were the wind, the rain, the snow, the sun, and the sound of waves touching the shore at night as I lay in my narrow bed on my sleeping porch.

In some ways, I had it pretty good after I was released by the military. I had a free place to live and my dad's old truck. I made spending money as a freelance writer for back-to-the-land periodicals and as an occasional firewood dealer, which brought in more cash than the writing. Everything took a severe turn for the worse, beginning late in the summer of 1978.

Uncle Oggie abandoned the commune for a couple months, driving off to parts unknown in his Thunderbird. He told the communards, "I've seen my burning bush." In his absence, there was no leader, and the commune did not thrive. Uncle Oggie returned to Red Shift late in the summer in a taxi laden with packages.

He had donated the Thunderbird to the Peoples Temple, the name of a church congregation that didn't mean much to me at the time.

By then there were only eight communards left. Five of those present were visitors who had lingered on because they had no better place to go. The only veterans remaining were Pete Shaughnessy, Jason Hinkley, who insisted on referring to himself as Jason the Anarchist, and 19-year-old Lizzy Rondoh, who Osgood Stone had entrusted with the Red Shift food and rent money. Jason tried to work his way into Lizzy's good graces, but she wouldn't sleep with him. Her loyalty was to Uncle Oggie.

Uncle Oggie did not seem to mind the degradation of his commune. In fact, he was in an effervescent mood as the communards gathered around the clearing between the barn and cabins on a warm sultry night. "I have an announcement to make," he spoke with great gravity. "I have found God's messenger. His name is Jim Jones. The breakthrough that I have been looking for all my life is Apostolic Socialism."

In Uncle Oggie's interpretation, Apostolic Socialism unified Biblical revelation with his own version of the counterculture. "The teachings of the old-time prophets and astrologers and all the holy men of the world are in perfect symmetry with the writings of Marx . . ."

Pete interrupted, "Who did you have in mind, Groucho or Harpo?" That got a laugh from the communards.

Uncle Oggie did not laugh, but he did not criticize Pete either. He looked

Pete in the eye and spoke in a warm, friendly way, "Pete, you were raised in a religion, how you must feel its loss. Jason, you were raised in a religion, how you must feel its loss. Lizzy, you were raised in a religion, you feel its loss, no?"

Lizzy nodded and bowed her head.

Pete's usual bluster seemed to drain out of him. His fallen state was so apparent and so unlike the Pete I knew that I went over to him and asked him if he was all right.

"No, I'm not all right," he said in a very low voice.

"What's the matter?" I whispered.

Pete waved me off, then as if he realized he had to say something, he looked at me and said, "Oggie got me thinking about my hopes and dreams back in high school, before . . ."

"Before what?"

"Before." he said and walked away.

I turned my attention back to Uncle Oggie, who spoke in a somber tone, "Whether you believe or don't believe in a deity or a religion, all of you surely believe in brotherly and sisterly love or else you would not be here with Red Shift."

Uncle Oggie let his words sink in, and when I thought there would be more speech-making, more serious talk, Uncle Oggie smiled and just like that his tone brightened. At that moment, a fortuitous breeze blew his long blond hair skyward for a moment.

"You've all been under a lot of stress because of my absence," Uncle Oggie said. "What we need is a celebration, so I've brought back some goodies."

He walked over to Pete, put his arm around his shoulders, and said, "Help me out, brother."

The two elders went into the school bus office and came out with beer, hard liquor, marijuana, and tabs of LSD.

"It's all on Red Shift, folks," Uncle Oggie said. "I propose that we party at the pagoda."

That relieved the tension—everybody was suddenly happy. "Welcome home, Uncle Oggie, let's party," said Jason.

Uncle Oggie turned to me while he spoke to the communards, "We have an unsung hero among us, the chronicler of our little experiment, Junie Blaise. Junie, I'm inviting you to party with us. I know your mother would not approve, but she is far away, and you are a man now. You can make your own decisions. I propose that we induct you into Red Shift as an honorary member."

Those words drew a cheer from the communards. I was swept away by the moment and agreed to be initiated. After that, my memory is foggy, and the notes I took in my journal afterward are thin and perhaps unreliable. This much I know to be true: at sunset Uncle Oggie gave me a beer, a shot, and a tab of LSD.

"You are finally ready—this will open your mind," Uncle Oggie said.

I rowed four communards out to Whirlybird Island, then returned to Shinbone Shack for Pete and his current girlfriend. Oggie took Lizzy and one of the new communards, a girl who looked no older than sixteen, to the island in the canoe. My clearest memory is that by the time it was dark Pete was already drunk.

We made a bonfire. I began to see the bright colors of the sunset slithering in the growing darkness. The LSD made everything seem grand and profound.

"You're stressed," I said to the great maple tree. The tree did not answer back.

There was dancing and singing. Time passed. Darkness engulfed the island. Pete made an ass of himself by arguing with everyone. Oggie told Pete he ought to take a swim to sober up. Was I initiated into Red Shift? Yes, or so I was told, but I have no memory of any ceremony.

It was a warm, starry night under a full moon that showed in fragments through the crown of the maple tree. In my state of mind, I thought that the glow of the bonfire made the tree shimmer with dread and expectation. Something signifying great meaning was going to happen.

I held out my arms, looked up at the sky through the tree's branches, and called out, "Oh, tree, you're dying."

"Get a load of that, Junie's talking to the tree," Lizzy said.

"It's the acid," Jason said.

"No, it's reality," Uncle Oggie said. "Concentrate, Junie—focus."

"Yes," I thought, concentrate and with the power of my will I would communicate with the tree.

I covered my one eye, and it was as if I could still see the tree with my eyeless socket.

"All those dead branches, are you dying, tree?"

"Of course I am dying. Aren't we all?"

"Is that you, tree? How come you sound like Pete?"

"Because I am Pete, you pitiful, hopeless fool," Pete said. The communards were all laughing, but I didn't care. My mundane conversation with the maple tree with occasional sarcastic commentary by Pete seemed quite profound and I didn't want it to end.

"Can we change places, tree?"

"Yes, of course, I've always sought mobility."

Suddenly, I was the tree. Squirrels ran across my limbs. Caterpillars feasted on my leaves. When a life form touched one of my branches, I took on the senses of that life form.

With the vision of a one-eyed crow, I watched the world of passing deer, green ferns, thunder bolts, Canada geese that had lost their bearing flying every which way, winking stars, nest-building birds, insect borers, and fungi spores that presently floated over my crown. I absorbed radiation from the Vernon, Vermont, nuclear power plant fifteen miles to the south and I glowed like a giant lightning bug.

I levitated to the top of the tree, and I could see my human incarnation below staring up. This new Junie suddenly sprouted a new eye. His scars smoothed out. Mother Nature spoke kindly to the new me, "All is forgiven, son."

Forgiven for what? I wasn't sure which transgression—there were so many.

It seemed to me that eons went by, but actually as I later learned it was maybe an hour. I remember, then, hearing Lizzy scream and thinking that it wasn't real, just extraneous neurons in my brain acting out. I don't remember rowing the body back to shore. But I do remember the moon darting in and out of clouds as if it were a living organism.

The medical examiner ruled that apparently a blow on the head had knocked Pete out and he'd drowned in three feet of water. The scenario seemed pretty clear to the authorities and everyone else. Pete, in his impaired state, had stripped to the buff and attempted to dive into shallow water and hit his head on one of the many rocks jutting out from the bottom.

Sadie returned to the pond for a brief memorial service, presided over by Uncle Oggie, who went out of his way to make the acquaintances of Maurice and Harry. Paul Shaughnessy drove up from his home in Lowell, Mass. I was surprised to find that he was very close to his big brother, and from the look on his face, mourned his loss.

I didn't tell her, but Sadie found out about my LSD trip. After the funeral, she announced to Uncle Oggie that Red Shift had broken a key term of its lease (no illegal drugs for her son) and she was evicting the communards. She gave Red Shift two months to clear out. What surprised me was that Uncle Oggie, who I thought was a fighter, seemed amused by Sadie's anger.

"I'll go quietly," he said. "My work here is done."

Lowell Connection

THE MORNING AFTER I emailed my report to Maurice and Trinity, I was brewing coffee when I heard the "doink" of a text message from Trinity, "Hello."

I texted back. "Coffee?"

"Of course."

I noticed that while Trinity had had a huge influence on me already, I'd had a very small influence on her. She was sending me grammatically correct text messages. We take our victories where we find them.

I watched from the summer kitchen as the door to Trinity's stone cabin opened, and slightly bow-legged, Trinity stepped out and started toward me, except this was not the same Trinity I'd gotten used to. Trinity was now a slender but muscled young man with closely cropped, russet-colored hair, a soul patch under the lower lip. He wore track shoes and a Western shirt tucked into blue jeans.

When he arrived, I noticed a shiny silver belt buckle embossed with the word ZENO.

Trinity sat down on one of the stump stools while I poured coffee. "Nice belt buckle," I said.

"Thank you. It's a body cam. Let me see your phone." Trinity's voice, like the walk and the mannerisms, was male.

I gave Trinity my phone and he fiddled with it for a few minutes.

"The camera in the belt buckle—like police wear?" I asked.

"Mine is higher quality," he said. "In a few years they'll be everywhere, and this one will be obsolete. I'll be mic-ed up. You'll hear and see whatever's going on, and you'll communicate with me because I'll hear you in my ear-buds. Check it out."

I looked at my phone and I could see a wide-angle view of myself, Shinbone Shack, the summer grill with the pagoda-style roof, transmitted from the camera to my phone. I looked closer at the belt buckle. Now I could see the camera lens in the center of the letter "O" in ZENO along with the name of a company embossed on the belt buckle, "Paradox Sight Lines, Inc."

41

Later as we were finishing our coffees, I said, "You look like a professional soccer player on his day off."

"I used to be pretty good, though I'm out of practice."

"In a pro league would you play as a woman or as a man?"

"I'm sure the rules would bar me either way, so the question is irrelevant. Gotta go. Bye." What did he mean that the rules would bar him? Was Trinity male or female? Both, an intersex person? I didn't have an answer. It was none of my business, but that didn't mean I should suppress my curiosity. All I had to go on was that word "shape-shifter." It wasn't as if Trinity was attempting to live without gender. The personas that Trinity presented were highly gendered. I decided to reduce the issue to pronouns. As long Trinity presented himself as male, I would refer to him as "he." When Trinity appeared to be female, I would refer to her as "she."

I watched as Trinity hurried to his homemade rig, put it in drive, and headed out way too fast on the bumpety-bump Shinbone Shack dirt driveway.

Trinity and I communicated over our mobile phones. Cameras on his rig let me see the road and environs in real time as he drove. The hands-free speaker phone allowed him to drive, talk to me, and browse the Internet.

After I'd finished my chores—hauling water, pulling weeds in the garden, checking myself for ticks—I connected with Trinity and his rig. I thought I would be seeing the road, but the view from the Zeno-Cam was from the prospect of a mountain top. Trinity was sitting on a granite ledge glittering with mica schist where the camera showed lakes and ponds in the forested hills below.

"What are you doing on top of Mount Monadnock?" I asked.

"I like to visit the local hot spots wherever I go. Nice little climb."

"You made it in two hours, including the drive."

"Yes, I took my time to study rocks and to take in the views."

Trinity snapped still shots with his smartphone—not of the vistas but of other hikers. "For my facial recognition database. I like people faces with a background vista as far as even a Cyclops can see."

"You have a cruel streak in you, Trinity."

"That's true. Many cruel people are naively damaging to other people, like cats batting around a chipmunk. But my cruelty is by design and for a purpose."

"You hurt people, maybe to relieve your own hurt?"

"No, to study them." I thought his following laugh mocked his answer, but maybe not. I was beginning to understand that I would only know as much about Trinity Landrieu as he wanted me to know.

Trinity and I found only two people in Lowell who knew Pete well and who would talk to us about him—Natalia Cominsky, Pete's high school sweetheart, and Paul Shaughnessy, Pete's kid brother who I met briefly at Pete's service decades ago. There were other Shaughnessy siblings, but they lived far away from Lowell and had nothing to say about their black-sheep brother.

Trinity met Natalia at the Worthen House Cafe in Lowell for a late breakfast. Trinity had made another change to his appearance. He was still in male form, but he looked ten years older with more padding around the middle, clothes partly formal, partly frumpy. The soul patch was gone, and he was clean shaven with a touch of gray in carefully combed hair from the natural part on the right side of his head. He looked like an ad man for a small-city radio station, and he talked with a slight nod to the Massachusetts diction.

"Why the big change in persona?" I asked Trinity.

"I shape-shift to gain the trust of sources. The right look varies from person to person."

"I think you just like to dress up," I said.

"That too, Uncle Cyclops. That too. Ha-ha."

Natalia appeared quite healthy, and what's that lame word used to describe able-bodied octogenarians? Oh, yeah, "spry." Natalia was spry with permed white hair and a whisper of blue, a craggy, wrinkled face but with good bones that suggested she'd been a beauty in her day. No bent back but plenty of arthritis in her lumpy ankles and swollen red knuckles.

They sat in a booth of aged wood with thick varnish over carvings, cigarette burns, and for all I know fossils from the Pleistocene era.

Natalia ordered clam chowder with extra crackers and dumped three sugars in her coffee. Trinity worked over a veggie omelet.

"This booth we're sitting in, guess what?" Natalia said.

"You added to the graffiti on the woodwork?" Trinity said.

"No, Pete did. See?" She showed Trinity a worn carving, the wood shellacked over and barely legible, read, "Pete Loves Latin, Jesus, and Natalia."

"That's sweet," Trinity said.

"Did you know that Edgar Allan Poe wrote *The Raven* in this very booth."

"Yes, I read that possibility online."

"Yeah, he had a girlfriend that worked in the mills,"

Natalia said.

"And Pete Shaughnessy romanced you here?"

"Well, sorta. Actually, nobody romanced me. Boys didn't do that in my day. Or maybe it was just me that they didn't do it to."

"Tell me some more about Pete."

Natalia described a Pete Shaughnessy that I did not know.

"When I met Pete in high school home room, he wasn't sure whether he wanted to be a priest or a Latin teacher. He was very studious and serious-minded. 'I'm a hick hike hock kind of guy,' he'd say." (Spelling conveys Natalia's meaning.) "His family was poor—well, whose wasn't? But his was especially bedraggled because his old man was a . . . how can I put this delicately?"

"It's okay, Mrs. Cominsky, this study won't include any names."

"In that case I'll tell you that Pete's pater was a lush, and I think the mother, she was a borderline Chablis-aholic. That happens you know in a marriage: one will drag down the other. I wasn't about to allow that to happen to me when I married that Cominsky bum. All the Cominskys are bums. Well, that's not fair you might say . . ."

"What was Pete's reaction to his parents' drinking?"

"Pete, he wouldn't touch the stuff. Not even altar wine. See, the altar boys were known for sneaking into the wine cabinet in the sacristy. We girls used to say that if you went steady with an altar boy somewhere along the line, he was going to give you sweet white wine. You'd ask yourself, 'Am I going to tattle in the confessional?' But Pete, he never slugged down altar wine, though maybe he did behind my back. I wonder… you know what? You can't trust a man to tell you the truth except maybe when he goes senile and forgets his tricks."

"How serious were you and Pete?"

"We didn't go out much after we graduated. I waitressed and Pete worked in the laundry room of the hospital. He didn't like the gooey part of the job. '*Look before you reach* is my motto,' he would say. I'm making it sound like he was a fuddy-duddy but actually he had a lot of potential."

"Potential for what?"

"I don't know—potential. I knew there was something more. And then everything changed. We went to war. And Pete, he joined up. Or maybe he got drafted—what difference does it make? Anyway, that was the end of that, and I ended up with that bum Cominsky. The Cominskys, they're all bums, even the women, or maybe especially the women. That's it—I never thought about it before. It was that bitch, Violet Davis, who thought she was hot stuff just because she was related to Bette Davis, who was a Lowell girl. It was Violet who corrupted the Cominskys. She was a Protestant. My mother used to say there was no future in a mixed marriage. She was right, I can see it now."

Natalia went on and on for another hour talking about her own life. How her people on her mother's side were among the builders of the mills that gave Lowell its reputation and brought in immigrants from all over the world and how they lost their fortune through bad luck. Like marrying into a Catholic family.

I admired Trinity. He didn't brush her off even though it was obvious early on that Natalia had little useful information about Pete Shaughnessy. All she knew were the rumors that Pete read too much Jack Kerouac, because he met Jack a couple times when they were teenagers and moved to California and became a beatnik. Far as she knew Pete never returned to Lowell after his stint with Uncle Sam. But he did return. And more than once. Or so said Pete's younger brother.

≈

Paul Shaughnessy could have passed for the grandfather of the Pete Shaughnessy I had known. Look at a person at birth, at ages 10, 20, 30, 40 all the way to the end, and you must conclude that Time is the great shape-shifter.

Paul was a semi-retired, successful, local businessman. He owned various rental properties and he was a principal in a car dealership. He had the look of a man used to wearing a suit and tie to work and who took pride in his appearance. The out-of-date suit was a little baggy on him, which suggested that he'd lost weight as some old folks do as their great decline begins to steepen.

Trinity and Paul met at Pete's gravesite at Edson cemetery in South Lowell. Trinity's Zeno-Cam revealed a simple upright granite slab (that Paul paid for) with Pete's name, dates of birth and death, and his status as a Korean War veteran. Beside the slab was an American flag and an empty bottle of Four Roses whiskey.

Trinity pointed at the bottle, "Your idea?"

Paul chuckled, "Pete's idea. Actually, he wanted it full and I complied. I came back a week later and it was still there but empty. I restock it once in a while."

"And it's always depleted when you return, because Pete comes out of the grave to partake."

"I like to think that's true," Paul said with a smile.

"It's death, disease, and the deity that gives us material for jokes, and without jokes there's no reason to go on day after day," Trinity said.

"Amen. My big brother was a philosopher in his own way. Pete used to say, 'Sometimes when you love a stranger, they applaud you, or you applaud them ... with the clap.'" Paul chuckled, made the sign of the cross, and bowed his head.

I laughed, too, but not for the same reason that Paul Shaughnessy laughed. Pete took his philosophical ideas from Jack Kerouac, but he stole that joke from his old buddy, G.I. Joe Blaise. It was one of dad's standards, making fun of his own Franco-American quirks with the English language.

After a pause, Trinity asked, "You think Pete knew he was going to die in the near future?"

Paul's facial expression changed from flippant to serious.

"Yes. He confided that somebody was after him, but he didn't know who. I thought you were coming here to investigate his murder."

"Murder?"

"Yeah, murder," Paul said with deep conviction in his voice.

"We're investigating his death, but we haven't settled on any theories yet," Trinity said. "What happened to lead you to believe that Pete was murdered?"

"Pete himself. I used to think he was just paranoid, because of those terrible substances he was putting into his body, but the way he died I couldn't help but think, 'You predicted it, brother!' One of those hippies did him in, mark my words."

"Let's back up for a minute. How would you describe your relationship with your brother?"

"When we were kids, he was my protector, my role model, and my hero. I loved him even after he went off the deep end."

"When he joined a commune?"

"No, it was before that. See, there were two Pete's. There was the Saint

Pete before he got drafted, and afterward the post-war Pete. The Saint Pete I grew up with wanted to be a priest to help other people find their way. Pete was a man, a real man, in the true sense of the word. I remember he faced-down Dad. He told him, 'You may be our earthly father, but the only father I answer to is our father who art in heaven.'"

"He protected you from the drunken rages of a disturbed father."

"Yes, that's right. He wasn't just my protector. He was every kid's protector in the neighborhood." Paul interrupted himself with a laugh. "I just got a flash from the past. Pete's looking at this big kid—huge kid—looking him right in the eye. He says, 'You're outnumbered. Me and Jesus Christ is going to kick your ass.'"

"So what was the bone of contention in that encounter, and was anybody's ass actually kicked?" Trinity asked with perhaps unintended sarcasm.

"Listen, buster, you shouldn't ask anybody over sixty multiple-part questions. They'll only remember the last thing you said, and nobody's ass was kicked because Mister Huge backed down."

"Do you want me to repeat part one?"

Paul shook his head. "Who knows, who cares, it was just Pete being Pete. He was tough, funny, serious, and pious all at the same time. And in those days a teetotaler."

"But something changed him," Trinity said. "He drank heavily, experimented with drugs, and lost his faith in his belief system. What was the cause?"

"No doubt the war, but I can't say what in particular."

"Because he didn't talk about it," Trinity said.

"Uh-huh. He didn't come home directly after the war. He went to San Fran, and we lost touch. He didn't show up when we buried dad, but he did when mama died. She and Pete were close.

"After that he'd pop in unannounced every once in a while, and we would talk."

"Let me guess, he asked you for money."

"Don't get wise with me."

"Sorry, Mister Shaughnessy. Snide remarks are a failing of mine."

"Your snide outflanks your sorry."

"You nailed it: another one of my failings. I apologize for my inability to properly apologize. Ha-ha."

The imitation laugh charmed Paul. He shook his head and smiled. "Okay, buddy, you're all right. You ever decide you want to live in Lowell, you'll fit right in. We're a town of wise-asses and proud of it."

"Does the name Gerard Stanton hold any meaning for you?"

"No, why?"

Trinity told Paul all about the dog tag and its appearance in the shallows where Pete drowned, but Paul had nothing new to say about the topic, except to repeat his theory that one of the communards was responsible for Pete's death.

"Bring me back to that moment when it became clear to you that Pete feared for his life," Trinity said.

"It wasn't any one thing. It was, I dunno, an accumulation of fears, doubts, and just craziness. He had this idea that he was being pursued—and deservingly so."

"Deservingly? You mean he believed that he deserved to be hunted down and killed?"

"Exactly. He used to joke about it. 'Maybe if they get me it'll be hell on earth, as if one time wasn't enough, and then I'll qualify for heaven.'"

"What did he mean by 'as if one time wasn't enough'?"

"I dunno."

"He must have an idea who was after him and why," Trinity said.

Paul shook his head. "If he did, he never shared it with me."

"But you still think that his death was not an accident, that one of the people in the commune killed him. Would you elaborate on that?"

"Yeah, I don't have any evidence—it's just a hunch. After we buried him, I hired an agency to look into it, but the results were inconclusive."

"Do you have the report from the agency, and could I look at it?"

There was a long pause. I could see Paul Shaughnessy screwing up his face. I think he was about to tell Trinity to take a flying copulation in a rolling pastry, but Trinity said the right thing at the right time. "Listen, Mr. Shaughnessy, when I contacted you, I told you I was the grandson of Maurice Landrieu. I should have mentioned that my partner is the son of another of Pete's Army buddies."

Trinity handed the earbuds to Paul.

"Remember me, Junie Blaise? We met at Pete's memorial service at the commune in New Hampshire," I said.

"With the facial scars, right? And the eye?"

"Yes."

Paul handed the earbuds back to Trinity.

"Like you, Mister Shaughnessy, we have a special interest in finding the truth," Trinity said. "I promise to let you know our findings."

"Okay, you can have the report," Paul said and he emailed the report to Trinity's phone.

The next day while Trinity headed for Washington State in his rig, I rowed over to the island. The pond was windy with whitecaps, not an ideal environment for a small, flat-bottomed boat, but I made it OK, though my little green and gold craft did take on water enough to wet a big toe.

I sat under the pagoda, which was partly shielded from the wind by the great maple tree, and I read the Shaughnessy report on my phone.

Either the detective agency was on a budget imposed by their client, or they were just shysters, because it was a cursory, even shabby, investigation. For one thing the agency never sent anyone to the site of the death. The report consisted mainly of notes by the coroner and a summary of the "accident" by Constable Godfrey Perkins, Darby's one-man police force at the time, now deceased.

There was no autopsy, and no tests for alcohol or drugs in his system, but Perkins did indulge in some professional guesswork. Cause of death was listed as drowning. Pete had sustained a blow on the right temple. The theory proposed by Constable Perkins was the one we all came up with at the time, that Pete knocked himself out while diving into shallow water where he hit his head on a rock or ledge.

There were no eyewitnesses, but several of the communards reported that Pete, who was known to mix alcohol with drugs, was even more intoxicated than usual. There was nothing in the report about Lizzy finding the body. There were no names in the report, except for Osgood Stone, who billed himself as the Executive Director of Red Shift Communal Living.

Uncle Oggie said that it was not the first time that Pete had jumped into the pond after a night of heavy drinking. I was not among those interviewed by the constable, because I was so messed up in the head myself that night that I had no evidence to offer. Sloppy case work, I realized. Constable Perkins, as well as the so-called detective agency, should have talked to everybody who was on Whirlybird Island that night.

I left the meditation space under the pagoda and walked to the scene of the crime, if that's what it was. I sat on pine needles and looked at the water. A notion popped into my head. I stripped down and, presumably, like Pete, dove in headfirst. My hands hit the bottom, but not my head. It was about waist deep

and I felt around with my feet. The bottom was sandy, no rocks. How did Pete get that head injury?

A few minutes later I was dressed and sitting in the pagoda trying to meditate my way into meaning, when Trinity called to inform me that except for an emergency he'd be unavailable for a couple or three days as he drove West to visit the Stanton Library and Research Center for the Study of Warfare in Bellevue, Washington. He had reservations at a dude ranch in the Black Hills of South Dakota. No doubt another rendezvous.

"Why a dude ranch?" I asked.

"Because that's where the dudes are."

"And you always wanted to ride a horse?"

"I do like to ride, yes."

Chief Seattle

FOR A COUPLE DAYS I thought my investigator had quit on me, because I didn't hear from him, nor did he respond to my emails. I was worried and about to query Grandfather Maurice when all of a sudden Trinity was there on my phone. The voice was female.

What I was seeing from her body camera was a small, pretty cemetery that looked like a familiar landscape, yet I knew I hadn't been there. Much of the Northwest is like that for us Northeast people. It's like our own landscape but on a grander scale.

"We seem to be specializing in graveyards," I said.

"You don't get much feedback from the clientele, but they don't complain either," Trinity said.

With the uneven ground, casually mowed lawn, and a few older wood-frame houses in the background the cemetery could have been in a New England town. "Where are we?" I asked.

"Suquamish, Washington. I had a very nice ride on the ferry from Seattle to get here."

"Why?"

"Why not? I'm early for my appointment with the Stanton Trust rep, so I thought I'd take in one of the area's claims to fame. Check it out." Trinity spoke in a slight East European accent as she walked to a stone monument topped by a cross. There was nothing special about the monument.

"Looks like any phallic marker to honor a local oligarch," I said. "What's so remarkable?"

"Read the inscription," Trinity walked closer so I could see better.

The inscription read: "Chief of the Suquamish, and Allied Tribes, Died June 7, 1866. The firm friend of the whites, and for him the City of Seattle was named by its Founders."

Underneath in big letters was the English equivalent to the chief's name, Sealth. On another face of the monument the name was repeated with an explanation that Sealth was his "baptismal" name, along with his approximate age at death, 80.

"Never mind Chief Seattle, what about you? Why do you sound like a girl now?"

"Not a girl, a young woman. Be respectful, please," she said.

I couldn't tell whether she was being serious or sarcastic. Once I got to know her better, I'd understand that Trinity's "serious" always had an edge of sarcasm, and her sarcasm was just another shape-shift to protect . . . what? I was never sure.

She took a selfie with her phone and sent it to me. She was now blonde, with no apparent make up, wearing hiking shorts and compatible foot ware. She looked ready to audition for a part in a Stoli ad.

"The Trust rep is an outdoorsy female from St. Petersburg, Russia, my first home sweet home," Trinity said.

"You were born in Russia?"

"No, Kazakhstan."

"And?"

"Maybe when I get to know you better, Uncle Cyclops, I'll share some of my tribulations with you. What do you think about the monument?"

"Quarried stone, Christian cross, obelisk aspect—seems all wrong to pay homage to a Native American leader."

"True enough. I bet if you exhume the body you'll see where it turned over in the grave. Listen to this from a speech the chief made. 'The white man will never be alone. Let him be just and deal kindly with my people, for the dead are not altogether powerless.'"

"It resonates, those last words, but so what?" I said.

Trinity stepped back from the monument so that I could take in the view of the background. There was a tall conifer and some young hardwoods, a house far away through breaks in the trees, and then Puget Sound.

Now I understood what Trinity was driving at. "The chief is giving us a mission statement for our investigation—'the dead are not altogether powerless,'" I said.

"You saddle the horses, Uncle Cyclops, and I'll be your Pony Express rider."

I didn't have to say what we both knew to be true at that moment, which was this ancient johnboat mariner and this young person whatever he or she or they were biologically, it mattered less now. We had found a calling for our enterprise: to learn what the dead want to tell us and deliver the message to history.

Russian for My Heart

AROUND 3 O'CLOCK IN THE AFTERNOON, Trinity was in Bellevue, Washington, her high-tech RV parked near the shores of Lake Washington. Her Zeno-Cam was showing me an exalted mansion, built along the lines of a European castle, dominated by a tower room. She had arrived at the Stanton Library and Research Center for the Study of Warfare, a private library open only to researchers with academic or government credentials approved by the Stanton board.

I don't know how she did it, but Trinity wangled an interview with Pauline Alvar, a Russian archivist who was also a trustee of the library. My first thought was how could Pauline Alvar be Russian and have that name. I found her on Wikipedia and LinkedIn. Pauline Alvar's grandfather had been an American soldier of color who had defected to the old Soviet Union and married a Russian woman.

I watched through the Zeno-Cam as Trinity ascended the stairs to a grand entryway. Just as she approached the door, some 12 feet high, I heard Trinity's snicker, "Get a load of this."

A sign with a permanence to it, almost like a plaque, read, "Please Enter at Annex on West Side of Building." Trinity tried the door anyway, but of course it was locked.

Annex—what annex? There was no separate building. The "annex" turned out to be a modest side door marked annex. Trinity pressed a buzzer, circa 1990.

I couldn't make out the tinny response from the buzzer, but I could tell it was female.

"It's Trinity Landrieu, I'm at your door," Trinity said to the buzzer.

Another tinny response.

"What did she say?" I asked Trinity.

"She said she'd let me in personally. You're going to need a hearing aid in four or five years, Uncle Cyclops."

Momentarily, the door opened, and I was looking at a very fit woman about Trinity's age, height and athletic build, dressed in casual office garb with a touch of elegance, long black hair that I'm guessing had been straightened. She looked to me like a ballet dancer getting off a bus to go to work. Pauline and Trinity shook hands in the doorway.

"You've got an old-fashioned buzzer system, but I noticed state-of-the art surveillance cameras," Trinity said.

"Yes, allocations of our budget do vary. We have noted that your body-cam is transmitting both audio and video to a destination unknown."

"Yes, my colleague on the East Coast is not altogether absent. Do you want me to shut it off? I can always brief him later."

Pauline answered in a generic American accent, as a foreign spy might learn. "Somewhere during the interview that may be necessary, yes. Do come in and I'll show you around."

I think Pauline meant her suggestion to Trinity as a subtle message to voluntarily shut off our communications system, but Trinity treated it as OK-for-now and kept it on.

The "annex" didn't look anything like a mansion on the inside. It resembled a modern library, which is to say a car dealership showroom with movable book stacks featuring metal crank cabinets, off-white walls, cool lighting, and metal trim around windows and doors. I got a nice tour as Pauline led Trinity past offices, conference rooms, and metal crank stacks painted the color of vanilla ice cream.

"We've squeezed in multiple stories of material here in the annex," Pauline said. "Books, videos, maps, etc. We specialize in diaries, journals, correspondence, and memoirs written by military figures, most of them unpublished."

"And all of it about warfare," Trinity said.

"Not all of it. Military figures have private lives like everybody else, so a good deal of their writings involves their acquaintances, loved ones, and their own personal—sometimes quirky—aspirations that they suppressed during their military careers."

"The human drama—it makes a cynic wish that universal entropy would hurry up and get here," Trinity said. "Will I have access to everything?"

"No, some government papers remain classified, and some of the memoirs are stamped with a future date set by the authors for public viewing."

"If this is the annex, what is the original library like? I tried to get in, but the door was locked, and there was a sign."

"Yes, I was watching."

"I know. I like being watched," Trinity said.

"Really?" There was a long pause when neither spoke. Finally, Pauline said, "Follow me, I'll show you the tower room."

There was no divider between the two areas except a curtain where you would normally find double doors. It reminded me a little of the drapery separating Uncle Oggie's office from the bedroom in his school-bus abode. Pauline pushed the curtain aside, and Trinity entered a different world. There was no ceiling as such. The dark wood walls seemed to rise up, close in, and disappear into a shaft of broken light, a phenomenon created by sky lights at the top of the spire.

The first-floor level was dominated by old style dark wooden bookshelves built into the walls. Here and there were oil paintings of war scenes. Later, Trinity told me her first sense awareness of the place was the smell of tobacco: "It was like walking into a Victorian era English men's club of smokers and whiskey sippers."

There was something odd about the books, all the same size. The background color of the spines of every volume was identical, colored olive drab. My attention shifted to book ladders on tracks that ran along bookshelves on octagonal walls. I pictured myself as a 12-year-old climbing a ladder to the top of this beanstalk of light to discover a book, say, *Swiss Family Robinson*.

"It's a magnificent space," Trinity said.

"Yes, and at one time the entire mansion looked like this, without these particular volumes of course," said Pauline. "The annex was gutted and rebuilt to serve as a modern library, except for this room, per order of our founder Sir Gwain Stanton."

Trinity pulled one of the books off a shelf and it disappeared from view of the Zeno-Cam. Trinity cracked it open. Returned the book to its place. Grabbed another. Opened it. The mocking laugh.

"Yes, I already figured, it's all the same book. What I don't know is how many?" Trinity asked.

"Yes, twenty-two thousand, three hundred and nineteen," Pauline said.

Trinity held the opened book in front of the Zeno-Cam so I could see it. The title was in olive drab letters on a plain white background, *A Life of Caliber: The Autobiography of Sir Gwain Stanton*.

"What's the difference between an autobiography and a memoir?" Trinity asked.

"While there is some crossover, an autobiography focuses on known facts, often with supported documentation, a memoir is one's recollection of the facts and events."

"As a vain person myself I can relate to the sadness behind Sir Gwain's act. What happened?"

"When our founder wrote his autobiography, he was determined to have a best-seller. Alas, the book buyers didn't cooperate, so Sir Gwain bought out the first edition to create a best-seller for a week and here they are."

Pauline grabbed one of the books and handed it to Trinity.

"I will read it, though not twenty-thousand times." Trinity said.

It was a typical smart-alecky Trinity Landrieu comment and a mistake that would alienate his source, I thought. But I was wrong. Pauline laughed out loud before she settled in with a stock answer.

"You may read the book, but it has to be here. According to Mr. Stanton's will, the volumes are not to leave this room."

"Fine with me," Trinity said. "I like this space. Could I conduct my interview with you here, too?"

"I was going to suggest the same thing, so if you will pardon me a bit of American word play, we are on the same page."

Trinity responded with a ha-ha, but there was no mockery in it.

"Do you mind if I smoke," Pauline said. "This is the only room in the library where smoking is permitted, because ..." Pauline paused to encourage Trinity to guess.

"Because Sir Gwain Stanton was a smoker. He bought a smoking room. Did he buy his knighthood, too?"

"He never had a formal knighthood. It was an honorary title. Have a seat." Pauline pointed to a couch in front of a low table with curved legs. Trinity sat down. Pauline reached into a drawer and removed a silver lighter and a blue pack of Gauloises cigarettes marked "Smoking Kills."

Trinity must have made a gesture that I couldn't see from the Zeno-Cam, because Pauline removed one of the cigarettes from the pack and gave it to Trinity who took it off camera.

"You're a smoker?" Pauline said.

"Only during extraordinary occasions with extraordinary company."

I heard a whoosh sound as Pauline flicked the lighter and lit Trinity's cigarette, then her own. Pauline walked away, but the camera didn't follow her. She returned with a bottle of Tito's Handmade Vodka.

"American vodka, you've betrayed your country," Trinity said.

"The transgressions we perpetrate to pleasure ourselves," Pauline said.

She poured two shots in two-ounce stainless steel shot cups. Then she sat with crossed legs beside Trinity on the couch. The two women smoked, sipped Tito, and chatted. Below is my edited version of the interview, minus most of the small talk.

"Is Gerard Stanton mentioned in Sir Gwain's autobiography?" Trinity asked.

"Oh, so Gerard is the reason you are here."

Trinity showed a picture of the dog tag to Pauline from her phone.

"This is quite a find. We have the other one in our collection, which came our way via an anonymous donor. Would you care to donate yours?"

"Perhaps upon conclusion of our work. Do you have any information regarding the donor?"

"All I can tell you is that it arrived in November of 1963 with a Los Angeles postmark. How did you acquire yours?" Pauline asked.

"The dog tag was found at the scene of what officially was described as an accidental drowning on a small pond in New Hampshire in 1978."

"New Hampshire, that's in Massachusetts, correct?"

"Yes, I can confirm that rumor," Trinity said.

It wasn't until I heard them laugh in unison that I realized they were sharing a joke.

"You think Gerard was at the scene?" Pauline asked.

"Unknown. What was the relationship between Gerard and the founder?"

Pauline thought for a moment, and said, "Gerard was Mr. Stanton's grandson."

"Was? You mean Gerard is dead?"

"We talk about him as if he's dead, but we don't really know. He is officially a missing person."

"Why is there so little about the Stantons on the Internet? It's as if all the Stantons are dead, or anyway dead to the world." Trinity said.

"Actually, they are all dead, but even when they were alive, they kept a . . . what is the phrase?"

"A low profile," Trinity said. "You knew that. You just wanted to hear it from me."

Pauline giggled. "I wanted to see your lips wiggle."

Trinity made a puckering sound, which elicited another giggle from Pauline. "Tell me some more about the Stantons," Trinity said.

"The Stanton family has a distinguished history of service in the military going back to Europe well before your bourgeois revolution. They were English loyalists in 1776, Confederates in 1861, supporters of the Kaiser in 1914, and Nazi sympathizers in 1939, though they did finally switch—more or less—to the Allied side in World War II, if just in time."

"Had a knack for picking the wrong causes," Trinity said.

"Acquired a fortune anyway in the arms trade," Pauline said. "Sir Gwain's son was a disappointment to our founder and died young, but grandson Gerard was, in the parlance of your extravagant metaphors, the apple of his eye—handsome, very bright, assertive, and destined for a distinguished career in the armed forces."

"Do you have a picture? I couldn't find one online."

"Yes, I do, the last one taken before he disappeared. I will upload it to your phone."

Pauline showed Trinity an image from the library photo collection on her phone. I couldn't see the portrait from Trinity's body camera, but later Trinity emailed me a sepia of a good-looking young Army lieutenant in uniform who bore a vague resemblance to Humphrey Bogart in the early years before the Captain Queeg twitch.

"He looks like a poster boy of the perfect American soldier," Trinity said.

"Well, he was."

"Until."

"Until he was court-martialed for disobeying orders that resulted in his men being killed. He was the only survivor. Some circumstantial evidence was presented in his trial that he deserted his men to save his own epidermis."

"A practical-minded man?" The mocking laugh.

"He was sentenced to prison, but jumped bail and absconded with a small fortune from the Stanton fund. He hasn't been seen since. If he's still alive he'd be in his twilight years."

Later, after Trinity and Pauline dined at Pogacha's in Bellevue on flat bread and greens, Pauline brought Trinity to her place in a modest residential neighborhood. Her house was small, California-style 20th century modernist with redwood siding, a shed roof, big windows, and many plantings in hand-thrown ceramic pots. Her tastes were eclectic and quirky. She collected African tribal masks, Russian nesting dolls, French calligraphy, and English equestrian paraphernalia, including a dozen or so riding crops hanging on walls from leather thongs.

"You own a horse?" asked Trinity.

"Yes, I stable him in the country. I see him on weekends. He is my passion."

"I love your stuff, but it looks like you have identity issues," Trinity said.

"Do not we all?"

"What's your horse's name?"

"Bitcoin," Pauline said.

"Named for the currency you bought him with. I like the concept."

The women went into a bedroom dominated by a queen-sized bed, mirrors, and equestrian artwork on the walls.

"This will be your room for the night," Pauline said. "Let me show you the bath." She led Trinity into a spacious bathroom that featured a horse watering trough that served as a bathtub.

There was a long pause, and I could see that Pauline was looking somewhere in the distance.

With a touch of humor but without the usual sardonic tone, Trinity said, "There's a lot of room in that tub."

"Yes, it is an awful waste of water for one person."

"But two, two would be just right."

"Yes, yes it would."

Trinity said something in Russian, and then followed up in English, "I hope my Russian doesn't offend you."

"It's not bad. You talk with a St. Petersburg accent."

"I was there as a child in the…" Trinity said something in Russian.

"Yes, the notorious psychiatric orphanage leftover from Soviet days."

"It was my home for the first five years of my life where I was treated healthfully if not humanely."

"I'm sorry," Pauline said.

"I was touched only to be moved, fed, and inspected. My grandparents brought me to the states, and I forgot most of the Russian I'd learned, but some of it came back to me when I spent some time in St. Petersburg in my university's foreign studies program. I'm moved by the emotion in the diction. I read somewhere that the author Vladimir Nabokov said, 'English for my head, French for my ear, and Russian for my heart.' Have you given your heart to anyone?"

"Not lately," Pauline said, and followed with a phrase in French that my phone translated as, "You have my ear."

Trinity clicked off the Zeno-Cam, and I was back on my porch in Shinbone Shack listening to water lapping on the shore.

Hornpout Interlude

LATE THAT NIGHT on my porch bed I was awakened by the "doink!" on my phone alerting me that I had a text message from Trinity. "Taking vacation to read Stanton book et cetera ha-ha bye-bye." The news left me with an odd, parental mixed feeling of pride, alarm, admiration, not to mention, curiosity. What happened in that bathtub? I wondered how a lover might relate to Trinity. As a woman? As a man? In some kind of physical relationship that I was unfamiliar with?

I remembered my dad talking about his family's religion that included three persons in one God—the Father, the Son, and the Holy Ghost. He used to joke that religion was the funniest of conspiracy theories. I thought at the time that the three persons in one God might make sense, but I didn't believe myself smart enough to understand the connectivity.

Now I was thinking that if the Father represented the male part of God, maybe the Holy Ghost represented the female part, while the Son was a gender transitional figure. If that was the case, the Blaise God of old French Canada actually was a transgendered supreme being. Since God created everything, how could it be otherwise? It occurred to me then that I never would have had that thought before I met Trinity Landrieu, a person whose gender to this day remains unknown to me.

It was 2 a.m., a warm sultry night, and I couldn't get back to sleep. Since I did not hear wave action from my bedroom porch, I knew without look-ing there would be no wind on the pond, and the surface would be calm. I decided to go fishing for hornpout, which is the local name for a small bottom feeder fish that inhabited ponds and lakes in my part of the world and that was most active at night.

It was an ugly creature, uniformly drab without colorful markings and slimy to the touch with a sharp bony protrusion sticking out of a blunt head with an eye on each side. Grab the fish wrong, and that horn could give you a nasty cut. The fish was also surprisingly pleasing to the palate.

Hornpout were easy to catch with worms, but I didn't have any worms handy, and I wasn't about to grub around in the dark on the ground. So, I grubbed around in my collection of my own hand-tied flies until I found a squiggly thing I built with two little hooks and some plastic ribbons back in the day. I had named this little whimsy the Anarchist, after Jason Hinkley. I owned two fly rods and I chose the one rigged with a sinking line and a short leader.

The moon was out, not quite full, so it didn't appear to look like a disk in the sky, but like a potato trying and failing to attain the status of a beach ball. That thought reminded me that Sadie used to call Harry Cromwell Potato Head behind his back. Of dad's friends, Harry was the only one for whom she felt any loathing. "He's one of those people that the more you know him, the more he scares you," Sadie had said.

Of the four Korean war buddies, two were dead. Maurice Landrieu was apparently thriving, indeed financing our investigation. What about Harry? I made a mental note to try to contact Harry in the off chance he might have come in contact with Gerard Stanton in their mutual war.

In the daytime I hardly noticed the sounds my little rowboat made, but on a windless night the clunking of oar locks and the gentle splashes of oars on disturbed water might have fitted well into one of those crazy twentieth-century atonal symphonies.

On that particular night I happened to go out during an hour when the mosquitos were taking a break from their mission to torment creatures that depend on blood flow for life. Even the smell of the night was different from the smell of the day, muskier, more personal, fecund.

I caught six hornpout on my Anarchist fly. Decades earlier back when I had caught a bunch of hornpout but didn't know what to do next, my father had taught me a secret to hornpout fishing that his father had taught him.

"Successful hornpouting is not in the catching or the cooking, which is easy," G.I. Joe had said. "It's in the cleaning. It is so unpleasant and messy to skin and clean an eight-inch hornpout the conventional way that there's no point in fishing for them. Now, watch."

My father grasped a fish, hand around the top of the blunt head, index and middle finger on each side of the horn. He made a twisting motion with his wrist and forearm and miraculously the head, guts, and skin slipped off leaving only the meat and spine. I tried the trick, but I couldn't do it and my father laughed at my efforts.

"You'll get it eventually, if you don't quit. You're not a quitter, are you?" he said. He was right. I did learn the technique, but only after much practice and after dad had died.

For a moment I fell into an ether zone. I grasped a hornpout and did the fish-clean trick. And then the demonic voice.

Good work, my boy, good work: He never said anything like that to you, did he?

I'm just a sixty-something man still searching for the right bait to catch up to myself.

You mixed your metaphor. You use bait to catch, not to catch up.

Who are you?

I am the returning host.

What are you trying to tell me?

No answer.

Next morning after a breakfast of hornpout sautéed in butter and olive oil with my own homemade bread, I hauled out my fly-tying kit and with crow feathers, blue jay feathers, Christmas tree tinsel, and colored yarn made years ago from a lamb raised by my adopted daughter, Piety, I created a fishing fly that I named the Pauline Alvar, a large, gaudy, attractor-streamer fly, a delight to the eye whether it caught fish or not.

My imagination was starting to run away from me. I was worried that Trinity had gotten involved with the wrong people. Even that she was in danger. I texted her and got an automatic response: "on break." I tried to reach Pauline through her telephone number at the library, but there was no answer, not even a voicemail. I contacted other people at the library. They all said the same thing. Miz Alvar was unavailable.

Троица

ANOTHER DAY WENT BY without word from Trinity. I was so worried about her that I emailed my report on the Russian connections to Maurice Landrieu along with my concerns about Trinity's whereabouts, asking if he had heard from her. He responded right away.

"Sounds like the Trinity I know and love," he wrote. "She disappears from time to time, often for weeks. She's like G.I. Joe that way. I trust she'll come out okay. Hang in there. I'll let you know if I hear anything."

"It might help if I knew a little more about Trinity," I texted.

"Fair enough. When Olivia and I married we never planned on having a family. We were a New York bohemian couple, or so we fancied ourselves. Also, I had mental health issues at the time. I didn't think I had the right stuff to be a father. Hell, I didn't think I had the right stuff to be anything. My art career certainly was not producing the kind of work that neither I nor the art world considered of value. And then, wouldn't you know it, Olivia became pregnant. She examined her options and we decided to keep the baby.

"Our son? What a son he was! From birth until his untimely death I swear he was the good soldier that his father never managed to be. He reminded me in some ways of your dad. He was a Green Beret and then chosen for a special unit that to this day I don't know the composition of nor its mission. Well, to make my long story short and not so sweet, on one of those special missions he fell in love with a girl in Kazakhstan. He insisted on marrying her and bringing her to the states, but that got him into trouble with the brass. They transferred him to Iraq where he was killed only weeks before Trinity's mother died giving birth.

"It took Olivia and I years to learn that the mother had died, and the child was sent to a special facility in St. Petersburg that treated and studied Chernobyl babies.

"The child didn't have a birth certificate name, but we found that she was referred to in documents as Троица which roughly translated into English, comes out as Trinity. The name clicked with us. It's no coincidence that this radiation mutant has the same name as the location of the first atomic bomb explosion, the Trinity site in New Mexico.

"By that time, I'd started my own business, so we had some money to spread around. We were able to bring Trinity home. She had just turned five.

"I want you to know, Junie, that I appreciated your long missive in your previous report. During this down time, you might want to look back into your past and include that history in future reports. The writing will keep your mind busy and the more we know the better our chances will be of identifying the components that will make those connections we all seek."

Maurice Landrieu's words inspired me to get to work. I ransacked my journal, and for the next three days put together those thoughts written by a younger Junie into a story that conveyed some meaning relative to our current inquiry.

The Grace Pond Monk

AFTER DAD DIED, and after an episode I am not ready to share, mom moved us out of the Keene apartment and into Shinbone Shack. That was the spring of 1969.

Let me now jump to an unusually warm early October evening in 1970 when my mother dropped me off at the local teen hangout. I was fifteen at the time. You'd order your food and dine in your vehicle or at picnic tables under an awning which featured a view of a field and a cow barn, abandoned when farmer Alphonse Kinsey sold his Holsteins, built Car-Hop Heavan (sic), sold Car-Hop Heavan (sic), ditched his wife of forty years, and moved to Las Vegas with one of the carhops.

Yes, I know "heaven" is misspelled, and of course everybody laughed when the sign went up to advertise the new business. What farmer Kinsey observed was that the mistake brought people into the parking lot, so he never corrected it and neither did the new owners. Farmer Kinsey may have been the butt of jokes, but he was laughing all the way to the casino.

I had just finished my hot fudge sundae when I encountered William "Wiley" Brewster. I knew him by reputation as a football player who had grown up on the east side in Keene. I was at an age that I hadn't caught up with myself. In my mind, like my father, I was rugged but somewhat undersized. But in fact, I was at the end of a growth spurt that set me at six feet tall, 170 pounds, a good size for my generation. I had developed a habit that I was unaware of, looking longingly at girls.

I was lost in this pain/pleasure when I heard a sardonic voice over my shoulder. "Hey, momma's boy, you like the goddamn stuff?" Everybody in the parking lot knew I was staring at Wiley Brewster's girlfriend—except me. I mean I knew I was focused on her. I didn't realize it was so blatantly obvious.

Wiley shoved me and I shoved him back. At this point Gary Hoover, a senior at our high school and the starting quarterback, intervened.

"Hey, guys," he said, "if you want to fight this is not the place for it. They'll call the cops."

Wiley and I went down into the field behind the old cow barn along with Gary and some other guys, our spectators, no girls allowed, and engaged in a classic fistfight where unconsciously and ceremoniously we followed the fight rules for teenage boys of that time period in our region. No hitting below the belt, no hitting when a man is down, no scratching, kicking, groin kneeing, biting, eye-gouging.

Wiley was built like a concrete building block, and he was stronger than I was, though not by much. I was quicker, though not by much. In stamina and determination, we were even-steven. The result was a fight that dragged on for quite a long time and that ended with two exhausted and bloody boys who decided to call it a draw.

After that, Wiley and I became best friends. In fact, we were so often seen together that we were known collectively as Wiley 'n Coyote. They called me Coyote at Keene High, because I lived in the woods. In fact, I could hear coyotes howling at night, but they had no interest in raiding Sadie's garden, so we rarely saw them, and then only on the pond on the ice. After I got my driver's license Wiley and I tooled around in my dad's GMC truck and talked about many serious things, though now decades later, I couldn't tell you what those "things" were.

The girl? In those days she was known as the Anita Ekberg of Keene High School, and she was destined to play important roles not only in Wiley's history, but in mine.

≈

One evening after supper at the drop-down table, my mother said, "There's something I want to talk to you about."

I nodded, but I was thinking, oh-oh, I don't like her tone of voice.

"Before dad died, did he have a heart-to-heart with you?" she said.

"What do you mean?" I said.

"You know, tweet-tweet, buzz buzz."

"Oh, you want to know if he talked to me about the . . ." I couldn't get the words out.

"The birds and the bees."

"He didn't say anything."

"That reprobate! He told me he was going to." My mother laughed at the look on my face. "Don't worry, I'm not going to get into male and female anatomy. I expect you've picked up the necessary knowledge around the schoolyard. But there's an awful lot more to male-female relationships and maybe I can help answer questions you might have."

"I don't want to think about it."

"I've noticed that you look at girls."

"You noticed that I notice?"

"Yes, it's normal for boys to be interested in girls, but you shouldn't stare. It makes them feel uncomfortable and it's not polite."

"Remember when I came home all bruised after the fight with Wiley, well, it was about staring too long at his girl."

"Are you more careful now?"

"I don't know."

"What do you mean?"

"I never know the expression on my face, because I can't see it."

"Do you talk to girls in school?"

"Not really."

"Tell me this. Would you rather know lots of girls and have lots of relationships or concentrate your libido on one girl?"

"What's a libido?"

My mother laughed again. She had a way of laughing at me without mockery or malice. She seemed to appreciate me as a comedy act.

She got up from the table, fetched our giant dictionary that we kept with the encyclopedias, and we looked up "libido." I still remember one of the definitions "PSYCHOANALYSIS: the energy of the sexual drive as a component of the life instinct." Defining libido with those words seemed to me a way of defining a feeling without defining the feeling.

"Mom, I don't know what to think about when I think about girls."

"Junie, you're doing the right thing for yourself by not going out with girls at this time in your life. There will come a day, but for the time being think of yourself as a monk in training."

The idea cheered me up. "The Grace Pond Monk," I said.

"The Grace Pond Monk—I like that," my mother said. "You have a knack with words. Real monks and nuns have a tryout period and eventually they decide whether the celibate life is right or wrong for them. So, think of this time in your life as a tryout. And, oh, one more thing. It's okay to keep doing what you've been doing to relieve tension."

My embarrassment must have gone neon, because my mother laughed for the third time in our conversation. "I'll tell you a little secret," she whispered. "Girls do the same thing."

I don't know if this little talk was my mother's intention to make me commit to an extended period of celibacy, but that's how it worked out. I could not have articulated it at the time, but I was waiting to mature and for some kind of moment with a future somebody.

Red Shift

AROUND THE SAME TIME PERIOD of my fight with Wiley Brewster, Pete Shaughnessy called my mother at her office and said the three surviving vets were having a reunion at Winding Brook Lodge in Keene and could they come to Shinbone Shack for a visit? Pete had something he wanted to talk about to my mother. An opportunity, he said.

Sadie was suspicious of anything coming from Pete or any of the "Army cohorts," but her curiosity got the best of her and she invited Pete, Maurice, and Harry for dinner. She served fish stew with her own home-baked bread. I was proud that I had caught the fish. The men sat around the drop-down table, drank Schaefer beer in my father's honor, toasted him, and yakked about old times for a while. I learned that Maurice had given up painting and started his own business, which was off to a good start. Pete was "looking for a high position in government," emphasis on the word "high," which drew a laugh from his Army buddies. Harry was still selling guns to dealerships in the Northwest quadrant of the country.

"I love scared people. They buy firearms and pay my salary," he said.

He'd married again, but this time around, it only lasted a month.

"I guess you married the wrong women," Sadie said, droll.

"No," Harry said, "they married the wrong man."

There was an intimacy that these men shared that to me in my teenage years seemed mysterious and thrilling. I wanted that experience of deep friendship based on profound experiences. I thought that the only way to get them was to go to war.

I went down to the pond to bring some water up to heat on the wood stove to do the dishes, which I cleaned with Maurice, who wiped. I could see that Pete and Sadie were deep in conversation, while Harry lay on the couch and napped. When he woke, he called me over to the couch. He gave me a ten, and said, "Don't tell your mother."

A hellgrammite seemed to crawl along my spine. Harry used the same words—-"don't tell your mother"—that my father had used on a fateful day he broke down in tears in front of me.

A week after the "Army cohorts" left, my mother told me that we were in for some changes on the property. She looked at me with mischief in her eyes and said, "Red Shift, Pete's commune, is coming to Grace Pond."

At the time, I did not know what to think. Maybe my mother had been swayed by persuasive arguments presented by Pete Shaughnessy, or maybe she had become a hippie, or maybe she had gone nuts. Later I learned that my mother had been swayed by economics. The Red Shift commune was well-funded, though the source was unclear. Sadie never got around to sharing any figures with me, but she did say, "They made me an offer I couldn't refuse." Red Shift signed a ten-year lease of our property that included the land, the shore front, and the barn, but not Shinbone Shack and not Sadie's garden.

Along with most local people, I assumed that the phrase "Red Shift" was a reference to left wing politics, and maybe in part it was, but when I took a physics class in high school, I figured out that the main meaning of Red Shift related to an expanding universe.

Rent from the new tenant allowed Sadie to reduce her work hours at the law office and enroll at Keene State College.

"College? It can't be all that hard," she not only repeated those words numerous times, but she also drew a poster featuring her motto and tacked it on one of the logs on the wall in Shinbone Shack.

Sadie started to develop a new life of her own, so I didn't see as much of her as I used to, which for a teenage boy with his own wheels, is ideal. So, I was content with this arrangement? Not quite. It seemed to me that my mother got over the death of her husband much too fast. Though I wouldn't have admitted it at the time, I wanted her to continue suffering.

Funny thing about grief: it hangs over the bereaved longer, maybe permanently when there is unfinished business, as inevitably there would be between a 14-year-old, unformed boy and his trick-or-treat father. You parents out there reading this, don't be cruel by dying when your children are in their formative years.

Red Shift arrived April 22, 1971, the first anniversary of the first Earth Day, a dozen men and seven women in a school bus with California plates.

The men wore long hair, scraggly beards, blue jeans and leather vests, the women jeans or long skirts, beads, frilly blouses but no bras, flowers in their hair, no make-up. One of the women was pregnant. With two exceptions the Red Shift communards, as they called themselves, were in their late teens and early twenties. The exceptions were Pete and the leader of Red Shift, Osgood "Uncle Oggie" Stone, who arrived in his own car, a blue Thunderbird.

Uncle Oggie was almost as tall as Pete, but built more solidly. He had long blond hair, a full beard, and blue eyes always on high beam. He carried himself with military bearing. It was as if General Patten and Timothy Leary had merged into one being who had grown a Zeusian beard. Even on that first day when Red Shift arrived, and even though I was not a particularly insightful youth, I understood that Osgood Stone had charisma that drew young people to his commune.

The communards were boisterous, joyful, and at the same time belligerent and smug. They brought out something contradictory in me. I wanted to jump in and join them, while at the same time, I wanted to run away from them, or better yet, gun them down.

That first night I watched from Shinbone Shack as they built a bonfire and danced around it. I heard guitar music and the sweet voices of women singing "we shall overcome" that made me realize all I was missing by not having a girlfriend, not belonging to a group, not being able to envision a future for myself, and the other et cetera's of juvenile self-pity.

Through the spring and summer of 1971, Red Shift converted my father's barn into a kitchen shack, dining hall, dormitory, and crash pad for visitors. They built outhouses and a yurt. In the years that followed, they installed a septic system and constructed five 10-by-10-foot cabins and a yurt.

The hippie school bus was converted to serve as Uncle Oggie's "office" and living quarters. Private cars were allowed for visitors but not for communards, but Uncle Oggie was very generous in allowing the Thunderbird to be used by the communards for shopping and joy rides. Red Shift created huge vegetable gardens, root cellars, and compost piles. Pond water was hauled into a cistern to flush toilets. Some of the communards drank the pond water "raw" and others boiled it to make coffee or tea.

There was a communal canoe that Uncle Oggie reserved for himself during his morning meditation. The communards had cleared a space in front of the huge maple tree on Whirlybird Island and built what Uncle Oggie called "my little pagoda," just four pine tree posts and a Japanese-style hip roof, no walls, inspired, as he eventually admitted, by Sadie's open-air cooking shack. On one of the posts, he'd hung a quilt in a plastic bag that he'd take out to keep warm when it was cold. He'd canoe out to the island, strip naked, and sit cross-legged on a mat in the center of the pagoda, and, in his words, "Contemplate space itself as it expands the universe into infinity."

When Pete was drunk, he'd mock Uncle Oggie's precious sayings. "Watch while I contemplate space expanding the universe into futility."

Uncle Oggie meditated at the island in all kinds of weather—sunshine, rain, snow, and fog. In winter he cross-country skied to the island on snow and ice. Except in the coldest weather, he always stripped down.

"Someday," Pete would say, "Uncle Oggie will walk on water. Ha-ha."

I admired Uncle Oggie because, while he could pop off at the communards if they displeased him, he never showed any rancor toward Pete. He'd smile and say, "Pete, have another beer and tell us more war stories. Was it as cold on the 38th parallel as Grace Pond?"

Sadie ordered me not to fraternize with Red Shift. "No drugs, no booze, no hanky-panky with girls—who knows what kind of diseases they're carrying. I've given these people a ten-year lease on the property to do as they please, but one of the stipulations in the contract is that they're not to give you wacky tobacky or any of that other stuff. Keep your distance."

In my Grace Pond Monk persona, I stayed away from Red Shift intoxicants and women, but I did not keep my distance. I was curious about Red Shift and its belief system, and I wanted to know more about those crazy young people. Once the novelty wore off, what kept me coming back was the commune's flashy founder, Osgood "Uncle Oggie" Stone, who almost immediately went out of his way to engage with me. He would invite me into his school bus office and lecture me. I loved listening to him.

"Red Shift believes that not just American but world institutions are outmoded," he'd say, repeating lines he preached to the communards. "National pride leads to useless wars. Democracy is a sham, because corporations exercise control in back rooms through bribes, coercion, and the mesmerizing influence of products. Western religion justifies exploitation of Third World countries and undermines their traditions, while science corrupts their core beliefs. Traditional marriage and so-called family values stultify creativity and human potential. As for race relations, get out of Darby and see for yourself. We believe in the freedom to love and honor, but never to obey without critical thinking."

In particular, Red Shift opposed the Vietnam War, denounced police brutality, criticized corporate and government policies that isolated and impoverished people of color and hillbilly whites. Red Shift promoted a peaceful revolution to replace Capitalism and Socialism with a new, grander but unspecified-ism.

It was relatively easy for even this clueless high school boy to figure out what Red Shift was against. It was harder for me to pin down what they were for. "Human potential" was a buzz phrase I heard a lot, though I never quite figured out what it meant. I was attracted to their idea that simple living close to nature was good, because I knew it was good for this Grace Pond Monk, but I didn't know enough to tuck that idea into an ideology.

"Ecology," the trendy word of those days, resonated with me, but I didn't know what I was supposed to do with it. To me it was just a scientific way to refer to Mother Nature, though if I had thought about it, which I didn't, I would have questioned just what was meant by the phrase "Mother Nature." I heard a lot of random talk about Capitalism and Socialism among the Red Shift communards, but I didn't know in any deep way the differences between the two -isms. I thought McDonald Restaurants were socialistic because the food and architecture were regimented, and the employees wore uniforms.

The Red Shift population increased rapidly at the beginning and then ebbed and flowed. While the members appeared committed to the commune, they varied in their beliefs. Some were self-described revolutionaries, some were West Coast left-over flower children from the sixties, some were druggies, some were Christian born-agains, but many were just sad drifters from broken homes. What they all had in common was dependence on the founder of Red Shift, Osgood Stone.

Over the next five years some of the original members would leave and be replaced by other hippie types. A huge number of visitors came to Red Shift, some to learn, some to teach, and maybe most, to party. The commune movement of the 1960s and 1970s is often regarded as an upper middle-class movement of spoiled youth. In fact, many of the members came from backgrounds with few financial resources. The commune offered them the comfort of like-minded folks that they lacked in their families. There were more men than women, and most of the men were draft dodgers of one kind or another and occasional messed-up-in-the-head Vietnam Veterans.

Uncle Oggie, however, belonged to my father's generation. He had much to say about Red Shift but nothing about himself. Sadie said he liked it that way. Part of his power as a leader was in the mystery of his origins. I didn't know until a few years into their lease that to join Red Shift straight women and gay men were charmed, or perhaps coerced, into having submissive sex with the Red Shift leader.

Uncle Oggie didn't sell Red Shift as permanent. It was, he said, "A ten-year experiment of human potential out of which we will create a new order." The communards were encouraged to expand the capabilities of their minds by experimenting with psychedelic drugs.

Uncle Oggie would repeat over and over again, "Live simply and close to the land. No TVs, no power grid, no newspapers. Do not join a formal religion. Find God within yourselves. Our values here at Red Shift include gardening, building, group conversing, and dancing. Oh, and lest we forget, loving. Ever-expanding universal free love."

Uncle Oggie was a great talker, but words failed him when he wrote—or maybe he was just lazy, which was Sadie's theory. I found I could please Uncle Oggie by coming up with handy phrases that he would post on the community bulletin board in the barn and by taking dictation and typing out the Red Shift newsletter on his standard Underwood manual typewriter. My role as a scribe for Red Shift began when Uncle Oggie helped me with my high school studies by teaching me to type.

Uncle Oggie showed me how to change the ribbon, introduced me to the qwerty keyboard, and demonstrated how to set the margins and place a paper in the crease behind the platen. I have a pleasant memory of Uncle Oggie standing behind me, hand on my shoulder while I sat at the desk he installed in the Red Shift bus when he converted it to his office, my fingers on the keys for the first time.

I also helped out with the commune's building projects, renovation of the barn, cabin building, even the yurt. A few years later, I was proud to inspire the construction of a bent-sapling sculpture that I christened "The Bucky: from Bucky Beaver to Buckminster Fuller."

Where many of the men and some of the women of Red Shift kept their hair in pony tails when they were working—gardening, gathering firewood, building crude cabins—Oggie kept his long blond hair clean, brushed and flowing over his shoulders all the time. The beard remained full, but trimmed, as if he were auditioning for a part in a toga movie. "He dyes it, hair and beard," Sadie insisted, but I couldn't bring myself to believe her.

Uncle Oggie was always "on." He didn't converse, he pontificated. Even so, I admired him very much, because he had a way of making me feel as if the knowledge he imparted was just for me.

Notes from my journal where I stitched together lines from various Uncle Oggie rants to his followers:

"They say we believe in free love, but that is not an accurate representation of our profound incongruence with the powers that be. We believe NOT in free love, for love is never free; we believe in the freedom to love whoever we wish to love and whoever wishes to reciprocate that love. You say if everyone is making love with everyone else, how will the children know the fathers? I say unto you that the fathers are merely the sperm donors. The fathers have little function in our society.

"Blood will tell, you say. If not the fathers then, who will the children look to for leadership, accurate information, and inspiration? The daughters will look to their mothers. And the sons, you ask, what of the sons? The sons will find their teachers in their maternal uncles. In our free-love revolution, a child may not know his father, but he knows his mother and he knows her brothers.

"No uncles, you say? I say let every man be an uncle to every child. That is the foundation upon which this experiment in communal living rests. I say, let the mothers and the uncles raise the children, for the fathers are irrelevant. Think of me, dear ones, as your most devoted uncle, for I pledge to be the uncle of all uncles to you."

Uncle Oggie reminded me of my father in the way he rambled on, but he was so much more self-assured, not to mention grammatical. My father would take off on some subject, and sometimes he made sense, but he lacked conviction. He professed never to believe anything, and of course such pronouncements sabotaged any wisdom he might have imparted. He covered up his insecurities with his corny sense of humor.

His pal Pete would say, "Joe, you're full of bat guano," and my father, amazingly to me, would agree with a bashful smile.

By contrast, Uncle Oggie came across as a man who was always sure he was right. He scorned any criticism thrown in his direction. The few that dared take him on were soon drummed out of the commune through the tried and true technique of shunning. It was not his words per se, but the apparent deep belief in himself that attracted the communards and me to Uncle Oggie. In my teenage mind I thought anybody so self-confident had to be more right than wrong, and certainly more right than I was.

Uncle Oggie was not what I would consider today a serious reader, but the few texts he did read he read very seriously—*The Mother Earth News*, *The Whole Earth Catalog*, *Living the Good Life*, and the writings of Timothy Leary. Red Shift was anti-war, pro-ecology, back to the land, but above all, "Red Shift is the Old Testament on acid."

The communards lived by a message of the times, "Turn on, tune in, drop out." Routinely, the members of the commune would gather around a bonfire to listen to music, sing, dance, sneak off to have sex, and somewhere in the evening listen to Uncle Oggie hold forth. It was the same "sermon" over and over again.

"When I came of age World War II was underway," he would say. "The Korean War followed, then the Cold War, and now the Vietnam War. There has never been a time in my forty-something years when we were not at war.

"What is the source of all this war, this unhappiness that comes with war? I'll tell you what it is, in a word, history. Human history has infiltrated the DNA of the species. I will confess that war has left its mark on me too, but that is not a story I am ready to tell. But I will give you a hint. On the outside I play the pacifist, but at heart I am an avenging angel.

"It doesn't have to be this way. A new day begins with the suppression of darkness, and dare I say it, with the concordance of the self and a greater power. If you get rid of the darkness, the dawn will come in naturally. Get rid of your formal religion, get rid of your family, get rid of your old ideas of morality. Do not get rid of your friends and feelings. Follow your bird of paradise and she will teach you to fly to the light. How to do this? It's not easy. You have to open your mind, your heart, and your entrails."

At the end of the oration, Uncle Oggie would pass around his own hand-built cannabis peace pipe for everyone to draw a breath from. In these early days of Red Shift, I was a witness to the rituals, but not a participant.

Jason the Anarchist

I FINALLY HEARD FROM TRINITY, audio only, on my phone. "Thanks for the reports, Uncle Cyclops." Same female voice speaking in an East European accent as before.

"You haven't answered my emails—I've been worried sick," I said, in the exact words that I used questioning my daughters and that my mother used questioning me.

"It's complicated. I was hit by a cyber-attack, and was afraid that the hackers would pinpoint the Grace Pond location, so I couldn't transmit without revealing our position."

"Why are they picking on you?"

"It's unclear."

"What is your current location, and how about some video from the car cams?"

"I'm in my RV, an hour or so from La Honda, California. I should arrive just in time for our interview with Jason the Anarchist."

≈

The Hinkley house in La Honda, California, was built of logs, not like the primitive, hand-hewn ones of Shinbone Shack and the Red Shift cabins, but machined like you'd see in a magazine with shiny paper. The house fit very nicely into an upscale neighborhood of five-acre lots, snuggled or maybe smuggled into a clearing of a redwood forest.

The yard was spacious with grass that needed mowing. I had never been to this country, and the view from Trinity's vehicle interested me. In my part of the world there's not much difference at first sight in the color of the grasses in the valleys and the grasses in the hills. In this region the valley grasses were dry, parched, the color of straw but in the uplands of La Honda the earth was moist, and the color of the grass made me think of questions by a forgotten poet writing about a conversation with his mother on her deathbed.

In the Spring
when dad burned the dead grasses,
do you remember that smell?
And the color of the new grass
growing through the black burn scar
after the rain, the brightest green
of the new season?

There was a plastic potting shed and two ruts made by a tractor that led somewhere into the woods behind the house. The driveway/parking lot, which consisted of gravel giving way to grass, included a three-quarter ton pickup truck, the tractor, and two all-wheel-drive compact cars from that continent larger than ours due west. Go west far enough and you've reached the Far East. Zeno, would you resolve this paradox for us?

The last structure in the yard, tucked into the trees, was what appeared to be a school bus that greatly resembled the Red Shift school bus on the Grace Pond property that I, in my perverse nostalgia, had maintained through the years.

Jason's bus had different markings than Red Shift's, some religious stuff, and some homilies from Red Shift—"Live simply and close to the land." "No TVs." "No Newspapers." Also Ken Kesey's evocative line, "La Honda is a slingshot at the sky." A closer look revealed that the bus had never been a bus but was actually a stay-put building designed to look like a hippie school bus, circa 1970s. So then, Jason too, was nostalgic for the old counter-culture days.

Trinity parked her rig in the driveway. When she stepped out of the vehicle I was switched over to her Zeno-Cam. Presently, Jason and two middle-aged, full-figured women came out of the house. The women had long hair tied up in buns, but no make-up. They were dressed in billowing skirts, white cotton blouses, and head gear somewhere between a bonnet and a turban. They looked like extras portraying pioneer women in an Old West movie.

My first thought upon seeing Jason was that time can sure shape-shift a body. The Jason I remembered was rangy with long greasy brown hair, and an asymmetrical scraggly beard. The current Jason had a shaved head, no facial hair, many tattoos, a pot belly, Oprah-styled glasses, a waddle that hung below his chin like a wet diaper, and the forced casual air of a man content with his current station in life, if not with himself.

Trinity had the same sexy female look of her visit to the Stanton Library, though she wore snug jeans instead of hiking shorts.

"Hi, I'm Trinity Landrieu, I called earlier. You must be Jason Hinkley?"

"Yep and this is Ruth and Victoria. Gwendolyn and Cicely are visiting grandchildren in Portola Valley." The women never said a word and melted away toward the rear of the house.

"Join me in my office," Jason pointed to the faux bus.

"There's another wife in the house that didn't come out, right?" Trinity said as they walked toward the "office."

"Yeah, how did you know?" Jason asked.

"Dancing light in one window, then another—she's watching us."

"That's my shy Maid Marian."

"You find it hard to control your wives?"

Jason shook his head. "Technically, they're not wives. You know, the law? But to answer your insipid question: I find it hard enough to control myself that I don't have any control left over for other people."

"I'm not exactly sure what that means, but I like the way insipid tickles my ear," Trinity said.

The office included a kitchenette, futon very much like the Red Shift ones, dresser, old style wooden file cabinet, computer desk, tie-dyed curtains on the windows, a small pellet stove for heat, and a few chairs. The interior, like the exterior, was not a clone of Uncle Oggie's office but it embodied the idea.

"You don't let the wives in here, do you?" Trinity said.

"Not unless it's an emergency, how did you know?"

"Dirty floor, dirty dishes, curtains drooping, sleeping bag askew on the futon, last year's calendar on the wall, no flowers, no family pics. This place doesn't exactly have a woman's touch."

"I think I'm going to like you," Jason said with a nervous chuckle as he opened a drawer in the desk. "What's your preference: mellow, music, glow, gems, gummies, tincture, something else?"

I didn't know what Jason was talking about, but Trinity did. "How about conversational?" she said.

"Of course," Jason said.

82

Jason and Trinity were quiet while they vaped "conversational" marijuana, only talking after they felt the effects.

I listened and took notes. Jason was an elder in a renegade offshoot of the Mormon church that allowed him to have multiple wives. From what I gathered he combined his family background in the Church of Latter-day Saints with his counterculture Red Shift experiences to create his own version of a commune/church. I thought about Uncle Oggie who may or may not have perished in the Jonestown massacre.

"Ask him if he thinks Uncle Oggie drank the Kool Aid," I said to Trinity's ear pods.

Trinity pointed to her body cam and said, "Junie wants to know if you believe that Osgood Stone died at Jonestown?"

After a long pause, Jason said, "No way, he wasn't the follower type." There was something in Jason's voice I couldn't quite nail down. A sudden fear. My fear was he was about to clam up. Trinity heard it, too, and changed the subject.

"You seem to live pretty well without being gainfully employed," Trinity said.

"I would say I live very well. We have a system. Each of the wives holds down a job. I act as property manager. When the kids were growing up, I was the homeroom teacher and school principal."

"You homeschooled your children?"

"Uh-huh."

"You didn't have any trouble with the law?"

"Of course, we had trouble with the law, still on-going, too."

"I find your lifestyle fascinating," Trinity said.

"Let me tell you about my great-great-grandfather Hyrum Hinkley," Jason said, at ease now that he was talking about his family. "He ran a small sawmill in the Wasatch Range of Utah. He had five wives, three of which he married after the church banned polygamy to get in line with the rest of United States. We Hinkley's are a stubborn bunch and old Hyrum, he wasn't about to abandon the women he loved and who loved him, but he didn't know what to do. Well, the wives did, and they came up with a plan.

"Hyrum borrowed money and bought the logging rights for a huge parcel of woods in the Wasatch and established five sawmills in key locations along the rivers. He divorced his wives to satisfy the law, then hired them and placed each one as a manager of one of his sawmills. Hyrum hired himself as superintendent, and he would visit each sawmill once every other week. The business thrived. So did the love lives. You see my point?"

"A wife prefers a husband she sees sparingly and vice versa?" Trinity said.

"You are a little smarty-pants, aren't you?"

"That I am. What's important to you, Jason?"

"Family and church, which are the most important institutions of human culture, but they're flexible."

"I want to talk to him," I said to Trinity.

Trinity handed the earbuds to Jason. "Here, put these on."

"Jason, it's Junie Blaise. Can you hear me?"

"A little tinny, but yeah. How you are doin', man?" Jason, in tone and diction, reverted to his Red Shift days.

"I'm doing fine, Jason. Thanks so much for talking to us. You remember that night on the island when I was initiated and Pete, you know?"

"There are days when I wish I could forget."

"We have reason to believe that there may have been someone else on that island who had something to do with Pete's death."

"Really? Well, that's a big relief to me."

"Is that so? Did you see somebody that night on the island who wasn't Red Shift?"

"I did and I didn't. See, I was pretty wasted that night from Uncle Oggie's freebies. I was wandering around in the blueberry bushes, and I heard voices. I could barely see them through the trees. I thought it had to be Oggie and Pete. They were arguing. But, since you mention it, maybe it was Pete and this other guy, because I recognized Pete's voice, but the other voice was muffled. It was like watching a TV show through a window in somebody else's house. Something happened that I couldn't see clearly. But I got crackles from the audio.

"One of the figures fell or was slammed on the ledge. I could actually hear a crunch against rock. Then no sounds for a while. Then the figures disappeared from view. Then a big splash sound. Later, after Missy found Pete's body, I hallucinated Oggie throwing Pete into the drink. Or maybe I didn't hallucinate. Maybe it's a memory. To this day, I can't find the reality in my head."

"You were young and strong—you could have saved Pete," Trinity said in a j'accuse voice.

"It was the acid—it fooled me," Jason said in a tone that told me his acid trip allowed him to forgive himself.

"Uncle Oggie was like a second father to you, like he was to all of the communards, and you couldn't bear to think of him as a murderer," Trinity said.

Jason seemed to shrink away from Trinity's words. Finally, he said, "After Uncle Oggie disappeared I left Red Shift, quit LSD, quit anarchy, and changed my life."

"You carried around this awful knowledge all these years," Trinity said. "You saw the struggle between two men, but because it was night and because you were pretty blasted and even though you didn't recognize the combatants you assumed the assailant was Osgood Stone. Tell us some more about the voices you heard."

"Pete's voice was obvious. Junie, remember how loud Pete was? But the other voice was low and I couldn't make out the words. Could have been anybody of the male persuasion, but I thought it had to be Uncle Oggie."

"Until now," Trinity said.

Trinity showed Jason the picture of Gerard Stanton in his military uniform, but Jason only shook his head. "I'm done. I don't want to talk anymore."

"What about the other men in the commune or even the women?" asked Trinity.

Jason shook his head, "No way. Look, I got things to do. Back off!"

"OK." Trinity said. "We won't ask any more questions about that night. I do have an off-topic question, which I hope you don't find disrespectful."

"I probably will."

"I'm going to ask it anyway. Let's say we have a population on Polygamy Island of 1,000 men and 1,000 women, the usual more or less fifty-fifty split. If, say, the average man has five wives, as you do, that would require five thousand women. Since there are only a thousand women, the math doesn't work to satisfy everybody. Some of the men will have multiple wives, but others will have no wives. In your religion, do you see this inevitable issue as a natural separation of gay, celibate, and straight men and women, a source of tension and conflict in the society, or a paradox that challenges the math?"

"I dunno. That question is beyond my pay grade. And anyway, I don't care. See, I got the wives." A nervous chuckle.

"The more wives a man accumulates the less need he has for introspection?"

"Yeah—I think that's right. The wives do the introspecting."

"Because they are the ones put under siege by the system?" Trinity said to nobody as she walked out.

How reliable was Jason's story about witnessing a murder while he was tripping? Should Jason, as well as Oggie, be on our suspect list?

On the drive out of La Honda back into the valley, Trinity said, "I have a reservation for a flight to Boston tomorrow with an Uber waiting to take me to Shinbone Shack. I'll arrive for supper, and I'd appreciate some of the fish gumbo."

"Of course. What are you going to do with your camper?"

"Ship it back by rail," Trinity said.

"You make all these arrangements on your phone?"

"Yes. And more. Easy-peasy. Uncle Cyclops, I think it's about time you spill your guts about how you lost that eye."

"Is that relevant?" I asked.

"Maybe. Also, while you're reminiscing, give me something more about Pete and Uncle Oggie. Their character."

"Let me guess. You want something to read on the flight," I said.

"Your powers of inferential logic are becoming more acute, yes."

Pete the Nomad

HERE'S WHAT I WROTE for Junie and Maurice.

Pete would disappear from Red Shift for weeks, sometimes months at a time, but he always came back and usually with a new girlfriend, who was usually too young. He told Sadie and me that Harry Cromwell these days lived entirely on the road in motels along his sales route. Gun sales were climbing steadily, and Harry was making good money. Harry was perfectly happy, he claimed, with no woman, no family, and no permanent address. Pass Landrieu's art business was thriving.

"What kind of art business?" I asked Pete.

"I dunno."

"You don't know the details?"

"Right. I don't like to overwhelm my enchiladas with too much sauce."

Pete returned to Red Shift when he was low on money, booze, and drugs. Uncle Oggie always took him back and reserved one of the cabins for him. In all the time I knew him, Pete pretty much remained in states of mind between feeling good, stoned, drunk, and shit faced. Because Sadie wouldn't allow alcohol in Shinbone Shack he'd hide his beer and Four Roses in our dank crawl space and under rocks outside, because he feared (and rightly so) that the communards would help themselves to his stash. In some former life no doubt Pete was a chipmunk, for he had this remnant instinct to hide his valuables all over the place.

While I honored my pledge to my mother not to use mind-altering substances with the communards, I rationalized that drinking with Pete didn't break the rule, because he had been G.I. Joe's comrade-in-arms. Drinking with Pete was my link to my departed pater.

Pete always made sure Sadie was gone when he'd show up at Shinbone Shack and of course after she left for Tulane University, it didn't matter. We'd sit around on the porch. Pete would give me a beer, and we'd talk.

One day sticks out in my memory. Pete picked up one of the Encyclopedia

Britannica volumes, and said, "This thing is so thick it might stop a bullet from Harry's man licker."

I must have given him my usual gob smacked look, because he laughed. "Man Licker is short for Mannlicher-Schoenauer."

"Oh, yeah, I remember now."

The reference to Harry got me thinking about my father and his Army buddies, "How come you and dad and Pass and Harry are so close?"

"We were in war together—that's not reason enough?"

"Yes, but why you four? You don't have anything in common. Was it something in the war that happened that brought you together?"

Pete was uncomfortable with my question. He seemed to struggle to come up with an answer. Finally, he laughed, a different and less confident laugh than usual.

"We do have two things in common," he said. "We got the gift from the devil to shoot straight, and we got simpatico mental illness from god-all-fucking-mighty."

"No kidding?" I said.

"You think I'm crazy, and you're right, but you don't think your dad is crazy, and Pass and Harry, but you'd be wrong," Pete said.

I gave him a noncommittal look. I was thinking that Pete was talking in the present tense as if my father were still alive.

"Me, the craziness is obvious. Look at me, a man my age acting like a twenty-year-old hippie. I'm not normal, OK, and it shows. Your dad, he's all sweetness and light one day, and the next day sour and dark—right?"

I wanted to disagree, not because I disagreed but because I wanted to defend the dead. But since I didn't know in those days how to argue countervailing positions of accepted norms, I just nodded.

"See, he's hiding his craziness from you and it's a strain." Pete paused, and I could see him struggling to say something. "Hiding his craziness on behalf of you. On behalf of Sadie." He paused.

I looked around, half believing that I'd see G.I. Joe's ghost.

Pete continued in the present tense, "I admire him. The way he fights to control himself to lessen the impact on his loved ones." Pete took a long drink, perhaps to gather his thoughts.

"Pass? You can see him trying to become an artist. He's blessed with all the smarts, talent, and education, but the art thing that happened to him before Korea didn't happen to him after Korea." Pete did something really unusual for him, then. He made the Catholic sign of the cross. "Something is holding him back, and I know what it is, and Harry knows, and G.I. Joe knows . . ." Pete paused for the third time.

"What about Harry? He doesn't seem crazy to me," I said.

Pete threw his head back and laughed without mirth. "Harry? Of the four of us he's the craziest." Pete pointed to his temple and made circling motions with his finger.

"The war, it was something in the war that made you all crazy?"

"Could be, garçon, could be."

Next day, Pete was gone. It was like that with him, an on-again, off-again communard. He left behind a couple bottles of Four Roses in those sneaky chipmunk places. For many nights I nipped away at the booze, alone, on my porch, looking out at the pond in contemplation.

After I'd written that little remembrance it struck me that Maurice Landrieu would know what Pete was talking about. I emailed my question to Maurice, copying Trinity.

Maurice emailed me back right away. "Golden Rule 2, WST."

I messaged Trinity, "What did your grandfather mean by WST, We Stick Together?"

"It means that the four vets made some kind of pact that you won't see shared on Facebook."

The Fourth Death

I DIDN'T REALLY WANT TO REMEMBER my excursion in military life and it's horrifying ending, but I realized I had to. So, I went back and looked over my notes. Here's the compilation I put together for Trinity and Maurice.

In my high school you had to pick sides on the issues of the day. Were you for the Vietnam War or against it? For the boys, the options were: join up, go to college, and get a deferment, take your chances with the draft lottery, or head for Canada. Or maybe you were one of the lucky guys that had a medical condition that would keep you out.

My pal Wiley Brewster was a love-it-or-leave-it kind of patriot. My own position was murky. I was still living with grief for a soldier and parent who died too young and the uncertainties surrounding that death. I saw the world in terms of sunshine and fog. The sunshine was my life as a boy-naturalist, The Grace Pond Monk. Everything else was in a patchy ground fog, including the war on the other side of the world. I had no clue how to find my way. I had no deep beliefs, no certitude. My tendency was to follow the leader: Sadie, Uncle Oggie, Wiley, even Pete. I had no idea how I truly felt about the Vietnam War, nor my possible role in it after I turned 18. That changed with the death of our high school quarterback Gary Hoover, a helicopter pilot and recent graduate of my high school.

I never knew Gary as a friend, but Wiley did. Wiley talked about avenging his quarterback's death and while he was at it saving the free world by joining the military right after high school. Wiley's anger and determination made the war real to him and by extension to me. Maybe if I went to war with Wiley my personal terrible fog of unreality would lift. Maybe loyalty to country and best friend could even make a person feel noble, and nobility could lead you into the sunlight of reality.

I had another private reason for thinking about joining the army that was so shameful I didn't even talk about it with Wiley. I had discovered back when I was fourteen that I could not shoot an animal, but I suspected that I could shoot a human being if that person was shooting at me. I secretly hoped I had the courage to be a killer. Such was my thinking in those days.

I know it sounds crazy that I half-embraced my best friend's pro-war stance and at same time the pacifism of Red Shift. It's the kind of thing you do when you are young and have no real beliefs, no real self.

Sadie was not a touchy-feely kind of mom. We didn't hug or converse much, but when we did talk, I valued her advice. In fact, she acted toward me like a father. She was the man as well as the woman of the house. So, when she broke down, as she did one day, it awed and frightened me.

"I don't know what's worse you getting on the hippie bus with all those druggies or getting on the Army bus with all those druggies," she said, and then she burst into tears.

One of the few times I saw my mother not only cry but fall apart was when I told her I was joining the Army.

In June of 1972, right after I turned 18 and graduated from high school, Wiley and I visited the local Army recruiter. We joined under the "buddy program." We were sent to Fort Dix, New Jersey, assigned to Company F (Roughest Fuckers Alive) for basic training. We were inseparable companions, so much so that Wiley 'n Coyote, how we were known in high school, in basic training turned into Willie and Joe, the Bill Mauldin World War II cartoon characters.

I was delighted. My dad's nickname came from a cartoon character, now me. I thought maybe—just maybe—G.I. Joe would be proud of me.

Most new soldiers don't like Army basic training. I loved it. What did I love? Regular hours. Rapport with my fellow soldiers. Breakfasts of bacon, sausages, scrambled eggs (so what that maybe they were a little chalky), pancakes, grits, toast, coffee. On the firing range with the M-16. Learning the manual of arms. The infiltration course, simulated combat, which I enjoyed. The call of the drill sergeant—ten-hut! Even KP (kitchen police). Marching. How I loved to march in "quick time," Army parlance for taking a 30-inch step. Even today, I'm pretty good at measuring distances as I walk, two steps equal five feet.

I qualified sharpshooter on the rifle range. A sergeant told me I was a natural. Willie and Joe were going to be sent to Fort Hood for advanced infantry training. Looking ahead, I thought I might be sent to sniper school. After advanced infantry training, the Army "buddy program" would terminate. Wiley and I were probably headed for Vietnam. There were a lot of rumors going around: We were going to sign a peace agreement with the North Vietnamese. I hoped not. I was itching for combat. We were going to invade Cambodia or was it Laos? Or maybe we already had, but it was a secret. I didn't care one way or another. I just wanted the war to last long enough that I could be part of it.

The fact was we didn't get much news during the two months of basic training in the summer of 1972, and I hardly paid attention to the news that did come our way. I'd heard all the arguments pro and con about the war, and none of it seemed real to me. What I was obsessed with was the idea of killing. Could I do it? Was I, as I suspected, a coward? A sissy? A fairy? Could this momma's boy rise above his chicken-shit pacifist instincts and become a warrior? I wasn't going to war to protect my country, I was going to war to discover who in my gut I was.

Back in high school Wiley and I used to have serious conversations. We were trying for depths of understanding and feeling. But now that we were in the Army we strived for superficiality. Unconsciously, we tried to become Willie and Joe—do our jobs as soldiers, but cultivated a don't-give-a-flying-fuck attitude. If you knew too much you'd probably get scared, and the worse thing we could imagine, even worse than death in combat, was getting so scared you would panic and lose the respect of your fellow soldiers.

When Wiley and I battled at Kinsey's barn we fought by the unwritten rules of our boyhood. We didn't have a slogan, but if we did it would have been, "Fight fair and in the end you will prevail." It hadn't dawned on us that the Army we had joined did not fight fair. Nor did the other side. Adults, as a rule, did not fight fair, they fought to win. Our friendship served to retard our maturity. We became soldiers at the same time that we remained boys among men.

Upon completion of basic training in September of 1972, we were given ten-day leaves before starting advanced infantry training at Fort Hood, Texas. I promised my mother I'd look up some of my Texas cousins among the locally famous Boyd family. Wiley headed for Oak Street in Keene to be with the Anita Ekberg of KHS.

Much as I had been happy at the decision I'd made to join the Army, there was never a day that I didn't miss Grace Pond, Whirlybird Island, Shinbone Shack, the trees, the critters, my fly rod, my green and gold boat, even you, evil ones: the black flies. Accordingly, I was in an upbeat mood to be back home in Shinbone Shack on Grace Pond, and I plunged into the work I loved. Uncle Oggie had a plan to build a yurt and I volunteered to clear a building site. Uncle Oggie liked to plan, but he rarely did any actual work.

I fetched my favorite tool, my father's Jonsered chainsaw. It started first pull. G.I. Joe used to say that it was bad luck when a chainsaw started with the first pull of the starter cord. Why? I asked him. He didn't supply an answer, just the usual dirty look he would give me when I would ask what he considered to be a stupid question.

I worked steadily for a couple hours. The trees were perfect size for firewood, mixed hardwoods four to eight inches in diameter. One of the many things I liked about burning wood for heat was that picking up a stick of firewood would remind me of where it had come from. I'd remember the landscape, the weather that day, even my mood. Firewood logs were the brothers I never had.

The trees included sugar maple, red maple, white birch, and black birch. I was cutting a black birch, enjoying the minty aroma that slumbers in this wood and wakens when its bark is bruised. I had worked up a sweat and I was loose, so maybe too cocksure of myself. I knew I had made a slight error with my felling notch that went in a little too deep, so what? The tree did not fall where I wanted it to but did a little pirouette that I found fun to watch, and toppled into my brush pile. No big deal.

It was best to cut from the top, because some branches lay on other branches creating stress. In my arrogance I decided to trust my experience and my chainsaw and cut a stressed branch under the fallen trunk of the tree. I knew it would snap away from me—and it did.

What I didn't see was another smaller branch. It snapped into me and knocked the chainsaw out of my hands. I was lucky that the blade missed my thigh, which can kill when it severs an artery so that you bleed out.

My face was not so lucky. The branch gouged the flesh from my lip upward until it scooped out most of my right eye.

The United States Army does not accept one-eyed soldiers. They don't see straight and likely don't shoot straight. I was given an honorable discharge for medical reasons, a Section 8 in Army talk. My military career was over.

I think maybe for some people, yours truly, for example, self-loathing and self-pity amount to the same thing. I convinced myself that my Army buddies, including Wiley, my best friend, were thinking that I had deliberately injured myself to get out of the service. Because, well, I half believed it myself. It was that shame, more than anything, that led me into a dark place.

It was weeks before I dared to look at myself in the mirror with my good eye. I saw the medically zippered window of the removed eyeball, the twisted upper lip, the lurid scar on the cheek bone. I wanted to turn away from that face, but I did not. I decided to love it, because finally I had revealed, yeah created, the real me.

The medical people had assured me a prosthetic eye could be installed. Cosmetic surgery could make me appear normal, except around the upper lip. Uncle Oggie recommended that I wear a patch to give myself an appealing pirate look. I opted to display the sewed-shut eye socket and let my ruined face stand out as a statement. I thought, God, fate, the genie in charge of shit-luck—whatever was out there—was punishing me for . . . what? I wasn't sure. All I knew was that I had gotten what I deserved.

It makes me smile thinking about it as I write these words, but at the time it infuriated me that my mother was wildly upbeat about my new situation, happy to see me out of the military and not going to war.

"Look," she said, "you're morose now, but your scars are only physical. Inside, in your heart, you will heal. Some people who go to war, all too many, come back but they don't heal. Or they don't come back."

Only a month after my accident Sadie brought home a copy of the local newspaper. William "Wiley" Brewster had been killed in war. I was still recovering from my wounds, so I had an excuse to avoid the funeral at St. James Church in Keene, but, really, I could have gone. I just didn't have the courage. I had this mad idea that I would get up before the congregation and shout, "I killed him, I killed my best friend."

My betrayal of my country, the compromise of my integrity, the defilement of my father's spirit—and most recently the loss of my comrade-in-arms—was now complete. I could see myself on the cover of *Mad Magazine*, a one-eyed, ripped-lip, scarred-cheek Alfred E. Newman.

After my physical wounds healed, my mother suggested I apply to the state college. "It's not all that hard," she said.

But I didn't want to go to college. I had a very real, if irrational, desire that burst out of a dream: I was waiting for the dead of Grace Pond to reveal truths of future as well as past events. That was my mindset at age eighteen.

In the years that followed, when Sadie went off to law school in New Orleans, I latched onto Uncle Oggie as parent, teacher, and counselor.

One afternoon in the summer of 1975 sticks out. Uncle Oggie invited me out to the island in his canoe "to talk." I wanted to please this man, but I hesitated at his invitation. I knew that one of his rituals was to meditate under the pagoda in the nude even in cold weather, and I knew that he often took communards to the island for sex. What to say, what to feel? It was as if I was fourteen years old again.

Uncle Oggie read my confusion and set my mind at ease. "I know where you're coming from, Junie. It's okay. We're just going to talk." His reassuring tone calmed me.

We sat on a ledge six feet up from the surface of the pond.

"Something is holding you back," he said.

"So what?"

"Look, I don't mean to pry into your psyche. I just want to help."

"I can't even help myself, what can you do?"

"I can make you strong," he said. He grabbed my hand and squeezed. I squeezed back real hard and he winced. "Okay," he laughed. "There—see? You're strong."

"I'm strong but I don't know how to be strong," I said.

"Your problem Junie is your brain is murky. Talk to me, tell Uncle Oggie everything and as you speak you'll begin to see a light shine into the murk."

I shook my head.

"OK," Uncle Oggie said, "I'll talk, then, it's something I like to do. I know this much about you. You think your trouble began when you got a Section 8 medical discharge from Uncle Sam's Army. You carry some emotional baggage regarding the death of your buddy, Willy."

"No, Wiley."

Uncle Oggie chuckled. "I stand corrected. You were going to win the war with him, right?"

"I guess."

"That burden you load on your shoulders has no real weight in the Newtonian world. It's not real." He paused, then said, "And you know it's not real. You need to red shift your way home."

Uncle Oggie's words broke the dam of emotion, and I began to talk, just let it gush out.

I told Uncle Oggie about the annual hunt staged by G.I. Joe and his Korean War buddies and how my father was killed by a random bullet from an unknown hunter's rifle. I went into great detail about my resentment for being left out of my father's life. How the week before his death we'd had a big blowout. And the worse thing was that morning of the accident when he was still alive, I believed I hated him. I even gloried in the feeling of hatred. It was only after he passed on that I realized that I loved him.

"I don't think you loved him, Junie. I think you wanted him to love you, and now that he was gone it would never happen."

Those words sent another charge of emotion through me, and I began to choke up and fight off tears.

"Your hate for him was honest, true, and earned," Uncle Oggie said. "It's your denial of your need for a father's acceptance that holds you back, even today."

"I can't get over the feeling that it wasn't that random bullet that killed him, it was me. I killed G.I. Joe with my hate. I have this fantasy and go over it in my head. I shoot him, and then I hypnotize myself to forget, and then I do it all over again. And the worst thing . . ." I paused to take a breath before I voiced my greatest shame. "The worst thing is that I enjoy this fantasy. The thought of killing brings me a surge of mastery, if only for a short time."

"You're saying there's a killer in you."

"Yes, that's it. Given certain circumstances—and I don't even know what they are—I would not only kill, I would revel in it."

Uncle Oggie put his arm around my shoulder and spoke in a soft voice. "It's ok, Junie. You were just a boy dealing with a grief that was too big to handle. You know what? He wanted you to hate him."

Uncle Oggie insight detonated another bomb inside of me.

"Yes, of course. Why?" I said.

Uncle Oggie shook his head. "The answer is guess work."

"What's your guess?"

"He had a premonition," Uncle Oggie said.

My somber mood faded while curiosity took hold.

"You mean that he knew he was going to die?" I said.

"No, no, nothing like that. He sensed that he was moving away from you. It's supposed to be that the son leaves the father, but when it's the father that does the leaving. It's ... well, you know ..." His pause took the breath out of me. Finally, he said, "It's a disruption of the natural order."

"Does it have to be?" I asked.

"Yes, because of the stars," he spoke in a whisper.

"I don't believe any of that astrology shit," I said.

"I'm not talking about astrology. Do you know what Red Shift refers to?"

I laughed. "Some people say it's because you want America to go communist, but I know that's not true. We had it in high school. Red shift is a wavelength thing. Red means one thing and blue means another, but I can't remember which was which and why."

"If we measure the light that comes to us from a star we know that if the wavelengths are on the blue side of the spectrum, the star is coming toward us, red shift means going away. The dominance of red shift in the Universe tells us that everything is moving away from everything else. Space itself is expanding."

"Yeah, it's in your motto: Our Universe is Expanding. Yours?"

"There's a kind of beauty and grandiosity about expansion but there's also ... go ahead, name it for me," Uncle Oggie said.

"Loneliness," I said. "If everything is rocketing away from everything else, it means that we are alone."

"That's right—that's dead right. In the last gasp of creation, we are alone. Your father knew he was leaving you, red shifting. He thought if you hated him, his leaving would be easier on you. That was as close to love as he could get."

"Okay, why was he moving away from me?"

"And from your mother. He was going to divorce Sadie and move who knows where."

"How do you know?"

"I don't know. I'm just putting pieces in puzzle slots, and the picture is coming clear."

"All those times when he'd sulk and insult my mother and take off for weeks at time. He was ..." I couldn't say the words.

"He was probably having an affair."

So that was Uncle Oggie. When he was one-on-one with you—and it wasn't just me, but maybe scores of young people who came and went from that commune—he had a genius for finding your vulnerabilities and exploiting them for reasons of his own.

TRINITY RETURNED FROM THE WEST COAST in male mode, handsome in a GQ way, late at night in a taxi and went right to his cabin. Next morning, he was still male, but entirely different from his travel guise. He now appeared older, a little gaunt, body language formal and deliberate, back slightly stooped, exuding controlled exuberance. He was wearing an outfit derived from a Silicon Valley executive pitching the latest computer gadget, pressed form-fitted blue jeans designed for the male body, solid colored shirt not tucked in, a trimmed full beard, brown hair with streaks of premature gray.

We went outside and strolled the grounds. As we walked, I told him about building Sadie's stone-walled garden from rocks on the property.

"To keep out the critters," Trinity said.

I couldn't help laughing at the memories. "Sadie was used to firearms from her upbringing in West Texas. Before we built the wall, she would shoot the raiders of her garden, mainly woodchucks, which would end up in her stewpot. Later, after we built the wall and after Red Shift, Lynn and the girls grew all manner of veggies, and Lynn and I wrote books about those exciting days of experimenting with organic produce."

"Your walled garden looks neglected," Trinity said.

"These days I grow just enough for my own needs."

"In the growing season you have plenty of vegetables and fruit, but what about other necessities and what do you do in the off seasons?" Trinity asked.

"It's unpleasant for me to leave the pond, but I can make myself do it to shop, though lately I call my Uber or an Ideal Taxi for deliveries."

"In other words, your agoraphobia is getting worse."

"Maybe."

Trinity pointed to the tower at the top of the hill. "I read your letters to the editor in the archives of the *Keene Sentinel* opposing the cell tower. But now that it's built you are taking advantage, thanks to me. Ha-ha. You have betrayed the Grace Pond Boy Wonder."

"Not Grace Pond Boy Wonder, Grace Pond Monk."

Trinity just laughed. "You are sensitive about the weirdest shit."

"And you are an asshole in your present male shape-shift," I said.

"Good point. I don't even know I'm doing it. I'm a pseudo asshole. I wonder if real assholes are aware of their assholeness."

"Sadie used to say that hypocrisy and practicality make compatible bed partners," I said.

"You mom's wisdom sometimes makes me flinch," Trinity said. "Speaking of which, the cell tower is kind of funny looking, cross-dressed."

"Yes, they try to disguise it as a tree by hanging phony branches and plastic pine needles. It doesn't fool anybody because it's so much taller than the surrounding trees."

"Looks like a giant California sequoia lording it over your piddly Northeast forest." That mocking laugh.

We sat at the pull-down table in Shinbone Shack and dined on a veggie medley from the garden and my own homemade French bread baked in the stone oven in the summer kitchen that Sadie and I built back in the day. Trinity brought a bottle of Themyscira Chardonnay.

What took getting used to more than Trinity's constant changing appearances was the voice—now male, mature, self-assured.

"Do you have a default mode you can fall back on when you're not shape-shifting?" I asked.

"You mean a real me? Haven't we had this conversation before?"

"Yes, but it was inconclusive."

Trinity shook his head. "Maybe at one time there was a real me—I can't say."

"Isn't it a chore to be acting all the time?"

"No, just the opposite. When I assume an identity it feels natural, and I'm invigorated. I'm not acting, I'm just being me. It's when I go for the default that I feel anxious and confused. . . . The vegetables are primo—what's the secret ingredient in the sauce?"

"A goat milk base from Sage Farm Goat Dairy. It's the secret ingredient in my chowders, too."

"Those chowders probably held your marriage together," Trinity said.

"Why do you always win these conversational bouts?"

"Because I'm an asshole."

And we both burst into spontaneous laughter.

After the chit chat, our discussion got serious as we shifted to our investigation.

"We can conclude that there was a struggle between Pete and another man that resulted in Pete's death," Trinity said. "We are now conducting a murder investigation with four prime suspects, Osgood Stone, the mysterious Gerard Stanton, then there's Jason, perhaps acting out his anarchy philosophy of that time period in his life."

"I'm not so sure about Jason, either as a philosopher or as a killer," I said. "He's more an opportunist than an initiator. He may have made up that story of seeing a fight between Pete and somebody else."

"No, he doesn't have the imagination. But I agree with your critique of his personality. I didn't see him possessing the kind of mad resolve it takes to provoke a life and death struggle. Also, he lacks a motive."

"Who's the fourth suspect?"

"That would be you, Uncle Cyclops. After all, you were under the influence that night Pete died. Maybe you thought Pete was one of your demons." That mocking laugh—it came through no matter what persona Trinity was in.

"I don't think I could kill a man, except maybe at long range."

"You have thought about it, though. Probably, Junie Blaise is not a killer, but maybe J.B. Nielson is," Trinity said.

"I thought we were having a serious conversation?" I asked.

"We are," Trinity said. "I'm trying to see if there's balance or an imbalance between your day-to-day and literary identities."

"You're too close for comfort for me," I said, determined to change the subject, though Trinity's musings did linger in the back of my mind. "If Uncle Oggie killed Pete the case is closed, because Oggie likely died in Jonestown."

"I think it's more unlikely than likely that he was a victim in that massacre," Trinity said. "Everybody leaves a trail. Not this guy. We have both pounded the Internet, and we have no direct evidence that Osgood Stone went anywhere."

"If Uncle Oggie didn't die at Jonestown where is he now? And if he survived why haven't we found a trace?" I asked.

"Good questions," Trinity said. "Do you know any more about his back story?"

"All I know is his connection with Red Shift," I said. "He talked about a shadowy past, but he never offered any specifics, except he hinted at making love to Jane Russel. You know—that poster hanging in his digs."

"I made a few inquiries and found nothing before Red Shift. It was as if he never existed until he launched his little commune," Trinity said.

I wonder why a West Coast guy would bring his people East, especially on the advice of somebody as wiggy as Pete," I said.

"Who was Uncle Oggie intimate with?" Trinity asked.

"He had a lot of affairs, but no steady lover," I said. "The person who was closest to him before he supposedly took off for Jonestown was Lizzy Rondoh. She handled Red Shift finances while he was gone. He trusted her."

"Okay, she's already in my database," Trinity said. "Runs a dress shop in White River Junction, Vermont. I'll set up an interview with her."

I decided to offer him use of my truck, but I never got around to it because our conversation veered off in another direction. "Your rig won't arrive for a few days," I said, "In the meantime . . ."

Trinity interrupted and said, "Satoshi. My rig, as you call it, now has a name, thanks to Pauline."

"Pauline Alvar named your camper Satoshi?"

"Uh-huh. After Satoshi Nakamoto, supposed founder of Bitcoin currency. Her hero."

Trinity's expression changed from wise guy to worry wart. Did something happen between Trinity and Pauline Alvar that was more than a casual encounter?

"Something wrong?" I asked.

"Of course not," he said with faint insecurity that seemed out of character.

Trinity spent the rest of the day and that evening in his 10-by-10 cabin with his travel bag and laptop, which was surprisingly bulky. It looked like an older device from the 1990s. He'd built it himself for his own purposes, and he assured me that it was the most powerful laptop in the world and would remain so, because he updated it every time newer, faster hardware became available.

Next morning after a breakfast of my homemade zucchini bread slathered with peanut butter and wild honey, we sat on the porch with our feet up on the railing and worked on a second cup of Lynn's Farm Stand Coffee. Trinity was still in male, semi-formal mode, although he had removed the phony beard.

≈

"You shaved," I said, but my joke fell flat.

There was a long pause. I could see that Trinity was working his way up to talking about something that was troubling him. Finally, he spoke.

"Uncle Cyclops, do you think a beta model for the future of our species ought to pursue love?"

"You're telling me you're in love with Pauline Alvar."

"You figured that—I'm impressed."

"It wasn't so hard. I can understand your infatuation for a new person in your life. The part I don't get is why you think of yourself as a beta model. A beta model of what? And why would that idea get in the way of falling in love? It all seems like a queer mixture of grandiosity and insecurity."

"Queer mixture, indeed. It's not just me who is a beta model, there are multitudes of us. The problem is beta models are by definition, defective. They have to be tested in real world settings to determine their flaws. Unfortunately, there is no cadre of engineers to test and repair us. We are on our own."

"From what I've seen in your shape-shifter guises, I'd say you're experimenting with gender identities."

"That's obvious, but there's more to it. It's not that I care to transition from one gender to another gender, it's that both genders are already deeply within me."

"In your DNA?"

"Not only in my DNA, but in my bodily structure, sensations, emotional responses, thought processes—everything."

I thought I understood Trinity better now. I said, "Children born with ambiguous genitalia traditionally are re-assigned as infants one way or another."

That mocking laugh. "You really think that I'm an intersex person? I'm flattered or maybe flattened."

"You intimated you were and were not intersex. That means you're either a man who pretends to be a woman or vice versa."

"Not necessarily. Maybe I'm an alien. Or a robot like in *Darby Doomsday*," Trinity said, referencing the video game created by Darby's premier business, Geek Chorus Software.

"I'm not an expert on the *Darby Doomsday* video game," I said. "But know there's a female Luci Robot and a male Wiqi robot. If you were a robot, which would you be?"

"If I were a robot, and, well, maybe I am, I'd be both."

"A double-gendered robot?"

There was a long pause, which I perhaps mistranslated as Trinity's uncertainty in dealing with my question. Finally, Trinity started, "My dad . . ." but did not finish expressing what he had intended to say. Instead, he went off in another direction. "It's absurd that I should refer to a man who would be a stranger to me as 'dad,' as if he suddenly came out of the grave, but that's the word in my head. You know the story. Grandpa Maurice told you."

"Yes, your father was killed in Iraq, but before that he was in Kazakhstan where he fell in love with your mother, but Maurice told me scant about her people."

"We don't know much. Hints in the paperwork suggest that her family disowned her after she became pregnant. I never knew my mother's name, but through DNA tests I did learn some information about her lineage. I share a random gene from Genghis Khan who passed through the area back in his days of world conquest. DNA evidence documents that Mister Kahn seeded his way across the known world."

"Does that mean your dating games are part of a mission to conquer the world?"

"Yes, that's exactly what it means." The mocking laugh.

Our conversation had wandered far away from gender, no doubt because Trinity wanted it that way. I had asked Maurice Landrieu in an email whether Trinity was a boy or a girl, and he had ghosted me. Now I realized that Trinity's gender was none of my business. I was trying to find a way to apologize. Instead, I went against my best instincts and perseverated.

"Here we are today, and you are what, mid-twenties, and still haven't made up your mind which is your primary gender."

Trinity shook his head. "You're assuming I'm weighing arguments against emotions. Do I want to be a man, a woman, or remain a shape-shifter freak?"

"I think you're in an experimental stage in your life. Your promiscuity is exhibit A."

"Not really, I'm just having fun."

"I don't believe you."

"I don't believe half the shit I say, either. What about you, Uncle Cyclops, are there days when you feel like a freak with your scars and sewed up eye socket?"

"Of course. It's kind of a comfort actually. It's something I have that makes me, me."

"I totally understand. Protection comes in different guises. There may come a day when you can be fixed, and I can be fixed without loss of . . . what?"

"Our identities," I said.

"Yes, that's it, isn't it? I'm a freak, you're a freak, we tell ourselves we'd rather not be freaks, but our freakiness defines us."

"Your problem has greater depths than mine," I said. "If I could have a real eye, I'd take it in a Darby minute."

"It may happen in your lifetime, Uncle Cyclops. Human civilization and its accompanying advances in technology is only about ten thousand years old, a blink in evolutionary time. Think ahead now, not ten years, not a hundred years, or a thousand. Think ten thousand years. Or a hundred thousand years. Or more. What will the ordinary human being look like? Probably more like the robots in the Darby Doomsday game than the anatomy that constitutes people today with their narrow biological demands of gender and mortality. And what about culture, values, religion, philosophies, and overriding all, technology that can change the human genome?"

"Not to mention hopes, dreams, ambitions, et cetera," I said.

"In other words, what will the et ceteras do to the human condition?" Trinity said. "Distinctions inevitably will lead to genetic changes through technologically-forced evolution."

"Does that bring us to a mono-type or a poly-type human?" I asked.

"Which of the beta models will prevail—that's a question I ask myself every day—well, maybe every other day," Trinity said.

"The mono-type might create a cyber culture of humans and machines, all connected with a single Belichickian motto, *Do Your Job* for team Homo sapiens, an attractive idea in a lot of ways. Look at the mono-type success stories down through the eons: ant colonies, termite colonies, dung beetles, and the New England Patriots."

"Mono-types would not be your choice?" I said.

Trinity nodded. "My desires are in the other direction," Trinity said. "We need different kinds of people, from throwbacks like you, Uncle Cyclops. To transitional figures like me, beta models. To immortals who have uploaded their identities to servers and who stride around in robotic parts, the investors in Geek Chorus Software. To the teeming masses of humanity who do the real work and are subject only to the random change of the natural selection model."

"I'm rooting for natural selection," I said.

"Following your scenario, nature likely will choose two brands of humans, masters and slaves, because it's not probable that different kinds of humans can co-exist as equals over great spans of time. Distinctions of gender will be an insignificant part of the story."

"We'll extinct ourselves via Hollywood-style cyber wars long before the evolutionary time frame plays out," I said.

"Extinction is possible, though more likely from non-human activities," Trinity said. "A random asteroid crash, radiation flares from the sun, a comet cleansing our atmosphere, any number of celestial events or inner Earth turmoil that we cannot now imagine, could end it all in an instant, but those events are not statistically likely during the current eon."

"What is likely? Another more serious global pandemic? A world war involving nuclear weapons that poison the planet with radiation? Exacerbation of climate change disasters that we've already brought on?"

"Those are the trendy cases being made," Trinity said. "But there's another way of looking at the threats. A perversely optimistic way. Right here in your hometown of Darby, New Hampshire."

"Really?"

"It's all in the video game, *Darby Doomsday*. Look at STW—Save The World."

"An environmental group?" I said.

"The minions of Save The World view themselves as environmentalists, yes. Check this out." Trinity held up his smartphone and I watched a pale, completely bald man, step on a stage to deliver a Ted Talk.

"That's Origen," Trinity said. "He works at Geek Chorus Software, but he's also a spokesperson for Save The World."

As Origen began an oration, I flashed back in my mind to Uncle Oggie—the confidence, the verbose diction, the message of radical change.

"Whatever man-made catastrophe befalls us, the human species will not destroy itself completely," Origen said. "There will be survivors who will benefit. Consider at the moment that we have too many people on our little planet. Following the coming catastrophe, whatever it maybe be, the numbers of our species will be crunched down to only a handful. The survivors will have a huge jump-start toward creating a new epoch. They will enjoy all the data of the past to build on, and there will be sufficient infrastructure and resources remaining to serve a greatly reduced population. The political, religious, and cultural institutions of the past that hold us back today could be more easily managed or dispensed with.

"Allow me now to introduce you to a radical idea that is the core belief of Save The World thought in consideration of, say, a nuclear world war as species cleansing . . ."

The video snippet ended, and Trinity put the phone back in his pocket. "Notice how the grammar in that last sentence falls apart, so that you're not sure just what it means. I think that was deliberate obfuscation by Origen. He and his followers take their motto—*Save the World Before Ourselves*—seriously. They want to kill off most of humanity for the good of the planet. Save The World looks like an environmental group, but it's actually a terrorist organization."

"So, what's your point? That we should abandon our own plans and investigate Save The World?"

"Maybe."

"I think your efforts to make a better world are best directed inward, rather than outward," I said. "I don't believe anything we can do will change Save The World. You and I, Trinity, are just two little people."

"In other words, stick to my beta model idea."

"Yes," I said.

"Okay, so I'm a human GMO?"

"Sounds almost like a revival of the Eugenics movement," I said.

"I hope not, but I see your point," Trinity laughed without mockery or mirth, then all smiles in his face fell away. The sudden change in demeanor from confident and sardonic to almost mournful, unsettled me. It was as if I was looking at the emotional core of my teenage self. Could Trinity Landrieu affect such subtle changes to someone's psyche as part of his shape-shifter abilities? Or was he just showing me his own vulnerability? It's a question that even today I can't answer with certainty.

All I could bring myself to say was, "What's funny?"

"I was thinking that female hyenas sometimes grow penises, not for reproduction purposes but for dominance," Trinity said.

"And?"

"I'll tell you one of my secrets, Uncle Cyclops. I am unable to reproduce. Accordingly, I have concluded that the best thing, the right thing, I can do for the human species, for Pauline, for all ordinary mortals out there in this land . . ." Trinity stopped, took a breath, held it in.

"What—what is the best thing you can do, the right thing?"

"Die."

He didn't give me time to respond but kept talking.

"I never should have survived my birth. Pauline and I planned to run away, me run away from you and your—our—crazy inquiries, Pauline from the Stanton Library and her Russian roots. But I thought, this can't be. Beta models are by definition, defective. I am defective. I cannot improve my species, because I cannot breed. Because of what I am, I will ruin her life. If I really love her, I have to choose NOT to be with her. So, I left without a goodbye, walked out on her so she'd have good cause to dispense with me. Here I am, back with you, Uncle Cyclops."

"And in despair."

"Yes."

I wanted to hug him, tell him everything was going to work out, but I didn't believe that thought. Given the parameters of our conversation, everything was NOT going to work out. I had no good advice to give. The result was that my lack of response created an awkward moment. We left it at that, issue unresolved, not just regarding Trinity's physical make up and love life, but our own positions relative to one another.

The Fifth Death

THE NEXT DAY TRINITY, still male in aspect, had a look on his face, like the angel Gabriel about to make a birth announcement from high. "You know what?" Trinity said, "I'd like another look at that maple tree."

I rowed out to Whirlybird Island while Trinity sat in the stern seat and shot video with his phone. He was in work mode, which meant part of him had left the planet. When we reached the island, I pulled the boat up on the ledge with the usual sound of aluminum complaining to granite about rough treatment.

Trinity looked up at the maple tree and walked directly to the pagoda, removed the quilt from the plastic bag hanging on one of the posts, spread it on the ground, and sat on it in lotus position.

"You're going to meditate?" I said.

"No, I'm going to investigate."

After a few minutes, Trinity said, "I've been thinking about the shore here, a lot closer to the conservancy land than from your place."

"Yeah, it's only about a hundred yards."

"Do I see a road through the trees?"

"Yes, it's an old logging road that the conservancy upgraded for visitors."

"Where does the road go?" Trinity asked.

"Don't go nowhere, stays right there."

There was just a splinter of a moment when Trinity blanched and where I could see a huge reservoir of uncertainty. If he didn't feel in complete command of the reality of a situation, he was fearful that destruction was at hand. Then he got the joke and laughed, perhaps a little too loud.

"Good one, Uncle Cyclops."

"Oldest local joke in Darby," I said.

"I know, but coming from you, well, it stopped me. To put my question with more precision: Does the conservancy road wrap around the pond to your property?"

I shook my head, and pointed, "It dead ends into a cliff face. A path goes up and around, but it's impassable to wheeled vehicles."

"Since there are no residences on the road, there's probably very little traffic beyond the conservancy parking lot."

"That's correct," I said.

"Someone coming to the conservancy could park, then boat or even swim to the island."

"Yes. Gerard Stanton or anybody would have no problem reaching the island. They wouldn't even need a boat. They could swim the distance."

Trinity stood, turned, and looked up at the giant maple tree with its great but crooked crown of leaves spreading shade over the pagoda.

"Wow, that's some kind of a wounded old warrior tree," Trinity said. "When I was researching the island, I read that it was hit by lightning more than once. I'm surprised it's still standing."

"Maple trees grow from the outside, the sapwood—that's where the life is. So even though part of the tree would crack and burn, eventually it would grow around the burn scar."

"What about the inside of the tree?"

"They call it the heartwood, but actually it's dead, so it's nothing like a beating heart," I said.

"If the tree was cracked open by lightning, that dead part would be exposed to insect damage and rot, no?" asked Trinity.

"That's true," I said. "By now the tree is probably hollow on the inside, a common occurrence in maple trees of great age."

"Let's take a look."

We walked around the tree through some bushes. About six feet up there was a gap about three feet long extending upward and eighteen inches or so across.

"Bend over so I can hop up on your shoulders," Trinity said. Trinity shimmied up my butt and sat on my shoulders, turned on the flashlight app on his phone and peered into the void of the tree.

"Okay, you can let me down now," Trinity said and slid off me.

"Anything interesting in there?" I said.

"Only if you consider a human skeleton of interest."

We exchanged places. Trinity standing, me sitting on his shoulders so I could have a look. I turned on my phone flashlight. The walls of the hollow were almost black, which made the bones stand out more. I could make out feet, pelvis, ribs, the shards of a shattered cranium.

Later we sat under the pagoda and conferred.

"I don't want to call in any authorities, not until we know more," I said.

"If we don't disturb anything, we may never have to notify anybody."

Trinity laid out a plan, and we followed it closely. We took many still photos and some video with our smartphone cameras of the remains of the body. There were no signs of wearing apparel. From the positions of the bones, we determined that someone of substantial strength probably had stacked some of the many rocks in the area to make a platform, then lifted the body and stuffed it head first in the hollow of the tree.

"The victim was shot in the head either with a powerful handgun at close range or a high-powered rifle, like maybe from the shore on the conservancy property," Trinity said. "The sound of a shot would have been heard at Shinbone Shack."

"In these parts sounds of gunshots in the woods are common, and nobody would pay attention."

Trinity took a chip of bone for DNA testing and made a few calls from his phone while I rowed us back to Shinbone Shack.

"It takes a fair amount of time to get the results of a DNA dab, unless you know somebody and deliver personally," Trinity said.

"In other words, you want to borrow my truck," I said.

"Wow, another very clever use of inferential logic, Uncle Cyclops."

"On the way back, pick up some toilet paper," I said.

Trinity returned two nights later with the toilet paper and the DNA results. The sample included markers from the West Coast Stanton family. We sat out on my porch with Geek Chorus Amber beers and watched the sun set over the pond. In male mode, Trinity preferred beer, in female mode, wine.

"I'd say it was a good bet that the skeleton in the tree belongs to Gerard Stanton," I said.

"You nailed it, Uncle Cyclops," Trinity said. "According to the DNA results, those bones belong to a Stanton family member."

"Where are we now?" I asked.

"In possession of unanswered questions."

"Let's suppose Gerard Stanton murdered Pete and lost a dog tag in the struggle, then who murdered Gerard—Uncle Oggie?" I said.

Trinity shook his head. "Maybe, but I don't like it."

"We can't be sure about anything," I said.

Alone in the World

I EMAILED MY REPORT to Trinity and Maurice, plus a copy to my mother along with an image of the dog tag and the photograph of Gerard Stanton in his Army uniform. "Any chance that somewhere along the line you might have met this man?" I asked.

Sadie called me on my smartphone an hour later.

"I just read your post," she said. "The picture you sent me of Gerard Stanton, I recognized him right away."

"You knew Gerard Stanton?"

"No, I never met a Gerard Stanton. I recognized the man in that picture as Osgood Stone."

"Uncle Oggie! It can't be. The hair color is different, and Uncle Oggie had a beard. How could you tell?"

"Because I was intimate with him."

"What?"

"I thought that by now you would have figured it out."

"I didn't."

"You always had a selective naïve streak."

That pushed my button, and I retaliated. "Well, you weren't so special. Uncle Oggie slept with everybody and he wasn't picky about gender."

"But not with you. I made him draw the line there."

Still in shock that my mother had been one of Uncle Oggie's many lovers, I said, "I didn't need your protection."

"Yes, you did."

I hung up on her. Lynn used to tell me that I was at my worst when I couldn't admit I was wrong. My petulance kept me from thinking straight for a couple hours. When I had cooled down, I called Sadie back.

"I'm sorry, Mom," I said.

"That's all right. I know I must have sent you glutei over tea kettle. Let's start over. You must have some questions, as do I."

"Okay, Mom, the Red Shift involvement began with Pete, right?"

113

"Yes and no. He had this girlfriend who was a hippie and belonged to a commune, so Pete joined. Then, let's see if I remember this right, Pete told Osgood about Grace Pond. One thing led to another and Red Shift ended up you know where."

"How much of Red Shift's history do you know?"

"Precious little. Osgood never talked about his old life, and he was vague about his motivations establishing a commune. Which didn't make a lot of sense to me, given his personality."

"One thing I never understood about Uncle Oggie was his relationship with Pete," I said. "They were such opposites."

"Yes, that puzzled me too. I can see it from Pete's perspective, because Red Shift provided what Pete wanted—access to intoxicants, young women, crazy living, freebies up the ying yang. But why Osgood put up with Pete, who was contrary, insulting, and a mooch, I cannot fathom."

At this point in the call I heard Trinity's voice. "Hi, I've been listening in."

"I should have known," Sadie said, voice droll.

"You tell it like Pete was using Osgood/Gerard, but maybe it was the other around," Trinity said. "Maybe Osgood/Gerard needed Pete for his own purposes."

"What purposes?" I asked.

"To be determined," Trinity said.

"Anyway," Sadie said, "Osgood learned about Grace Pond and Shinbone Shack from Pete. That's when I came into the picture. It seemed peculiar to me that a hippie commune run by a CEO kind of personality would want to leave California for the hills of a little Northeast state. My first thought was 'no way,' but at the time we were iffy on finances and I had a dream to go to college, so I thought, 'I wonder how much I can squeeze out of this bird?' That's when I came up with the ridiculous ten-year lease idea that included enough rent money to let me cut my secretary hours at the firm and go to school. Oggie never blinked at the terms. I was suspicious, seemed too good to be true. So, then . . ."

"Probably it *was* too true to be good," Trinity said.

"Trinity, interrupting is an art form that you have yet to master," Sadie said.

"Gee, and I thought I was perfect."

"You're more perfect in your girly than in your manly incarnation," Sadie said.

I was enjoying the repartee between Sadie and Trinity. One-on-one I was over-matched by each of them, but between themselves they were almost even-steven, though I'd give Sadie the tiebreaker. I didn't know I was going to blurt out a question of my own, "Mom, why did you sleep with him?"

"Curiosity."

"There has to be more to it than that," Trinity said.

"No, there doesn't. Curiosity got me involved with the wrong man and with liquor when I was eighteen. Daring-do happens to me every once in a while. Enhances even when it appears to impoverish and, alas, vice versa."

"Curiosity and horniness go together for you," Trinity said.

"I wouldn't put it so crudely, but you're downwind from the perfume," Sadie said.

"Mom, since Uncle Oggie and Lieutenant Stanton are the same person, and since he, like Pete, was an Army veteran of the Korean War . . . see what I'm driving at?" I said.

"Yes, you're looking for a fit, and I use that word in both its meanings," Sadie said. "Osgood never intimated that he was in the service. However, he did have a lot of questions about Joseph and his Army experiences. He was always probing. When I called him on it, he told me this outlandish tale about researching for a movie. Pete believed that Osgood was a secret warmonger or maybe even a narc who had infiltrated the peace movement. Since Pete and Osgood were both full of bullcorn, I didn't know who or what to believe."

"Can you be more specific about what Pete meant about Uncle Oggie being a warmonger?" I asked.

"I'm afraid not. You know Pete, he never got down to brass tacks. I . . ."

Trinity interrupted. "This is from American Heritage online dictionary. I had to look up *brass tacks*: The origin of the first phrase, dating from the late 1800s, is disputed. Some believe it alludes to the brass tacks used under fine upholstery, others that it is Cockney rhyming slang for 'hard facts,' and still others that it alludes to 'tacks hammered into a sales counter to indicate precise measuring points.' So, then . . ."

Sadie interrupted Trinity. "Maybe how Osgood and I broke up has some relevance. I got tired of his questions. One day I said, 'You want something from me, what is it?' He said, 'Your magic touch.' I said, 'No, something else besides that.' Maybe I'm flattering myself, but I now think he was afraid of me, afraid I'd find out too much about him. Anyway, I could see him thinking. Finally, he said, 'You're a little too perceptive for my taste, Sadie.'

"After that we didn't see each other anymore. I started to suspect him, but I didn't know of what. Eventually, I let it go. Removed him and my suspicions from my mind. No doubt it was my dependence on the rent money that made me stupid."

"Mom, I'm not entirely convinced that you're right about Gerard Stanton and Uncle Oggie being one and the same person."

"Could be," Sadie said.

"No, no, you're right, Sadie," Trinity said. "Junie wants to keep his Uncle Oggie's memory pure in his heart. Remember that poster of the Jane Russell movie, *The Outlaw*, that Osgood Stone took such an interest in? Well, there are twin mountains in Korea where battles were fought during the Korean War. The G.I.'s referred to those mountains as the Jane Russell hills."

"Oh, my God," I said. "That seals it. Uncle Oggie and Lieutenant Stanton are one and the same."

After a pause, I asked Trinity to hang up so I could talk to Sadie about something personal.

"No problem," Trinity signed off.

"What is it?" my mother asked.

"You and dad had to get married, didn't you?"

"Well, yeah. That's common knowledge."

"You never told me the details."

"It was nothing special. Happened all the time in our day," Sadie said. "The first time I had sex was with Joseph when I was eighteen. He had just returned from Korea on temporary assignment at Fort Sill, Oklahoma, due to be released in a couple weeks. I had just started my first job in Lawton. As the daughter of a farm family in Texas I had lived a sheltered life, and to tell the truth, I was looking to whoop it up.

"I met Joseph on the street. He was with Potato Head Cromwell, and he was very forward in a charming, non-threatening way. I was carrying a sack, on my way to one of the new laundromats. We had a two-week romance until he was discharged and headed for New England and out of my life, or so I thought."

"That doesn't tell me what happened," I said.

"In the middle of week two he brought some liquor to my apartment. My roommate was out of town, so he knew we'd be alone. I wasn't used to drinking and it did something to me that encouraged him. I have to tell you, Junie, our encounter, which is how I think of it, wasn't exactly a rape in the legal sense of the word, but it wasn't entirely consensual either. I was naive and unsure of myself, and the alcohol knocked me for a loop. I can't say to this day exactly what happened. "When I came to, your father and Potato Head were leaning over me asking if I was OK. I wasn't sure if I was OK or not. I remember pointing at Harry and saying to Joseph, 'What is he doing here?'

"Potato Head said, 'I think I'll leave you lovebirds alone,' and he stalked off but with a smirk. It was all a big joke to him. Joseph said he was sorry, that he didn't know I was a virgin. A few months later I called the farm and told him I was pregnant, and he had to marry me. There was no thought in those days of ending the pregnancy. I was either going to have the baby and give it up for adoption or marry the bum. That's the way it was in the 1950s. In the end we got married by a justice of the peace in Tennessee, about halfway between my hometown of Tahoka and here. Joseph and I hardly knew each other. I had to leave the only part of the world I knew and settle in your teensy state."

"Sounds pretty awful the way you tell it," I said.

"Actually, it was an enlivening time for me. Your father was touchy, but he could be a lot of fun, too. He had a Bugs Bunny way about him, and he awakened my womanhood. When you were born, I was thrilled. You made a couple out of us, Junie."

In response to my mother's story I asked her a question that came from movies and *The Romance of Helen Trent*, which my mother used to listen to on the radio. I said, "Were you in love with him, and was he in love with you?"

"Well, you got me on that one. I think I did fall in love with him and you know why? Because I realized that he had fallen in love with me. Even with the booze and the sneaking off, and the harsh words, I could feel it. The man, on some level, adored me."

I was thinking of Uncle Oggie's words, his suspicion that G.I. Joe was having an affair, but I kept that knowledge locked in. I didn't want to hurt my mother.

≈

Next day Trinity was in female mode, dressed casually but conservatively, with long straight black hair. She could have been a grad student from India going to lunch with her American dissertation advisor. I drove her to the local rail yard to pick up her Satoshi camper. I thought that because I had a passenger it might be easier to deal with my demon who always showed up when I left Grace Pond. Nope. I tried to hide my panic, but Trinity picked up on it immediately.

"Your agoraphobia, what does it feel like?" she asked.

"I don't want to talk about it."

"Of course, you do."

"So, now you're my therapist?" I said.

"No, I'm just a young PI with a brass-tack personality collecting information for my database on human emotions. I've experienced many feelings, but I don't know much—emotionally—about phobias, because I've never had the experience. Give it to me in great detail. Think of it as data sharing."

The absurdity of Trinity's nerdy request somewhat calmed my wrought-up state of mind.

"I love you, Trinity, because you are so earnest an idiot."

"That's a brass tack if I ever heard one." The mocking laugh.

"The bad feelings started, I dunno, right after my father got shot in a hunting accident. I never quite felt comfortable away from Shinbone Shack and the pond. It wasn't all that important—just a vague discomfort. I thought I'd outgrow it. And I did, kinda, in my brief time in the Army. After I lost the eye, it came back in a vague way and stayed with me. I just thought I was a home boy."

"But it hit you hard after your wife was killed."

"Yes. After Lynn died, I didn't experience the mad, lingering grief that I felt when G.I. Joe died. It was more like a detached feeling, like I had left my body. I thought the feeling would go away, but it only got worse and all mixed up with fearfulness when I would leave the pond. Eventually, the panic attacks started."

"And where are you today?" Trinity asked. "The feeling. Tell me about the feeling at this moment, what a panic attack means to you."

"When I leave Grace Pond it's like I'm walking on a path that winds up a mountain and gets narrower and narrower until it's only about six inches wide and the drop off is into eternity."

"So just turn around and go back," Trinity said.

"Yes, so you do that, and you find the way blocked and you enter the second more grievous phase of the panic attack. You're not on a cliff edge anymore. You're in a coffin. You hear them nail it shut. You feel the coffin being lowered into the grave. You hear them throwing dirt on top of you. You cry out in terror, but there is no one to hear you. At the same time, you know this is only a feeling. It's not real. Your life is not in danger. This realization is not a comfort, but a door opening into another emotion: shame for being so weak willed."

"From your description, I'd say your phobic reaction is like a bad LSD trip?" Trinity said.

"I wouldn't know."

"You had one, didn't you? The night you were initiated into Red Shift, the night Pete Shaughnessy died."

"To tell you the truth, the LSD trip wasn't all that bad. Confusing, yes. Scary, yes. Bad? I wouldn't say so."

"I think you're hiding from your truths." Trinity put her hand over my heart and then over her own. Her touch felt like the touch of a daughter.

"Maybe you're right, it's all connected," I said.

"Your hallucinogenic experience was a rehearsal for your panic attacks."

I tapped my right temple with my right index finger. "I've had the experience of being buried alive without actually being buried alive. What is your big scare, Trinity? You have not experienced a phobia, but I believe you're carrying around a big scare."

She shook her head, and I laughed at her. "Come on, you goaded me into revealing my vulnerability, now it's your turn."

"OK, Uncle Cyclops. I call it my holy shit benediction. It comes to me only once in a while, but it's real disturbing, because it hits me when I least expect it, a waking dream. Pretty real, almost like a vision from hell. I'm in my mother's belly, but my X-ray vision allows me to see the midwife attending to her. My mother is in pain hollering that I'm killing her. This goes on for some time until finally I shoot out of her womb into the world. Like the alien in the movie, I scamper away crying but my mother goes silent. I look around, but there's nothing to see. The midwife is gone. My mother is gone. The walls around me have opened into a great, vast nothingness, like that image from another *Alien* movie, where Ripley casts out the creature into outer space."

"You're alone in the multiverse."

"That's right. It's not my mother's death or even the fact that I killed her by being born, that terrifies me. It's the alone part. It scares me even talking about it now. In those *Alien* movies I never identified with the people but with the creature. Alone in a world not its own."

"And you fill this void with . . . what?"

"Data."

≈

Later that night, as I pondered over this huge philosophical question Trinity raised, I distracted myself by going through my fly-tying supplies, which gave me an idea that might help make things right between Trinity and me. I found a pair of green and gold earrings that Sadie decided she could do without. I hung wires on the loops and added two new streamer fly hooks to the ends of the wires.

Lizzy Rondoh

WHEN TRINITY EMERGED from her cabin for her trip to White River Junction, Vermont, to meet with Lizzy Rondoh she was in female guise but with a twist. She wore high-heeled shoes, a hip-hugging dress as a woman might wear to a pick-up joint, too much makeup, and an obvious blonde wig. Something about her walk and voice was designed not to seem right.

"You don't look like a woman, more like a male crossdresser trying too hard," I said.

"That's the idea," Trinity said. "It'll relax Lizzy and she'll talk more freely."

"You really believe that?"

"I am a believer," Trinity said, imparting a tone vaguer even than the words.

"I think you pick your outfits for personal reasons only marginally related to our work."

"So what?"

"I'll be honest with you, Trinity . . ."

She interrupted me with, "Oh-oh, now I know I'm in for it."

"Part of me believes that, really, you're physically a man working your way toward being a woman," I said.

"And that my current shape-shift is the real me, CD sissy at heart."

"Yes, that's what I half-believe."

"You're more of a momma's boy than I am, Uncle Cyclops." The mocking laugh.

I laughed, attempting to mock the mocking laugh.

Trinity laughed without mockery.

We laughed together as if to conjoin our contrariness.

After a moment of relative normality, I said, "I got us off to a bad start this morning," and held out the streamer earrings. "I made these last night. Maybe you can use them in a future personality."

Trinity accepted the gift in the palm of her hand. "You have names for them?" she asked.

"Yes, Truth and Clarity."

"Rare commodities. See you later." And she was off.

Twenty or so miles from her destination, Trinity turned on the vehicle cameras and audio. "I want to check to make sure nothing got screwed up in transit on the train. Everything working on Satoshi?" she asked.

"Just fine. You're not on the Interstate, you're on old highway 5."

"I wanted to get a feel for the river."

"Yes, it divides our twin states."

"Sibling rivalry?"

"Pretty much, yes."

"What do you know about White River Junction that's not on the Internet?" Trinity asked.

"The famous scene in D.W. Griffith's movie *Way Down East* where Lillian Gish is filmed on an actual ice floe took place on the White River on an actual ice floe."

"That information is on the Internet," Trinity said.

"The downtown of wrj is basically one square block," I said. "I used to take Uncle Oggie's Underwood to Twin State Typewriter periodically for cleaning and tune-ups. Tell you the truth, I don't know what wrj is like today."

"Because your current world has shrunk. What are you going to do when you can't leave the pond?"

"I'm going to swim out to Whirlybird Island and crawl into that dark hole with Lieutenant Stanton."

"He might resent the incursion into his private space. The dead are not altogether powerless," Trinity said.

≈

It was easy to form a profile of Lizzy Rondoh strictly from information that she had generated herself on social media. Lizzy, like Jason, had incorporated communal living into her mature lifestyle. She lived in a sprawling Victorian house with three men that she referred to as "my husbands," an older man who was her business partner, a confidante close to her own age, and a younger lover boy. One of her daughters, from an early marriage, lived with her partner and two children in a separate apartment in the house. Lizzy reigned over that house and her business with queenly airs.

The one block of wrj was dominated by an old-fashioned hotel, a restaurant, a coffee shop, a theater for stage plays, and a few specialty shops, one of which was Lizzy Rondoh's place of business. I got a good look from the Zeno-Cam at her sign over the door: "RED SHIFT Casuals and Costumes," with a logo of a model wearing a 1920s-style red chemise.

The dress shop was small and picturesque in a flea-market chic kind of way, but I knew from my research that it was not profitable. Most of Lizzy's income came from her costume business. Lizzy would buy basic off-the-shelf cloth from Asian countries, which she would move to local seamstresses who would do alterations to meet contracts that Lizzy made with theater groups and university drama departments.

It was obvious that not many people wandered into Lizzy's dress shop, because there was a retriever dog of mixed heritage napping in the doorway. Trinity stepped over the dog and into the shop.

Plump but inviting, Lizzy sat behind a big, cluttered desk. She looked familiar, but not like the Lizzy I knew as a 19-year-old back in the late 1970s. I never would have recognized her on the street. She wore full skirts and a headdress with a tiny crown on top. It took me a few minutes, but it soon dawned on me that Lizzy was riffing on the famous Alexander Bassano painting of Queen Victoria. No doubt Trinity was impressed.

Lizzy got up from her desk and came over to shake hands.

"So, you're Trinity Landrieu—I was wondering," she said.

"Yes, I'm Trinity Landrieu and your quote unquote, guard dog, is Rose, right?"

"Glad to meet you, Miss Landrieu. Thanks for connecting with Red Shift. How did you know my dog was named Rose?"

"Facebook, Twitter, Instagram, and of course the color of the collar. You've created a celebrity that never leaves your front stoop," Trinity said.

Lizzy laughed. I could see that Trinity had already scaled one barrier of trust.

Trinity bought some clothes until finally Lizzy said, "You don't have to butter me up by buying, I don't mind answering the questions you posed in your email."

"No, no, my buying spree is genuine," Trinity said. "I knew I'd love this place when I saw it on your website. I adore—just adore—clothes with a whiff of bye-gone days."

Lizzy brought Rose in, turned the OPEN sign to CLOSED, and shut the door. She already had some tea brewing, which presently she poured for Trinity and herself, and served with scones. She sat for Trinity's interview behind her desk. It was clear the desk and the position behind it was her throne.

Trinity sat on an Empire style chair against the wall very close to the desk and pretended to take notes on a tablet with her index finger. Rose jumped on the couch.

"How's Junie?" Lizzy said. "Did he ever have sex?"

"I can't confirm that," Trinity said, "but I know he was married for many years."

"Was married?"

"Yes, was. Remember that news story about the organic gardening author who was shot by her ex-boyfriend and war hero?"

"No, I don't pay attention to the news. But anyway, tell Junie I'm sorry to hear about his loss, and give him a hug for me when you see him. Your email said you were investigating Pete Shaughnessy's death."

"That's correct. Did you like Pete?"

"Not particularly. I was young then, and in my mind, he was an old man trying to act like a hippie, when in reality he was just a drunk and a blowhard."

"Wasn't Osgood Stone a blowhard, too? But you liked him."

"Uncle Oggie was not a blowhard, Uncle Oggie was a visionary." Lizzy's tone verified my belief that Uncle Oggie was the love of her life and that she would remain true to that love no matter what.

"You found Pete's body, right? Did you see anybody else in the area or hear anything?"

"No, we had a bonfire going and we were singing, so I didn't hear anything, and then I went for a walk to be alone. I liked the island and I always liked to walk around it. That 'peaceful, easy feeling.' When I saw what I thought was the back of a snapping turtle which turned out to be Pete's butt. I hollered and then I pulled his head out of the water and tried to give him mouth to mouth."

"When you left to take your walk do you remember if Osgood Stone was among those sitting around the bonfire?" Trinity asked.

"The cop asked me that and I didn't have an answer for him, and I don't have one for you."

"Who was the first to arrive at the scene when you screamed?" Trinity asked.

"There was no first. It was like everybody came running."

"Including Osgood Stone?"

"I think so. Why do you keep asking me about Uncle Oggie?"

"We have reason to believe that he killed Pete," Trinity said.

"I don't believe that, but if he did, Pete had it coming. He was not a good communard—he was a leech and an instigator. What I don't understand is why Uncle Oggie put up with him."

"Maybe it was because they were both veterans of the Korean War."

"Well, that's funny, not funny ha-ha, but funny. Uncle Oggie never talked about the military, but sometimes he'd use Army lingo. Like, for example, he called our composting toilet experiment a latrine. And he referred to meditation as mental PT."

"PT, Army expression for physical training?"

"Right. I didn't know what it meant until after I married my first husband, who had been in Nam." She put a thumb down, apparently a reference to the first husband. I was hoping for a follow up question from Trinity regarding Lizzy's first marriage, but Trinity ignored the gesture.

"What can you tell me about Osgood Stone's life before Red Shift and the forces that drove him to begin a free-love commune."

"There was more to it than free love, OK?"

"My apologies."

"Apology accepted—you're kind of little cupcake in your own way, aren't you, Miss Landrieu?" Lizzy said.

"I'm more frosting than filling. Please continue."

"Uncle Oggie didn't like talking about his old life unless it was talking to the group. Mesmerizing. I gotta say, though, he wasn't all that consistent in his stories. I know because I paid attention."

"That was his public self. What about when you were alone with him?"

"In private he was focused on the now. There was something about him that appealed to a woman. Hard to explain. Call it mystery and comfort. You knew he was holding something back, what was it? At the same time, you felt special in his presence. And safe."

"Did he share stories about parents, childhood friends, places, episodes, stories from his past, the kind of stuff we all talk about?"

"Never. His talk was kind of bass-ackwards religious and philosophical stuff related to Red Shift. He appealed to me, but the talk was over my head."

"What about your personal relationship with him?"

"There was more to it than the physical. There was a point when he decided I was special, and he spent a lot of time teaching me how business works." Lizzy stopped talking abruptly.

I watched her face. Her businesswoman's no-nonsense expression didn't change, but tears bubbled out of her eyes, and stained with mascara and foundation, streamed down her cheeks. She didn't make a sound. There was something strange, futile, but beautiful in her silent weeping that made me tear up. The leader of the Red Shift commune may have been a shape-shifter in his own right but many of us loved him in his Uncle Oggie incarnation.

Finally, Lizzy resumed talking. "I learned that Red Shift was a business registered offshore. In its own way—and this is a laugh—RED SHIFT Casuals and Costumes, in tax and corporate terms, is legally Red Shift the commune. Or so my accountant husband tells me. Ha-ha. I just used all the same info when I started my business. I own it, phony baloney and all. Ha-ha."

Lizzy talked on, but none of the information was helpful.

Trinity took a two-hour lunch break at the Tuckerbox Cafe during which she cut off communications with me and worked on her super laptop. We talked next on her drive back to Grace Pond.

"I was able to get into Red Shift company records," Trinity said. "There was nothing in there that was remarkable except a few references to the Stanton library. With the exception of Lizzy, it's a company with only ghosts on its board. I had a hunch and made a few inquiries."

"A few inquiries? Let me guess. You were back in touch with Pauline Alvar."

"Actually, she was in touch with me," Trinity said with a laugh that touched me, because it was free of mockery. "Seems as if there was still quite a bit of Gerard Stanton remaining in Osgood Stone. At the very time that he had stolen from his family—abandoned them—he was depositing that missing dog tag into the Stanton library archives along with a handwritten letter from the founder praising his commitment to military life."

"He must have greatly valued his time in the Army," I said.

"Yes, so, given that he had a sentimental streak, you can see that he would be embittered and shamed when he was court-martialed."

"Right," I said. "The experience must have motivated him to an extended vendetta."

"People who love hard, especially when they're ga-ga over their own self-worth, have a capacity to hate hard," Trinity said.

"Something happened in that war that slopped over," I said.

"It was a slop-over war. Gerard/Oggie was using you, Uncle Cyclops. He was a very smart and careful adversary, but he had a weakness."

"His ego," I said.

"Let's call it his human frailty—he wanted to be remembered. His last deposit to the archives is dated November 1978."

Trinity showed me a phone photo of typewriter paper that I recognized as typed on Uncle Oggie's Underwood: "Frequent meditation allows my normally fevered and vengeful demon to access and utilize the mind of the meek."

"The meek—I think he's talking about you, Uncle Cyclops," Trinity said and zoomed in on the handwriting.

"Oh, my God," I said.

The note had four names, two of which were crossed out with x's and v's typed over the original characters, but you could still make out the words underneath: Joseph Blaise and P. Shaughnessy. The other names were not crossed out, Harry Cromwell and Maurice Landrieu.

"He crossed out Pete's name, and since we're 99 percent sure he killed Pete, that lends importance to the fact that he crossed out my dad's name. Was it Uncle Oggie and not some random hunter who shot G.I. Joe?"

"Maybe, but we're a long way from proving it," Trinity said. "He might have eliminated G.I. Joe knowing that his prey had already died."

"I don't doubt that Uncle Oggie was stalking my father and his buddies."

"Big question is why," Trinity said.

"Something in the war?"

"The details are missing."

"Did Harry and Maurice catch on and assassinate Uncle Oggie in retaliation?" I said.

"That worries me a little," Trinity said. "Well, more than a little. I don't want to do anything that would hurt my grandfather."

Trinity and I had stumbled into the personal equivalent of a Soviet-era checkpoint in our investigation.

The crisis wasn't in learning what happened in that distant past. It was in what the wreckage of subsequent knowledge might impart to our individual psyches and to our loved ones, in particular, Maurice "Pass" Landrieu, Trinity's grandfather, and Sarah "Sadie" Boyd Blaise who I suspected factored into this developing story. Neither Trinity nor I spoke for quite a long time. Finally, I said, "Let's sleep on it."

"ok," Trinity said.

The Ad Infinitum of Self

NEXT MORNING Trinity came over to Shinbone Shack for breakfast dressed in blue jeans, denim shirt, and scuffed work boots. Her hair was short and a little helter-skelter, and yet she was female in the way she walked, in the reveal-curve of her buttocks, in just a suggestion of a bust underneath the shirt, her voice in contemporary Sedaris-speak mixed with hints of 1990s Valley Girl. She sounded like one of my recent discoveries on YouTube, the dazzling cellist, Tina Guo.

I marveled that despite being dressed in traditional men's clothing, Trinity looked and sounded more persuasively female than when she'd been dolled up as a male crossdresser for her interview with Lizzy Rondoh.

"What's that Shakespeare play where the girl disguises herself as a boy trying to act like a girl or maybe I got it backwards?" I asked.

There was a pause. Trinity wasn't trying to formulate an answer to my question; her thoughts were more to the point of our inquiry. Finally, she said, "*Twelfth Night*. I'm not ready to talk about whether my grandpa should be on our agenda. I need a couple or three days to quiet my mind. Meanwhile I want to make some changes to one of the cabins you loaned me. The work will calm me so I can think."

"The stone cabin?"

"Yes."

"The cabin was not a loan, it was a gift," I said. "You earned it."

"Not yet, but I will."

Over the next week Trinity installed a black-white, checker-board tile floor in her stone cabin, plastic silver panels over the plywood inner walls, and deep black-and-white prefab cabinets. She ditched the futon and brought in a recliner that she adjusted at different angles to type on her laptop from the supine position or to doze off. She removed the curtains from the windows, because "I like to imagine that people are watching me."

The most prominent furnishing in the room was a makeup "studio" with a stone countertop, drawer space, and the mirror on the wall that faced the existing full-length mirror.

"When I stand between the mirrors, I can see the ad infinitum of myself," she said.

In the center of the room was a square table with Trinity's Zeno-Cam logo stamped at the corners. Across from the tiny table were two simple straight-back chairs, with black legs, a checkerboard seat and a white back, no arms. The other chair reversed the colors. It wasn't until the renovation was complete that I understood what Trinity was trying to do. When you entered her cabin, it was like walking onto the set of a 1940s film noir shot in black and white.

In those new chairs we sat, looking at ourselves in the ad infinitum mirrors, sipping green tea and discussing the state of our investigation.

"Have you ever run into a situation like this, where the investigative team has a personal stake in the outcome?" I asked.

Trinity shook her head. "The problem is bound to crop up when the investigators are also the clients."

"I've had this terrible sense of unease ever since my father supposedly was killed by a random hunter who was never found."

"Your unease was there even before he died."

"But it got worse after G.I. Joe was shot."

"It probably didn't get worse. You were at an age where you began to notice your inner self." Trinity pointed at the mirrors. "Recognition enhances mood."

"You're probably right."

"Even though you were happy all those years after you married, your malaise was still there, hiding. It's playing itself out now in your agoraphobia. You've been living with the Uncanny, Uncle Cyclops, capital "U." I know Uncanny because I was born with Uncanny. It's with me all the time. You can get over your Uncanny. Me? Never, because Uncanny is my natural state."

There was a long moment when neither of us seemed able to articulate thoughts. I broke the silence.

"We've already discovered that Uncle Oggie was not who he pretended to be. We're pretty sure that as Gerard Stanton he murdered Pete Shaughnessy. But we don't know why. We know that somebody killed Stanton. Maybe Harry Cromwell? Maybe your granddad? Maybe the two of them working together?"

I could see Trinity wince when again I raised the possibility that her grandfather might be involved in the mess we had found.

"Maybe somebody we don't know," Trinity snapped.

"Odds are whoever killed Uncle Oggie actually was targeting Gerard Stanton," I said. "If that's the case, the mess gets messier and possibly uglier."

"I'm looking at the current situation as a challenge to our collective imagination," Trinity said.

"Remember your grandfather is part . . ." I didn't finish my thought, because Trinity interrupted.

"I can't make myself believe that Grandpa Maurice . . ." Trinity didn't finish her thought, because it was my turn to interrupt.

"This situation we're in relates somehow to war and to the death of G.I. Joe," I said.

"All we've done so far is create more unease, more angst."

"I have to pursue this story to the end no matter where it takes me," I said. "Remember our motto from Chief Seattle?"

"The dead are not altogether powerless."

I was wrought up now, and I said, "Yes, and if we back out now, the dead will haunt us for the rest of our lives for our dereliction of duty."

"No, Uncle Cyclops, only one of us has the vulnerability to be haunted. I've dealt with my ghosts. I will protect my grandfather no matter what, including taking you down if necessary."

I laughed, mimicking Trinity's mocking laugh. "You just redecorated your cabin, and now you're threatening me?"

There was a long pause where we both understood that events could separate our partnership. Finally, Trinity spoke in an even voice.

"I really can't imagine that Grandpa Maurice got himself involved in a murder," she said. "Did you know that he had a breakdown at the end of the Korean War so severe that he had to be hospitalized?"

I nodded. "My father hinted at it," I said, speaking softly. There was another long pause.

"I propose that for the time being, we forget Grandpa Maurice and concentrate our efforts on the most likely suspect," Trinity said. "From what I know of Harry Cromwell, I think he should be moved to the center of our investigation."

"OK, but if the trail leads back to Pass Landrieu . . ."

"Yes, yes, I know," Trinity said, and turned her head away from me.

So that was that. I had a partner who I was very fond of and who was far more capable than I. But it was a limited partnership. If our inquiries brought us to her grandfather, would my partner, as she put it, "take me down?" And what did that mean?

I changed the subject, "You've been wearing the denim outfit for three days—you have any plans for changes?"

"Not at the moment. I'm comfortable in this guise. It suits me. I don't want to break up, Uncle Cyclops. Can we try something?"

"Sure, what do you mean?"

"I have mixed feelings about the idea of a Divinity deeply interested in human affairs, but my Grandma Olivia, who is a believer, taught me that belief in prayer does not require a deity. Only the belief has value because belief is wired directly to the human heart. Would you say a prayer with me?"

I nodded. I knew what Trinity was driving at. As secular people we assumed that prayer was a variant of what we call today the placebo effect, but maybe it's the other way around. Maybe the placebo effect is a variant of prayer.

Trinity rose from the table, turned, and faced the full-length mirror, and got down on her knees. I joined her on my knees beside her. She took my hand in hers. Her touch had that dual feminine and masculine quality.

"We should pray to the dead," I said, staring at the endless figures in the mirror.

"Yes, to hear their voices," Trinity said.

I shut my eyes and prayed silently.

So did Trinity until suddenly she began to pray aloud. It took a beat before I realized she had memorized parts of Chief Seattle's speech when he addressed the people who had displaced his people.

"Every part of this country is sacred to my people," Trinity spoke, but I was hearing the voice of the old native leader. "Every hillside, every valley, every plain and grove has been hallowed by some fond memory or some sad experience of my tribe.

"Even the rocks that seem to lie dumb as they swelter in the sun along the silent seashore in solemn grandeur thrill with memories of past events connected with the fate of my people, and the very dust under your feet responds more lovingly to our footsteps than to yours, because it is the ashes of our ancestors, and our bare feet are conscious of the sympathetic touch, for the soil is rich with the life of our kindred . . .

"When the last red man shall have perished from the earth and his memory among white men shall have become a myth, these shores shall swarm with the invisible dead of my tribe, and when your children's children shall think themselves alone in the field, the store, the shop, upon the highway or in the silence of the woods, they will not be alone.

"At night, when the streets of your cities and villages shall be silent and you think them deserted, they will throng with the returning hosts that once filled and still love this beautiful land, for the dead are not altogether powerless."

I pictured Grace Pond in my mind—"this beautiful land"—as Trinity recited the old chief's lament.

Piety and Desire

TRINITY AND MAURICE didn't ask for a report, but I sent them one anyway. I had found myself thinking about Lynn. I went back to my notes and cobbled together our story.

≈

Shocking news came on a raw November night in 1978 on the battery-powered radio I listened to when I ate supper. The Reverend Jim Jones and hundreds were dead in a mass murder-suicide episode at the Peoples Temple in Guyana.

I hurried to the village store in town and called my mother in New Orleans and asked her if she had been in touch with Uncle Oggie.

"I haven't heard a word since I kicked Red Shift off our property for giving you those nasty drugs, and I really don't know how to contact him," she said.

"Wouldn't his particulars be on the lease you gave him?"

"I checked, and the originating address given for Osgood Stone and Red Shift is fictional. I always thought he was shady."

"Since we haven't heard anything, can we assume . . ." I couldn't voice the rest of my thoughts, but my mother knew what I was saying.

"It may be years before all the victims in Jonestown are identified. We may never get all the answers, Junie."

"What was left of the communards cleared out. I'm all alone here."

"You need to get away from Grace Pond for a while."

I laughed, though there was no mirth in me. "That's what Uncle Oggie told me."

"Close up Shinbone Shack and stay with me in New Orleans for Thanksgiving. I've been meaning to ask you to visit anyway, so this timing is serendipitous. There are three people I want you to see here in my crazy crescent city."

"Really, who?"

134

Sadie laughed with an edge of absurdity in her voice. "Let me put it this way. You'll know one of the parties, but you never met the other two."

"Well, that's a mystery."

"You'll have to come to New Orleans to crack the case."

I left G.I. Joe's battered fifteen-year-old GMC truck at Shinbone Shack and hitchhiked to the train station in Brattleboro, Vermont. All day and all night on the train brought me to New Orleans.

After my mother joined Fulton, Chambers, Canal, and Spring legal firm in New Orleans she traded for a new Ford Bronco and bought a "creole cottage" on Laurel Street between Milan (local pronunciation "Myl'n") and Marengo streets near Napoleon Avenue.

Whoever named these streets must have had a sense of humor, since Marengo was Napoleon's horse.

My mother always looked stylish, to me anyway, probably because she had worked in an office where everybody had to dress well to go to work. She wore formal clothes well because she was tall with good posture and long legs. Dad used to call her Hepburn because she bore a resemblance to Katharine Hepburn. Now that she'd turned forty-two, she had gained more than a little weight around the middle, and she'd cut her hair so that it barely touched her shoulders.

Sadie's "creole cottage" consisted of a big room with tall ceilings, and a kitchen and living room divided by a fireplace converted to use gas. Off the kitchen was a wing that included the bathroom and the only bedroom. As one who had grown up with no running water, no electricity, and wood for heat I found the place quite luxurious. Instead of making a fire that snapped, crackled, and popped in the warmer colors of the rainbow, I could flick a switch, listen to the whoosh, and enjoy a fire that played the blues. On the night of my arrival, I slept on the couch.

Light from the street poured through big windows with thin curtains but no shades. Sounds of the fireplace fan whispered in the voice of a drill sergeant—fool, failure, freak, fraud, fuckup. From the outside I heard train whistles and the rumble and clanks from nearby ship docks on the Mississippi River.

It took me forever to fall asleep without the comforting sounds of Grace

Pond, and I didn't wake until 8 a.m. It was the Tuesday before Thanksgiving. Sadie was already up and dressed for her law office on St. Charles Avenue, which opened at 10 o'clock. She brought me a cup of coffee. "It has chicory in it," she said. "If you don't like it, spit it out in the sink."

"Thanks, mom. I've always admired your solutions."

We laughed at each other's silliness.

"For breakfast, how about we get some beignets at the Cafe Du Monde in the French Quarter?" Sadie said. "There's those people I want you to meet."

"One that I know, two that I don't—why the tease, mom?"

"Can't help myself, I like mischief."

Sadie drove us in her new Ford Bronco to the French Quarter. I liked Jackson Square, from the dignified church, to the brick shops street side, to the artwork and sidewalk artists that framed the square. I liked the view from the river-front park of the mighty river, ocean liners, cargo freighters, tugboats. I liked the Jax Beer sign on the Jax building. I liked the Jackass-propelled tourist wagons. I did not like the crush of humanity.

Sadie and I had just sat down with our beignets spiked with a mysterious white powder when a beautiful woman caught my lone 20/15 eye. My first thought was: Wow! A movie star, Anita Ekberg. Second thought: She's looking at me, her smile a lighthouse beacon on a stormy night.

"Hi, Lynn," Sadie said. "So glad you brought the girls."

We were joined by Lynn Nielson and her twin daughters, introduced to me as Piety and Desire.

"They're going to hate me someday for naming them after NOLA streets in the neighborhood where they were born three and a half years ago," Lynn said with a warm laugh that gave me a little thrill. Of the people who occupied my memory house—Sadie, Pete, Harry, Pass, Uncle Oggie, G.I. Joe, Grandma Isabelle, and, yes, Wiley Brewster, laughter always had an edge of sarcasm or irony or despair to it. But Lynn's laugh was all about the joy of life. She was one of those people with a capacity to appreciate whatever came her way.

I could see a familiar likeness in the twins. "These are Wiley's girls, aren't they?" I said.

"Well, I guess," she said. "When he joined up, we went our separate ways, but when he returned on leave I realized, yeah, and we sneaked off. Then he went back to the stupid war and got himself killed. When I found out I was pregnant my parents wanted me to . . . you know. But I never thought of my pregnancy as a problem. To me it was a solution."

"I was too chicken to go to the funeral," I said.

"So I noticed," she said, and when she saw the look on my face, whatever it was, added, "It's all right, Junie. I understand—you're sensitive."

I could have wept. I wanted to say, I can't even shoot a frog. Instead, I said, "Do you know how Wiley died?"

"Reading between the lines of the official explanation, I'd say his fellow soldiers fragged him."

"Oh, my God. He was too gung-ho. If I had been there, I would have had his back. I would have saved him."

"Maybe, maybe not. Why dwell on it? After the shit hits the fan it dries out and blows in the wind like the song."

Lynn talked about Wiley in a matter-of-fact voice. Some people not familiar with the death of a loved one are sometimes disconcerted when the bereaved recall their dead like they're reading a to-do list. But I understood grief because I went through it. You wring out the upfront emotions early on. After a couple years you have no problems acting normal. Without you noticing, the grief hides like a stuck-deep-in-the-ground undetonated bomb.

Back in high school everybody said Lynn was the Anita Ekberg of our town. Look a little closer and there were distinct differences. Lynn was not as voluptuous. Lynn, like Anita, was fair skinned with blue eyes in that Nordic way but with a suggestion around the eyes that she had an Asian ancestor way back when.

In high school I believed I didn't deserve a girl like Lynn Nielson. I still felt that way at the Cafe du Monde that morning in New Orleans.

"Lynn, why don't you show Junie around?" Sadie said. "I'll watch the girls."

So, the next day Sadie drove me to a small hotel in the Marigny neighborhood. We met Lynn in the lobby with Piety and Desire, who went off with Sadie. Lynn and I were alone.

"You don't have your own place?" I asked.

"I did have my own place, an apartment in Riverbend, relatively near my work at DePaul Hospital."

I looked at her, waiting for an explanation of why she left her apartment to move into a hotel room. None was forthcoming. Finally, Lynn said, "It's a long story."

I dropped the subject.

We walked around those funky streets in the Marigny and Bywater neighborhoods of New Orleans just talking.

Lynn stopped on North Ramparts Street between Piety and Desire Streets, where one and two-story houses were as close together as lovers on a toboggan run. Lynn sent a shock wave through me as she took my hand and walked me a few feet into a narrow dirt lane that dead-ended a short way into shadow.

"This is Rosalie Alley. It has a history of voodoo and hoodoo, and means a lot to me personally," Lynn said. "My daughters were born here prematurely. I was walking down North Ramparts and my water broke. Next thing I knew I was in the alley giving birth alone. A couple of women originally from the islands seemed to come out of nowhere and brought me inside into a room lit by votive candles. They were my midwives. Every time I light a candle, I think of them.

"Born in Rosalie Alley between Piety and Desire, no doubt Wiley's twins are destined for great things," I said. "What were you doing in this neighborhood anyway?

"I was visiting Sadie, who was staying with her boyfriend on Desire Street."

"Really? My mother had a boyfriend. Imagine that."

"Has."

"Really?"

"You didn't know?"

≈

Sadie and I had a quiet Thanksgiving dinner at her creole cottage.

When we sat down to eat at the little table between the kitchen and the living space that Sadie called The Library, I remarked on a statuette carved from a dark piece of wood, out of Africa no doubt.

"I never thought much of fertility goddesses until I started to look like one," Sadie said with a laugh.

"How come you never mentioned you had a man friend."

"Well, he's a little bit married."

"What does that mean?" I asked.

"It means it's none of your beeswax, Junie."

"I know but you'll tell me anyway."

"His wife has a house in Toronto. They've got kids. They're trying to work it out. I hope they do. That's all I'm going to say."

"Okay, mom, sorry I pried into your private life."

"No, you're not," she said with the chip of a laugh.

We dined on her homemade turkey and alligator gumbo served with salad and a traditional bread stuffing.

"Delicious," I said.

"Closest I could come to the Grace Pond stew that I made from the critters I shot. Which is one of the things I miss from our Shinbone Shack days. You can't get that Grace Pond flavor, even in New Orleans."

"Is it the shooting you miss or the stew?"

"For the public, I'll say it's the stew, but really? A little bit of one and a lot of the other. I'll let you guess on the proportions."

"So is that where I get it from, this mixed message of peace and pissed off?"

"Who knows?" she said, and then added. "Sometimes I miss that Baptist God and my slack Bible reading habits I grew up with to help me out with puzzling questions."

It was only when we were working on dessert, Sadie's version of a Car-Hop Heavan (sic) hot fudge sundae, that the conversation turned in a direction I did not anticipate.

"Junie, I had another reason for inviting you down here, and it's serious business."

"No kidding?"

"No kidding. I think Lynn's life might be in danger, maybe even the girls."

"How can that be?"

"Lynn had a boyfriend, goes by the stage name of Sig Howl, singer in a band. He left, or maybe they kicked him out. Anyway, he wanted to take Lynn and the girls out West to some kind of survivalist encampment. When she said no, he got abusive, and she walked out on him. He did not respond in a gentlemanly manner. He's got a rep."

"How did she get involved with somebody like that?"

"I think maybe she liked the idea of simple living on the land, just not his version of it. She can't stay at the Olde Town Inn much longer. Eventually, he'll find her if she remains in New Orleans. I told her you'd drive her and the girls and their stuff in the Bronco to her parents' place in Keene."

"Mom, do I have a choice?"

"Of course not."

We both laughed.

"I'll drop them at the Nielson house and return the Bronco to you," I said.

"I don't want it. Keep it. It's too much vehicle for me in the city. I'm going to get one that's little and more parkable." That was mom. She knew my truck had had it. She did things for people, and especially for me, and made it seem as if you were doing her the favor.

Next day I headed north with Lynn, the girls, and their baggage. Lynn talked about the twins and her adventures as a night attendant at DePaul Psychiatric Hospital. Having to put people in restraints in "control rooms." Assisting in shock treatments where you had to hold patients down while they had seizures. Watching a 13-year-old girl endure a hellish psychotic episode.

She talked about her memories of Wiley as a madcap guy who used to amuse her with an imitation of Groucho Marx when he was host on the *You Bet Your Life* tv show: "Say the secret *woid*, win a hundred *dollahs*." It struck me that this was a Wiley Brewster that I never knew. Isn't it like that with all of us? Different people bring out different parts of our personality, the good, the bad, and the et cetera.

I talked about writing in my journal on Uncle Oggie's Underwood typewriter, how I started my personal journal with Bics but graduated to the Underwood after he gave me the machine.

"I satisfy myself when I write, but I don't know how to write for a reader," I said.

"Pretend you're writing a love letter."

That was Lynn. She would come up with ideas outside of my spheres of knowledge and feeling. We took turns at the wheel, stayed a night at a motel that had a pool so the girls could swim.

Next night I dropped Lynn and the twins at her parents' place. They still lived on 19 Oak Street, in Keene, in a little white house with green shutters and a front porch with white peeling-paint pillars, in Lynn's words, "Perfect on a hot summer evening for listening to the Red Sox on the radio before TV ruined the world."

There was a very nice reunion. The grandparents were charmed by Piety and Desire, and Lynn was happy to see her parents. I drove back to Grace Pond alone, tired, sad, elated, dejected, and discombobulated.

Months went by until it was June. My birthday was coming up. I heard that Lynn was waitressing at Lindy's Diner in Keene. Any sane man who was in love would have not only kept in touch but would have asked the object of his affection to lunch or a movie. Anything. I reverted to old habits—did nothing.

I got a postcard from Sadie. Sig Howl had shot and seriously wounded one of the members of his former band and was in jail. He was sure to spend many years in a Louisiana prison. Lynn had been notified that it was OK for her to return to New Orleans and her job at DePaul Hospital. Frantic with desire to see Lynn, but alas, immobilized perhaps by misplaced piety, I hustled to the Darby Village Store pay phone and called my mother.

"I bumped into Lynn at Lindy's Diner," I said. "She's debating whether to return to New Orleans."

"And?" Sadie said.

"And she asked to see Grace Pond," I said. "I'm going to pick her up tomorrow. What should I do? Should I wear dark glasses or maybe get a patch for my eye socket?"

Sadie laughed at me. "Junie, she's seen your scars. Go with what you got. What should you do? I'll tell you what you should do. First, listen, I mean like listen for real, and then listen some more and when it's your turn to speak tell her about the things you love in the most loving way you can."

I picked up Lynn in the Bronco. Her parents took care of the twins, and Lynn and I drove off with a picnic basket and a bottle of white wine that Lynn brought.

I followed my mother's advice and listened to Lynn talk about her life. I knew some of the stories, because she'd told them before on our escape from New Orleans. It was less the content than the sound of her voice, rich with music, that made me weak in the knees.

I showed Lynn Shinbone Shack and Uncle Oggie's Standard Underwood typewriter, my father's barn where I stored Uncle Oggie's canoe and where

Red Shift had installed a communal bathroom and the septic system, though the water to flush the toilets still had to be brought in manually from the pond to fill the cistern above the shower. I showed her the 10-by-10 Red Shift cabins, the Red Shift school bus, my dad's GMC truck which sat idle since Sadie's gift of the Bronco.

"You think I should junk the school bus and the truck?" I said.

Lynn shook her head. "No way, they are monuments to a time gone by and to folks laid to rest. And what's that funny structure of bent sticks?"

"That's the Bucky, from Bucky Beaver to Buckminster Fuller. It has no practical purpose."

"Wonderful! I love it." And she talked about her dream to personify the idea of the earth mother in her lifestyle as a grower of good food.

We went for a walk in the woods where, I realized, it was my turn to talk about the things I loved.

"This is a grey birch," I said. "It's a short-lived tree, poor quality wood for stove and sawmill, unlike white birch which has value."

"Like for what?"

"Like to make Scrabble tiles. White birch is a very stable wood, does not splinter and the bark is full of oil, great fire starter even on a rainy day."

"The gray birch and the white birch look more or less the same, so how can you tell the difference?"

"By the way they behave," I said.

"Yes, yes, we keep our secret heart to ourselves, but our behavior is what we give to other people. Plants do it, too. And that one?"

"That's a black birch. It's not flashy. It doesn't possess grand proportions. It's a Joe Schmo kind of tree."

"The Mrs. Schmos are the backbone of the human world," Lynn said.

"I took my Swiss army knife out of my right front pocket, opened the long blade, and made a tiny slice in the bark.

"Check out the aroma," I said.

Lynn sniffed the tree where I made the cut. "It's like some magical mint," she said.

I didn't mention that it was a black birch branch that had put my eye out and that at the instant the branch ripped my face apart the minty aroma hit me before the pain and stayed with me on the ambulance ride to the hospital.

Back at Shinbone Shack, I showed Lynn my fly rod and the flies I'd made from found materials.

She picked one up.

"That's the Maurice Landrieu," I said, "made from a wild turkey feather and Christmas tree tinsel."

"How do you hold it all together?"

"With dental floss and epoxy glue."

"Let me guess, you broke the barb to make it easier to release the fish."

"Exactly. How about a tour of the pond and a little bit of fishing?" I said.

"I'd like that. And maybe we could have our picnic at the island."

"Great idea," I said.

We packed the basket, along with a blanket and my fly rod, and headed out in the johnboat. I rowed and Lynn sat in the stern seat facing me.

"Why did you paint the boat green and gold?" she asked.

"It's a long story," I said.

"You'll tell me when we know each other better."

In the shallows I showed Lynn the nest of a great blue heron at the top of a dead pine tree in two feet of water.

"I could see it from your cabin but it was so far away I didn't know what it was," Lynn said.

I brought in the oars and just let the boat go where the iffy breeze willed it. For a while we were quiet and then Lynn spoke.

She loved New Orleans, but she didn't want to live out her days there. She missed the changing seasons of New England. She'd read the Rodale books and she dreamed of a huge vegetable garden, a place where her girls could grow up close to the earth and far away from television. She confessed that if she didn't have the girls, she might have joined a commune.

I stood, not a smart thing to do in a little boat, but my balance was primo in those days. I showed off my casting abilities with the fly rod. A little small-mouth bass hit the fly right away and jumped all over the place. I brought it in, then flipped it off the barbless hook and it swam away.

"Let me try," Lynn said.

"Sure, but I have to tell you, it takes some practice to cast well with a fly rod."

Lynn took the fly rod and cast expertly.

"Hey, where did you learn how to do that?"

"My dad is a mad fly fisherman and he taught me. Number 7 weight floating line, right?"

I shocked myself with words that jumped out of my mouth. "Wow, I guess you're the girl for me."

Perhaps in deference to the embarrassment she saw on my face, Lynn didn't say anything.

When we reached Whirlybird Island, Lynn laid out the blanket, and underneath Uncle Oggie's pagoda we drank wine and dined.

Lynn looked at the maple tree. "It's beautiful in a ruined kind of way—nature does that," she said in that grand earth-mother manner that so enslaved my libido.

"The heartwood is rotted out," I said.

"It's all about the heart, isn't it," Lynn said.

"Those are the exact words my father used once upon time," I said.

Lynn nodded to acknowledge my words, then said, "Look how the live part of that tree surrounds the dead part in an embrace."

We talked some more, but I don't remember the subject matter. What did we eat? I can't remember. The contents of the picnic basket do not appear in my journal or my memory. What I do remember is the aroma that arose from sunlight on pine needles. Crawl of ants. Flight of a monarch butterfly. Sounds of bees. Grace Pond Monk losing his virginity, on that blanket, under the pagoda, in the shadow of the great maple tree, on his twenty-fifth birthday.

Lynn never returned to New Orleans. She and the twins moved into Shinbone Shack. Years later, Lynn said the sweetest thing anybody ever said to me, "Momma's boys make the best men."

Breakthrough

IT WAS NOW AUGUST on Grace Pond, mainly hot and muggy, but we had a couple of cool nights that included a cold rain. A few swamp maples had a touch of color. Just a hint of fall. I love the seasons in my world. Just about the time you get bored by the weather, and the show that nature offers looks a little dreary, everything changes, often dramatically.

Much to my delight, Trinity had taken to the pond. She Commandeered Uncle Oggie's canoe and did some exploring and proved to be a natural with the paddle. At one point near the beaver lodge I watched as she rolled out of the canoe into the water without tipping it over—quite a trick. She dove into the depths, came up for air, dove again.

I didn't see her surface, so I was getting a little anxious. I saw a splash, but it wasn't Trinity. It was a beaver. Another splash. Another beaver. Presently, my phone buzzed in my pocket. It was Trinity.

"Where are you?" I asked.

"I'm in the beaver lodge."

"What is it like in there?" I asked.

"It's like a movie theater just before they dim the lights. Smells like veggies that have been in the fridge too long."

"I think you surprised a couple beavers."

"Yes, they were not happy to see me barging in. I apologized for not knocking, but they splashed me and took off, insensitive of them. Then again it was insensitive of me to violate their fourth amendment rights. I won't be coming back."

"Why did you do it in the first place—curiosity?"

"Yeah, that was part of it, but I wanted to test my waterproof smartphone. Also, it struck me that a beaver lodge would be a good place for a felon to hide something."

"And?"

"I don't see anything here that will help our investigation."

≈

It was later, at the tail end of the cool spell, that we had a breakthrough.

I had been searching the Internet looking for information about Harry Cromwell. He and Maurice stayed in touch over email, but Maurice said he'd promised not to divulge Harry's personal information. I learned that Harry had retired from his job as a firearms salesman in 2006. Harry never owned any property. Following his last failed marriage, he lived on the road. After he retired, I assumed he'd kept the same habits, because I never found a permanent address for him.

His few remaining family members had lost touch with him even before he retired.

One cousin described him as, "A funny duck but not in a quack quack kind of way." I asked if he was abusive, and her answer was, "No, just cold-hearted."

One of his ex-wives had died and the other was not forthcoming. She wouldn't share details, though she did describe him as a "wolf in Peter's Gunn's clothing."

I tried his former place of employment. Nobody who worked with him was still employed or available to talk to me. The only interesting tidbit I managed to gather was that on several occasions he'd refused promotions to the home office in Flatonia, Texas. I reasoned that if he were alive today, he'd be settled in the northern climes of his sales territory. Of course, I was wrong.

Trinity took a different tack in her research. She discovered a website called Wild About Harry.

The site went back to the old Myspace days, though in recent times it had shifted to a closed Facebook page, which Trinity was able to access. She communicated with the founder, Myra Blake Bornstein, a woman about my age. Myra was a successful real estate broker in Denver, but she had gone through some hard times growing up in Medora, North Dakota.

Here's what she had to say. "I was just a kid, had a baby out of wedlock and was living with my parents. I was making a marginal living as a waitress in a diner. One day this guy comes in. I knew he was from out of town because

146

he was so well dressed, suit and tie. It passed through my mind that he might tip a little more than the locals, like maybe 15 percent. Lo and behold he left a hundred-dollar bill under the coffee cup.

"I thought it was a mistake and I ran outside to tell him. He was just getting into his van. He smiled and said, 'Enjoy.' I was flabbergasted. Next time he came in a couple months later it was 3 p.m., real slow, and he gave me another hundred. I was in a particularly sad state of mind, which always made me talkative. I told him about my baby. He said, 'Show me a picture of that daughter of yours.' I did and he gave me another hundred and said, 'Do something for the little girl.'

"Third time same thing. We talked. Even though he was much older than I and not at all handsome, there was something solid about him that I liked. And no, we didn't have an affair. But he inspired me, gave me confidence to change my life. I never saw him again, but his generosity and kindness stayed in my heart.

"Back in 2005 after I'd had some success, I was in the hospital for a couple weeks after a car crash—not my fault, thank you very much—I was bored and had nothing to do. And I was starting to think about Harry. At the same time, I'd discovered Myspace and the Internet and all the things you could do.

"Well, Harry had talked about his sales route and the towns he hit in Washington, Montana, the Dakotas, Minnesota, Wisconsin. I looked up diners and cafes in those towns and clicked around. Holy smoke! Harry was well-known and an admired tipper everywhere he went.

"He touched so many lives and never asked anything in return. One woman in Billings wrote that she told Harry she was living in fear of her ex and Harry said, 'I'm going to wave a magic wand and poof! He'll disappear.' That guy apparently left town and was never heard from again.

"Harry is every working woman's superhero. I tried reaching out to him—I mean he's gotta know about today's Facebook page, right? But he never responded. My guess is that he has passed on."

Trinity contacted some of the women who thanked Harry. A pattern developed. Several, and no doubt more of the women, had difficult relationships with boyfriends, husbands, ex-husbands, and employers. These men often just vanished.

Trinity and I discussed the case in the boat while I cast my line. It was a sultry afternoon, a little buggy, because the wind was down. Trinity liked to dangle a hand in the water as we drifted.

Trinity had done further research through law enforcement, discovering that missing persons were reported along Harry's sales route.

"Police have recovered a couple bodies stashed in odd places, the victims shot in the head from long range by a high-powered rifle," she said.

"Oh, my God!" I said. "No doubt there are other victims out there."

"It's a good bet Harry Cromwell is a serial killer," Trinity said. "I made a timeline. Harry's extravagant tipping and killing started in 1979, a little after Gerard Stanton/Osgood Stone disappeared. Get it?"

"Yes," I said. "It's likely that Uncle Oggie was Harry's first victim."

"And like most serial killers, he developed his own special murder motif: Male victims with reputations as abusers. Victims dispatched at long range with a rifle. Bodies stashed."

"So how does this relate to our own investigation?" I asked.

"We don't know for sure, but we have to imagine that Lieutenant Stanton killed Pete because of some animus he bore toward him."

"Tied in with the Korean War."

"Correct," Trinity said.

"And that the four buddies—G.I. Joe, Pete, Maurice, and Harry—were on his hit list," I said. "Gerard Stanton went through the trouble of changing his identity and acquiring a commune, just so he could pump information out of Pete and Sadie."

"Yes, and you."

"Now we have a good idea why he bought plane tickets to Trinidad," I said. "He probably learned at Pete's funeral when Maurice would be in Trinidad, and he made plans to assassinate him there."

"No doubt," Trinity said, "and somehow Harry got wind of the situation, and after Pete was killed, he killed Stanton."

"In retribution!"

"Maybe. We don't know for sure the motive."

"Seems like Harry got a taste for killing after shooting Uncle Oggie," I said.

"Or before that, in the war. We have to talk to him."

"Maurice wouldn't say where Harry was living, but I bet he knows," I said.

"Yes, you want me to interrogate Grandpa Maurice."

"Where is he now, his New York apartment on Sutton Place?"

Trinity shook her head. "I'm not going to tell you, ha-ha. Hey, I think you got a bite."

It was a nice smallmouth bass, three pounds, I guessed. Two and a quarter pounds, Trinity guessed. We didn't weigh the fish.

Trinity didn't eat supper with me that night. She went out and didn't return until late. I was afraid that Trinity and I were on the verge of a big blow up related to her Grandpa Landrieu, but something happened that night that changed everything.

Next morning Trinity came over from her cabin to Shinbone Shack for breakfast. I wasn't very good at acting, because she spotted my smug look right away. "What is it?" she asked.

"I got a call last night from Harry Cromwell," I said.

"No!"

"Apparently, he follows his Facebook fan club, because he knows all about you and me, and he got my number from Maurice. He wants to tell his story."

For once Trinity was speechless, though only for thirty seconds. Finally, she said, "Where can I find him?"

"In an RV in Port Mansfield, Texas."

The Sixth Death

LATE THAT AFTERNOON Trinity was on a plane to Atlanta, then San Antonio. Before she left, she took a couple hours to change her appearance. She looked older, a little worn, dressed neatly but plainly in baggy shorts, old-style sneakers, no socks, and a T-shirt that said, "Hope Is a Four-Letter Word," hair mousey brown with bangs. An old-fashioned girl. From her clothes and demeanor, she might have been a carhop at a New Hampshire ice creamery in the 1960s.

She didn't want to arouse suspicions at the airports, so she didn't bring her Zeno-Cam. No problem for my daring and resourceful investigator. She was able to rent a unit and pick it up that night in San Antonio. She was also able to get in a good meal at a Brazilian Steakhouse before retiring to her hotel room. Did she wangle a date? I didn't ask. She didn't tell.

She left early in the morning in a rental car for Port Mansfield, a tiny town of maybe four or five hundred people, some of them retired and living in RV's, the town located on the Gulf of Mexico near the bottom coast of Texas. What was the closest big city? There wasn't any. Port Mansfield is surrounded by range land that from the look of it didn't seem fit for cows or cowpokes. The town itself was built around a small dredged harbor in the endless Padre Island lagoon.

Trinity was supposed to meet Harry at the harbor. When she parked and got out of the air-conditioned rental car, I asked her how the weather was.

"It's very hot and very humid, no breeze," she said.

The rental Zeno-Cam gave me a nice view of the harbor. It was lovely. Small boats. Modest size condos on twelve-foot piers. If a serial murderer wanted to retire to a pretty spot with a sweetheart winter climate in the middle of nowhere, Port Mansfield would be ideal. Not in August, though.

Moments later Trinity's body cam showed a healthy looking, sturdy octogenarian with a sun-darkened face that had so many wrinkles it might have been mistaken for a mummy at an archaeological dig. He sported a shaved head wearing a straw Panama Hat, with a white band, white Bermuda shorts, black flip flops, and a black T-shirt with white lettering that said, "BE KIND/ You Asshole." He looked Trinity over as he approached.

"You must be Harry, I'm Trinity, and I work with Junie Blaise." She reached out a hand for Harry to shake, but he didn't take it.

"You're a trans, right?" Harry said.

"Not exactly but close, how did you know?" Trinity said.

I had to smile. Harry had seen through Trinity's shape-shift in an instant.

Harry laughed. "Because in my day I was a daddy to a number of persons like you. I like 'em better than real women."

"Really, why?"

Harry shook his head. He wasn't about to answer. He pointed to the belt and buckle around Trinity's waist. "Let me guess, surveillance rig."

"Do you want me to shut it off?"

"No way—I want to be on camera. Nobody cares about old people. I'm glad somebody's paying attention."

"I guess leaving a trail of dead bodies behind will perk up a resume," Trinity said.

Harry laughed. It wasn't a mocking laugh like Trinity's. More like a sad chortle, like you laugh at the insignificant absurdities that take place every hour on our little, endangered goldilocks planet.

"Let's get to work," she said. "Shall we go to your place?"

"I don't think it would suit you. I don't have air."

"Really? Seems like a masochistic choice in this kind of climate."

"Hey, that's good, you nailed it. I can afford air-conditioning, but I like the discomfort. It takes my mind off my dreadful life."

"There's no dread in your voice."

"My problem is not emotional, it's intellectual. I don't feel my awfulness, but I think it." Harry pointed at the harbor.

"That black and white one, that's my boat—the Peter Gunn. We'll talk on the water."

"I like black and white," Trinity said.

The boat was a hybrid craft, somewhere between a traditional Boston whaler and a bass boat with fish wells, inboard engine with a tiny outboard motor for backup, no cabin, no sun protection. Not a vessel you would take out into the open ocean during inclement weather. But Port Mansfield was protected by a barrier island, so that here in the lagoon on a day with no wind it was like boating on a great big pond.

As they went farther and farther from the port, Harry pointed. "See that gap in the island, that's the channel. Go out there and it's a different world."

"Yes, I can hear the breakers crashing on the far shore," Trinity said.

"I got bad skin cancer that I'm not treating," Harry said. "One of these days when a big storm comes in from the Gulf, I'm going to take the Peter Gunn through the channel and head for jolly old England."

"You'll be lucky to get through the channel, and I don't mean the English Channel."

"That's the idea."

Harry cut the engine near the shore of the barrier island and let the boat drift on the flat water. He talked to Trinity for quite a long time. There were many digressions, so I've stitched together their words into a narrative.

"My people are from the South, but I was actually raised in the Seattle area, because that son-of-bitch father of mine took a job with Boeing." Harry was very animated, no doubt he wanted to look good on the video.

"Did you ever go to Chief Seattle's gravesite?"

"I don't care about that shit. I was a Washington all-state football player in high school. I played fullback on offense and linebacker on defense. I had a football scholarship to VMI but was kicked out in the first week after slugging an upperclassman. He had it coming and I was secretly glad to be on my own. I hated schools of all kind, because of the uppity la-dee-da bullshit, and to tell you the truth, learning came easy to me."

"You didn't need school."

"Shut up and let me talk. Mainly, what I hated was the boredom. I didn't abide the coaches either, but I did miss football. I really didn't care whether we won or lost. What I liked was banging into people. I didn't know how much I'd miss that until it was taken from me.

"I worked at Boeing for a while and married a nice girl, but if there's one thing I learned about myself during that first marriage, it's that I'm not a nice man. Generous in many ways, but not nice. I enjoyed pleasing myself, rather repeatedly I might add, but I wasn't interested in pleasing the wife. In fact, I experienced a high when I didn't please her.

"It was a little bit like the thrill you feel when you bang into somebody on the football field. You don't dislike the person you hit. What you like is the actual hit itself and the hurt it puts on the hurtee. Anyway, she filed for divorce after six months. Who could blame her? I mean the only reason I married in the first place was steady nookie. The women wouldn't put out in those days without a ring. At that age I would have fucked a rock pile if I thought there was a snake in it.

"I didn't wait to get drafted. I joined the Army. It wasn't until I was in combat that I learned who I was on the inside. Who I *really* was. The only thing that ever scared me in my entire life was that moment of self-knowledge.

"They tell you in basic training that they're going to make killers out of you, but they don't mean it. What the Army is really telling you is that killing is a temporary and disgusting job you have to do for God, country, self-preservation, and peer group support. You get over the killing when you're a civilian. But for some of us, we don't get over it. We like the killing. It's the ultimate banging thrill.

"When I got out of the Army, I knew that I wasn't over with killing. I could have been a contract killer for an organization, like the CIA or the Mafia or some lame religion, etc. But I couldn't do that kind of killing. You see I'm moral in my own way. I couldn't kill strictly for money, somebody who may or may not deserve killing. I didn't want to kill on behalf of another person, and certainly not on behalf of an entity.

"My kills had to be people I chose who deserved to be executed. In other words, it's OK in football to bang into a stranger and enjoy the thrill, but when that banging is extended to taking a life, it ought to have some moral component to it. I didn't act on my impulses. I spent a lot of time in contemplation of future acts.

"Look, I know you think I'm bullshitting you. I know because I realize I'm bullshitting myself but only partially. The more important reason for my lifetime commitment to... how can I put this? Let's say there's a pearly gate, well I'm not going to be allowed in, I understand that. But let's imagine that I get to argue my case.

"I'm going to say, 'Listen, Mr. Archangel, I was just following my urges. I didn't create the urges. You—through creationism or evolutionism, whatever you want to call it—you made me who and what I am. Why should I be punished for doing what cometh naturally?'" Harry paused. "Where was I going with this?"

"A lifetime commitment to executing assholes," Trinity reminded him.

"Oh, yeah. I not only kept the moral component up front I cultivated it. Thought long and hard. I worked on the road. I slept in rooming houses, rundown hotels, Motels 6 through 8, and in my vehicle if I was out of money. Why would a single man making a good living and picking up an expense check from his employer run out of money?"

Harry waited for Trinity to supply the answer. But she didn't say anything, so Harry answered his own question. "Because I gave away all my money to waitresses, motel maids, and down-and-out sissies. It was my way of making friends in new places, and I did get a kick out of it. But I had another agenda. After you've given 'em two or three hundred bucks they start talking. You learn all about their lives, hopes, and dreams. I never cared about that shit. What interested me was who were the bad guys messing up their lives. I made sure to get corroboration. I had to be sure the guy was an asshole. Then I acted. Setting up was the fun part.

"Junie, you are listening to this, right? Remember that G.I. Joe used to stalk his deer year-round? Well, I got the idea from him. It was harder than anything he ever did. I not only had to walk the edges to set up the kill and get away with it. I had to dispose of the body. That's the hard part but also a big fun part.

"I worked for days, weeks and sometimes months. Some guys I never got. There were just too many assholes to kill off. Now watch this."

Harry opened one of the fish wells. Harry pulled out a rifle with a telescopic sight on it. In a split second the Zeno-Cam went blurry and now Trinity was holding the rifle.

"Wow!" Harry said. "You got some kind of quick. If I had reflexes like that, I'd be a bully."

Trinity emptied the rounds from the magazine, cleared the breech, and handed the weapon back to Harry. "Forgive me, Harry. It was just a precaution."

"That's okay, if I'd a been in your shoes I'd a done the same thing," Harry said. "I'm grateful for the humility. That's what getting old is all about, you little fucking sissy, one humiliation after another. You gotta learn to like the drool when they spit in your face. Do I understand why you did it? Yes. Do I forgive you? No."

Harry aimed the rifle at the harbor. "Sometimes I come here with my man licker and I get this urge to pick off as many of my fellow retirees as I can find in my sights—mercy killing has its moral component. Then I wait for the state police helicopter to blow me out of the water."

"But you don't do it."

"Naw, I retired. Retired serial killer. Ha-ha."

"And the Mannlicher-Schoenauer, the Hemingway rifle, that was your preferred weapon. Why?"

"It's got feel, man—it's got feel. It's accurate, reliable, powerful, and untraceable. I bought it from a guy at a yard sale. He didn't know what he had and didn't know who I was. Sometimes when things go around, they don't necessarily come around. It gave me a chuckle that I never actually read anything by Ernest Hemorrhoids. See? Get it? Even us serial killers have a sense of humor. Junie, that brand of humor sounds like G.I. Joe, does it not?"

There was something about the way Harry called my name, an intimacy. He was bringing me back to those days my father hosted the annual deer hunt with his Army buddies and Harry would sneak me ten-dollar bills.

"Harry," Trinity said, "I wonder if you would tell us about that first kill."

"In the war?"

Trinity shook her head. "I think you know what I mean. First kill with the man licker."

"Yeah, sure. It began with that urge to kill I told you about, which did come from the war. I had it big time for a long time. The feeling made me philosophical. Somebody was going down. I didn't know who. I hadn't formed my modus operandi yet about killing men who were assholes. All I knew was I wanted to kill a man who had it coming. I had nothing personal against killing women, but I thought it would be more satisfying to kill a man. More of a challenge. Killing a woman is like playing tackle football against girls—it's just too easy. I prayed for a worthy victim."

"Maybe 'pray' isn't quite the right word, Harry."

"What's your definition of prayer?"

"For me it's an SOS. For you it's a call of the wild, right?" Trinity said.

"I could learn to like you, you sissy. I was waiting for an opportunity. It came when I was having a drink with my buddy, Pete Shaughnessy. He was telling me about this windbag asshole who ran this hysterical commune on G.I. Joe's property. I thought, 'I'd like to kill that asshole,' but I wasn't about to do it. It was just a loose thought over a couple beers with Pete. I loved Pete. He was such an idiot. He never got over the terrible things we did in the war. None of us did."

"What terrible things?"

"That's another story best left to the trench rats in Korea to chew on. Anyway, I didn't take action, but I should have because the next thing I knew Pete was dead. I didn't believe for one minute that he drowned all by himself."

"So, you killed Osgood Stone to gain justice for your friend and because he was an asshole?"

"That was part of it, but there was another more important reason."

"Really? I'm all ears."

"I can't tell you. It's private."

"Oh, come on Harry," Trinity said. "You're going to be dead pretty soon when that cancer spreads to your organs. Do the right thing. What was the personal reason that inspired you to plan and execute that first kill?"

"Fuck you, fairy."

"OK, let's forget the why. Tell me the how, how you managed to kill the leader of a commune surrounded by many people almost all the time."

"I told you that the planning was the fun part. First, I learned as much as I could about Red Shift. The a-hole was going to take some volunteers to Jonestown. I thought, I better get this done pronto. I wasn't about to go to South America.

"I took some vacation time from my job and got a room at Winding Brook Lodge and a rental car from West Street Texaco in Keene. Every day I'd go to the nature conservancy with my binoculars and watch the island. The asshole was a man of habits. He'd canoe out to the island, strip down until he was bare ass, even when the weather was chill. I know the type—vigor idiots. He'd sit real still under that shelter. But you know what, he cheated. He'd wrap himself in a quilt if it was too chilly for him.

"The easy part was shooting him. Only a hundred yards. Stationary target. My bullet hit right where I aimed, between the eyes. The hard part was swimming naked in that cold water to the island. But I was pumped, and I made it, no problem. I dressed in his clothes. Boy, that coat felt good."

"What gave you the idea of stuffing the body into the hollow of the tree?" Trinity asked.

"You found the body—I'm impressed and disappointed at the same time. Isn't that what a man's life is about? I liked thinking about the asshole in his final resting place."

"If it makes you feel better, Harry, we left the bones undisturbed and have not contacted the authorities."

"Thank you, I'm grateful, you little fucking fairy."

"How did you know about the cavity in the tree?"

"Back in the day, G.I. Joe took us out to the island a couple times where we'd make a fire and get drunk, and he showed us the cave in the tree. Just moved rocks a couple feet high to stand on so you could actually look into the hole. So, I knew ahead of time what I was going to do with the body."

Harry tapped his head and said, "Planning is everything. It was no big deal to canoe to shore in the asshole's clothes. By the way, I didn't cheat and use the quilt to warm up. Luckily, I didn't see anybody and hiked back to my car. It was an extremely exhilarating experience. I was high for a week. I knew I would be chasing down that experience again. You have any more questions? I'm an old man, and you're interrupting my nap."

"Yes," said Trinity. "Did you know that Osgood Stone, or Uncle Oggie as he was known by the Red Shift communards, was not his real name, that he had an entirely different identity as an officer in the United States Army during the Korean War, Lieutenant Gerard Stanton?"

"No shit," Harry said, and I could tell by his tone and the surprised look on his face that he had no knowledge that Uncle Oggie was Gerard Stanton. Harry's secret reason for killing Oggie wasn't about vengeance or the war. I knew that Trinity must have been relieved that her grandfather was not implicated in Harry's first civilian blood, since Harry made it clear that his secret reason was private.

"I do have one more question," Trinity said. "When you grabbed your rifle a few minutes ago did you plan on using it against me?"

"It did cross my mind."

≈

Back at Grace Pond a couple days later, Trinity and I sat outside at one of the Red Shift picnic tables with uninvited mosquitos to drink a bottle of wine and talk about the Harry Cromwell interview and to decide where we were going next in our investigation. Trinity was in the same "working girl" persona that she had devised to meet Harry with, though she had changed her outfit into a frumpy two-piece bathing suit from that time period before Bridget Bardot brought the bikini to North America.

There was a bulge in the crotch area of that baggy bottom piece. Was it produced by male genitalia, my imagination, a prosthesis designed to confound and confuse this observer? These were questions I couldn't stop thinking about, even though I knew the answers were, as Sadie would say, none of my beeswax.

"There's nothing like a cyclopean stare to get my attention?" Trinity said.

"Blatant staring is one of my character flaws. I apologize for being so obvious."

The mocking laugh. "No doubt a result of your own questionable sexuality."

I didn't respond, but Trinity must have seen me blush, because she followed up with, "It's okay, Junie. We're brothers and sisters under the skin. Only difference between us is that I'm more manifest."

"And younger," I said.

At that point Trinity jumped from the table, raced to the pond, ran in until she was knee deep, then dove flat and swam far. She came back a few minutes later, obviously refreshed and pleased with herself. Without bothering to towel off, she sat down dripping wet at the picnic table.

Then suddenly she stood. "Hey, look at this—on my belly?"

I went to pull it off.

"No, no, leave it on," Trinity said. "It's a leech, right?"

"I don't know the proper name. Locally, we don't call them leeches, we call them bloodsuckers."

"Interesting, it's feeding on my blood," she said.

"Just like mosquitos, though with different bio operating systems," I said. "They use your blood to make their babies."

"So, even though I'm infertile as a woman and sterile as a man I can—in my own way—assist in the propagation of various other species."

"It's an irony," I said.

"Maybe for you. For me it's a comfort. I feel useful." Trinity let the bloodsucker have its meal before gently transporting it back to the pond.

The wine bottle was almost empty before the conversation turned to our investigation.

"What did you think about Harry?" I asked.

"I liked him. He's one of those people who is bad but not deceitful. Like some serial killers, he was born with an unbalanced IQ. His reasoning powers are far above average, but he lacks the ability to imagine, to fantasize, to synthesize what he knows to create a mental playground. The result is that he is subject to profound bouts of boredom with outbreaks of overwhelming urges. If you don't have the ability to fantasize, your urges possess you. You must act upon their behalf in the material world. In his own way, Harry has the attributes, good and bad, of a comic book superhero."

"Harry Cromwell is one of the few people that my mother loathes. She calls him Potato Head behind his back."

"Sadie has great instincts."

"So, what do we know now that we didn't know before your conversation with Harry?" I asked.

"We know that Grandpa Landrieu wasn't in on the kill of Gerard Stanton."

"I'm relieved for my own selfish reasons. I didn't want to go to war with you, Trinity."

"We were saved this time by circumstances, but in the future—well, who knows."

There was a long pause while Trinity and I contemplated our peculiar partnership. Finally, I spoke. "I was disappointed that Harry had no knowledge of Uncle Oggie's dual identity," I said. "I could have sworn that there was a direct connection between the murder of Pete and the Korean War."

"If there was, Harry didn't know about it," Trinity said.

"And yet Harry insisted his primary reason for offing Uncle Oggie was personal. So now what?"

"I want to go back to the Stanton War Library," Trinity said. "You're probably right that there's a Korean war connection. I'm betting there's more Gerard Stanton material in the library that I can get my hands on. What are you going to do?"

"I plan to go back in time and take a close look at the supposed accidental shooting of my father," I said. "We have reason to suspect that Uncle Oggie may have made him his first victim."

"If that's the case and if a revenge motive is at play here, it must have been very satisfying for Oggie to bed the widow. Ha-ha."

That line put my teeth on edge, and I lashed out at Trinity. "Your cruel streak is acting up again."

"It's a failing, I admit. Some people stare, some people mouth off, I inflict emotional pinpricks." Trinity spoke in a lowered voice that was as close to an apology as she was going to give. The steam went out of my indignation.

Trinity left the next morning in Satoshi for the airport in Boston. His clothes were male-casual, uninspired, imitation baggy NBA shorts, cut-off sweatshirt, box store dirty track shoes, maroon socks. He was going to infiltrate the Stanton Library under an assumed name, Stephen Boone, a research assistant from PLC (Paradise Lots Covenant), a corporation whose CEO, H.C. Wentworth, was a Darby native. Stephen was a little clumsy, a little spacey, balding, thick around the middle, a bit of a slob, the kind of young man Pauline Alvar would not take note of.

"Do you think you'll fool her?" I asked.

"Sure. Heck, I've already fooled myself."

His use of the word "heck" got a snicker out of me, which perhaps was his intent, or maybe he was just talking in the character of Stephen Boone.

"If you're not going to wear a wire, message me once in a while," I said. "I worry about you."

"Yes, sir, Uncle Cyclops," and Trinity spontaneously gave me a little daughterly kiss on the cheek, which felt touching but strange coming from a young man.

≈

Harry Cromwell died a day later, though not in the way he envisioned for himself, on the Peter Gunn boat in a storm. Harry was taking a walk on range land when he was bit on the foot by a rattlesnake. So much for flip-flops. He might have survived had he made his way to a public place where he would have received medical attention. Instead, Harry went back to his RV and medicated himself with whiskey, Seagram's VO. His body was found by a neighbor who noticed that the door to his rig was open.

According to his wishes, expressed in his very short will, Harry Cromwell was cremated, his ashes scattered in the lagoon, the notice posted on Facebook. What followed was extraordinary. His Wild About Harry Facebook site organized an online memorial service where Harry was eulogized as the Legendary Tipper of Interstate 90.

Re-enactment

I STARTED MY "RE-ENACTMENT" of G.I. Joe's last hours by drawing a map of the area where he was killed. Then I photographed it for reference on my phone.

"Ready to go," I said aloud as if to Trinity on her Zeno-Cam. But of course, we were not connected. A wave of loneliness broke over me as I set out on the trail that four hunters traversed on that terrible day. I tried to imagine my dad and his war buddies preparing for their hunt. They had spent the night in Shinbone Shack and were up later the next morning than more serious hunters.

Never mind that it was high summer on my walk and I was sweating from the heat and humidity as I followed the hunters' history. In my mind it was December 1968.

Pete, Pass, and Harry sit around the drop-down table drinking coffee, while G.I. Joe cooks bacon and eggs in a cast iron skillet on the top of the wood stove.

The men talk about the hunting plan for the day and during this session they abide by "Golden Rule 1: No discussions of contemporary issues."

While they are bonded closer than brothers because of their experiences in war, they have wildly different personalities, family backgrounds, education, and political views. Nineteen-sixty-eight has been a tumultuous year world-wide with street protests all over Europe, Mexico, Brazil, and of course, the United States. Martin Luther King and Robert Kennedy, two of America's most well-known political leaders, have been murdered by assassins. The war in Vietnam continues to demoralize the American psyche.

The men's politics place them in two equally matched factions: G.I. Joe and Harry representing one perspective, and Pete and Pass, another. The men know that eventually, like always, they will break their Golden Rule and there will be a time of raucous argumentation, but that will not come until the evening drinking session following the first day of the hunt.

They are in no hurry to kill their deer. This is a week-long retreat and very rarely do all four men shoot a deer. Only G.I. Joe always kills his deer and always alone before the buddy hunt, except for 1968 when for reasons unclear, he chose not to kill. Nobody questions him. It's as if his buddies already know the reason, though not Sadie, not me, no one outside the four veterans.

As he cooks the bacon, with very careful attention to each strip, G.I. Joe gives his buddies a detailed account of his "patrols" in the preceding months to find and evaluate the deer herds. Habits of the animals vary from year to year to deal with weather, predators, access to feed, and changes in the land. Joseph Blaise makes it his business to keep track of these changes.

First day of hunting usually produces no kills, because the men stay together to walk the paths, and check out hunting stands that Joe has set up. They also take time to sight in their rifles, do a little target practice, and even help out with work around the camp. It's a day of catching up and preparation.

Starting on Day 2, the actual hunt will begin. One of the men will position himself in a tree stand, another on a camouflage stand on the ridge line, for G.I. Joe has determined that Rock Ridge is the best place to start the hunt. Joe and one of the other hunters will act as drivers. The idea is to locate the deer and drive them in the direction of the ambush stands.

Day 3 and Day 4 are repeats of Day 2. Day 5 is, in Pass Landrieu's words, a "meditation hunt." The men will hunt alone and return to camp at Shinbone Shack to compare notes. Day 6 they will sleep late, help G.I. Joe with chores around Shinbone Shack, and return to the Blaise apartment in Keene for showers, a meal prepared by Sadie, errands, and an evening of drinking and conversation before departure early on Day 7.

When one of the hunters kills a deer, the men make a big communal deal out of the occasion. They field dress the animal, haul it in Joe's truck to the state's deer-kill station at the Darby Village Store, then bring the animal to a butcher shop in Keene for processing for the freezer. The successful hunter will return to the hunt with his buddies, but without his rifle. "Golden Rule 2: WST" (We Stick Together).

It's a good day to be walking in the woods, though not for hunting. The temperature hangs around the freezing mark, the sky is clear, but there is no tracking snow, nor wind to throw off the scent of hunters. There has been some snow, a thaw and melt off, and now the weather is turning cold again. Bloodsucker Brook is still running fast through breaks in the ice.

The men walk spread out but within sight as if on patrol in the Army. Harry carries his recently acquired man licker. He has removed the scope because except for the expanse of the pond, the surrounding landscape consists mainly of mixed hardwoods and conifers, steep hillsides, narrow valleys, and narrower ravines. There will be few opportunities for long-distance shots. Pete and Pass carry almost identical Winchester 94s, and Joe as usual is unarmed. He has long ago identified with the deer family he stalks during the year. The killing has been part of a ritual going back to his family heritage in French Canada, back to the forests of Europe, perhaps back to ancient times and the source of the hunting instinct itself.

So, why didn't he kill his deer this year? Maybe he is trying to break the ceremony. Or maybe Artemis, pagan goddess of the hunt and wild animals, is onto him and is arranging an accident to honor her own ritual of blood-letting.

It ends at probably the prettiest spot in the vicinity, what Joe calls Rock Ridge, and where one of the hunting stands has been set up. The ridge runs for almost half a mile but the stone wall that gives it its name, is much shorter, only about fifty yards in length.

At first glance it looks like any of many falling-down stonewalls you find in New England, random stones gathered by the builders from the local area and stacked on lines three to four feet high. Removing stones to make the walls helped prepare land for growing crops. The walls penned in farm animals, acted as property boundaries between lots, and fences along roadsides. Or so the speculation goes. There's no consensus among interested parties for why the walls were built.

Rock Ridge wall is different. It isn't part of a longer wall, nor is it an enclosure, it sets there for no obvious reason. About the only commonsensical thing you can say about it, is that it is pleasant to look at and makes a nice place to sit while you gaze at the meanderings of Bloodsucker Brook below as it cascades over rock outcroppings in the ravine. G.I. Joe believes the wall has been built not by the colonists but by native people for their own purposes. He offers no proof. His belief is that an opinion expressed with passion and sincerity is worth more than known facts and scientific measurements, because, "In the end, nobody knows nuthn.'"

Another of Joe Blaise's favorite sayings is, "Avoid the places where you would not want to die." No doubt Rock Ridge and Bloodsucker Brook have met with his approval of good places to die.

The position at the wall provides an excellent field of fire of the brook below. The men are having a smoke at the ridge enjoying the view and chatting. In a time when many men smoke and when the military actually sets aside "smoke break" minutes on the hour, the Korean War vets associate smoking with relaxation and casual conversation.

G.I. Joe, the lone non-smoker in the group, takes a moment to hike down the steep incline to the brook to fill his canteen, another one of his rituals. He kneels on the ledge near some fast water just below a pool where deer are known to drink (and get shot by hunters). Local people are advised not to drink surface water in the woods, because it could be contaminated from the droppings of wild animals. It is a warning that G.I. Joe laughs at.

"The best drinking water flows over ledge. The arsenic in the granite kills the bacteria," G.I. Joe says, cracking one of his standard jokes.

He removes his gloves, sets them down, unscrews the top of his canteen, and holds it into the flow of a mini waterfall, which is how he always fills a canteen. Joe claims that fast water provides the best taste because it is "aired out."

He never hears the sound of the shot that kills him, because the bullet penetrates his brain before the sound arrives. Joe pitches head-first into the fast water. It is about 10:15 in the morning.

≈

According to Constable Godfrey Perkin's report, the killing shot likely was fired somewhere from the top of the ridge.

I scrambled down the long banking to the brook, very quiet at this dry time of year. So many changes in the ensuing decades. Different flora, even a different brook. "Water changes everything from one fucking moment to the next," Dad would say, so I couldn't find the exact spot where he had died. All I had to go on were the police reports and my imagination.

The bullet had entered the side of the head just above the right ear. They call it the "temple," perhaps because the ancients believed that was the part of the brain devoted to religious observance. The bullet plowed through the brain carrying shards of bone, and blew out the other side, leaving the face intact. The body tumbled downstream a few feet. The bullet was never found. The buddies pulled G.I. Joe's body out of the water and rested it on a table-like rock under a balsam fir tree. Pete stayed with the body while Harry and Pass left to notify the authorities.

I looked around for that balsam fir tree. The area was full of red spruce and white pine trees. You often can't tell at a glance differences between balsam fir and a red spruce tree. I walked along feeling the branches of trees. Balsam fir trees have soft needles, red spruce tree needles are prickly. I could not find any balsam fir trees.

Pete recalled that he picked up Joe's canteen. "I take a drink," he was quoted as saying. "It's like holy water to me, like I am an altar boy again back in Lowell, and Father Spike Morrisette is saying mass." Pete was a man who liked the present tense.

I knelt by the water's edge and tried to imagine myself as my dad, but the gesture felt false. I wasn't him, he wasn't me. Then was not now. Imagination can only bring you so far. History is unreliable because historians are unreliable. And memory? Ha! "Close enough" has to be good enough, because you can never actually get back to a there there. Reality confounds the comfort of a Zeno Paradox, because despite mathematical calculations based on theory, the bullet always arrives at its destination.

The town constable, the state fish and game office, and the state police all tried their hands finding where that stray shot came from. They talked to local hunters, everybody who had registered a deer that day, and they interrogated local suspicious characters. The only thing close to a lead were several reports that out-of-state hunters had been sighted who had left the public parking area on the conservancy shortly before noon. The authorities couldn't even find the bullet that killed Joseph Blaise. They theorized that the force of the moving water brought it far downstream or tucked it into a rock crevice.

The investigators talked at length to dad's buddies. The constable inspected their weapons, discovering that all three rifles of my dad's buddies had been fired recently. They explained that as occasional hunters their weapons needed to be sighted in before the hunt. I seemed to recall that in previous years dad sighted in the weapons in the days before his buddies arrived, but I wasn't sure.

I tried to think like the killer. I could conjure scenarios where a hunter's stray bullet might have hit dad, but only if it had been fired downslope from the ridge line, in which case the hunter in pursuit of the deer he missed would have come upon Pete guarding dad's body. Maybe that's exactly what happened and he had backed off, not wanting to take responsibility for his actions. The police pursued a similar scenario. No one ever came forward.

The other possibility, one more likely in my current thinking, was that my father had been targeted by Lieutenant Gerard Stanton. But why? I shouted my thought in the direction of the cell tower. "Uncle Oggie, you bastard, what was your motive?"

Something in war, my demon replied.

I took another hour to hike to the crest of the next hill for a look at the cell tower on the conservatory property. It was surprisingly populated. A logging road traversing down the other side of the hill to the Salmon Estate had been improved to allow trucks to drive to the site of the antenna. A couple of men in hard hats were standing around talking. I could see surveying equipment. They told me they were doing site preparations to build windmills. That was the only info they had.

I headed back to Shinbone Shack, typed out my notes, and sent them to Trinity and Maurice Landrieu, in hopes Trinity would immediately get back to me. But he didn't.

Compatible Fuckedupness

TWO DAYS WENT BY before I finally connected with Trinity. Late in the afternoon I heard Satoshi coming down my long driveway. I watched Trinity get out of his vehicle carrying a twelve-pack of Geek Chorus Amber. It was raining and he bounded up the stairs about as fast as a human being could move without looking like he was trying.

"I'm starved—do you have anything to eat?" he said in his Stephen Boone voice.

"How about a big stonewall garden salad and my homemade bread with Sage Farm goat cheese?"

"Great. It's been a long day."

We sat on the porch drinking and watching the rain fall on the pond.

"Why didn't you call or text me?" I asked.

"I was fighting off somebody trying to hack into my device. For all I know, they're trying to kill me."

"Your life may be in danger—you don't seem upset or even vindictive."

"No, the opposite, I'm grateful. I live for this kind of excitement, all too rare."

"Who's trying to hack into you?"

"I'm not sure. Which is part of the excitement," Trinity said.

"Does Pauline Alvar figure into this?"

"Probably, though her role is unclear," Trinity said. "Could be Save The World. Could be Geek Chorus Software. More likely the NSA? Quite the sophisticated cyber-attack. Which is the reason I couldn't contact you. I had to change all my passwords and reroute my stuff through a different array of servers. Not hard to do, but a lot of donkey-style labor. These government people are very persistent."

"What—the NSA wants to prosecute you for cyber crimes?"

"No, they want to recruit me. One way of coercing me is to ruin my life online. It's also their way of testing to see if I'm as good as my rep."

"Why not go to work for them? It would be a way to serve your country as well as your own interests."

"It's not that I'm unpatriotic, it's that I value my independence, which you don't have when you work for somebody else, especially a government agency with motivation to keep you under their thumb."

"'I value my independence' are the exact words that my father used over and over."

Trinity responded with her mocking laugh. "I dunno, Uncle Cyclops, from what you've told me about G.I. Joe, he sounds like a guy whose archenemy was himself."

"Maybe. What did you find on Gerard Stanton?" I asked.

"Nothing new. His archive has been moved to an undisclosed location. As long as the Stanton Library people refuse to digitize their materials and create an online presence, I have no way of tracking down any additional info."

"Trinity, you knew all this when you left."

"So what?"

"You didn't go all the way to the West Coast for the investigation. You had another agenda. Romance."

"You've become a better investigator, Uncle Cyclops."

"I'm worried about you."

"Really? Why?"

"For one thing, you're still in your frumpy Stephen Boone persona."

"Yeah, well, the fact is I don't know how to get out. It's me. I am Stephen Boone. See, I bumped into Pauline and just as I predicted she never gave me a second look, which means the Stephen Boone identity worked the way I wanted it too. And you know what?"

"Heartbreak!" I said, and Trinity responded with a bare nod of agreement, as if to show more would bring on more of the hurt.

"Consider your mood a message," I said. "You blew her off supposedly for her own good. Sometimes making a sacrifice is the right thing to do, but other times it kicks everybody in the teeth including the kickee. You need to admit you made a mistake and try to win her back. If it doesn't work, you'll know you gave it your best shot, and there will be no unfinished business."

"I get that. Problem is another possible scenario is that Pauline actually did recognize my Stephen Boone persona and that she's an agent working for some foreign entity.

"I'm sorry to hear that."

"It's OK. On one level I'm thrilled, because if she's trying to harm me it would mean she cares."

"You vacillate between bravado and despair. You're smart, logical, and insightful when you're dealing with a case, and you claim to be commonsensical about your life, but you're as . . ."

Trinity interrupted with a laugh that had no mockery in it and spoke his own take on what I was about to say, "I'm as fucked up as you are . . ."

It was my turn to interrupt, and I said, "But in your own way."

"We don't have competitive fuckedupness, we have compatible fuckedupness," Trinity said, and we both exploded into shared mirth. It was as if we had accidentally created an in-joke that included only the two of us.

I realized that finally I knew Trinity well enough to unburden myself of that awful scene I'd kept private all these years.

Soon as darkness fell, I rowed my boat out into the middle of the pond and typed a report on my tablet keyboard. I finished at dawn.

Momma's Boy

IN MY MEMORY it was a perfect fall day in 1968—a late Saturday morning—
when my father approached me at the kitchen table as I finished my breakfast.

"It's foliage galore out there," he said. "Let's play tourist and go leaf peeping."

Leaf peeping? An invitation to do something with his son. Very peculiar
of Dad, I thought. But I was thrilled to be with him.

It was a ten-mile drive from the city to Shinbone Shack, me riding shotgun in my father's GMC three-quarter ton truck that he used to deliver firewood to customers.

A couple miles before the long hill that would bring us to Grace Pond and
the hunting camp, we drove past what once had been the Blaise family farm.
My father never took his eyes off the road, and his blank glower enforced a
silence. At an early age I understood that G.I. Joe missed out on his calling to
work the family farm like his father and grandfather before him. At the top
of the hill, we turned off the blacktop onto the dirt road to Shinbone Shack.
One of my father's standard jokes was that our road devolved into a path
that ended up a tree into a hole hollowed out by Woody Woodpecker, the
joke followed by a fairly accurate imitation of the *Woody Woodpecker* laugh.

I can still see and feel the fall colors in the leaves that day: sugar maples
orange and yellow, with streaks of red. Red maples almost solid red with
streaks of green. Birches in shades of yellow. Oaks just starting to turn rus-
set. Beeches still green. Ash trees already bare of leaves crisp on the ground
because it hadn't rained for a week. Evergreens of balsam fir, red spruce, white
pine, and hemlock. Whirlybirds on the surface of the pond.

My father's ten-foot-long aluminum johnboat, dull silver in those days,
was tied to our rickety wooden dock. A cove beside the open water in front
of Shinbone Shack was dominated by lily pads whose white blooms had died
with the summer.

It was colder in Shinbone Shack than it was outside that sunny October
day in 1968, and dad sent me to bail rainwater out of the johnboat while he
started a fire in the old-fashioned box-style wood burning stove. Whirlybirds

were strewn about the boat, which meant that some weeks earlier dad must have rowed out to the island where the whirlybirds fell from the great tree into his boat. When I returned to the camp the room was warmer and dad was sitting at the drop-down dining table on which sat two cans of Schaefer Beer.

My father opened the cans with the "church key" he carried on his belt keyring. "I think you're ready for this stuff. Don't tell your mother."

I was shocked. I had never tasted an alcoholic beverage before, and I couldn't think of an appropriate response. I ended up blurting out lines from a TV jingle. "Schaefer, the one beer to have when you're having more than one."

My father laughed much too loud. "And to think I never figured you to be a chip off the old block!" My father downed his beer in two long gulps.

"I found whirlybirds in the boat. Do they actually fly?"

"Sure, why not," he said with that grin that told me he meant the opposite of what he said.

I took a drink, and the fizz came back out my nose.

I thought my father would laugh at me again, but he spoke kindly, "It's OK, Junie, you'll get used to it. Meanwhile, take it easy until your liver adjusts."

We didn't talk much for a while. I took my father's advice and drank very slowly while I contemplated my liver, wondering where it was in the body, what it looked like and what it did. By the time I'd drunk about two-thirds of the beer Dad was working on his third or maybe fourth. I wasn't keeping track. I felt pretty good. The room had warmed pleasantly, and it was as if that warmth was now within me. I don't remember what I was thinking at the time, but I knew there would be more beers in the life that lay ahead.

Finally, my father began to speak in a measured, formal way that I had never heard before, or maybe I was just reacting to this new substance in my system.

"You're probably wondering why I brought you here today," he said. "No, that's all right, don't answer. Hear me out. I know I haven't been the greatest family man. I can't help myself. You think it's the booze talking, well, OK it's the booze talking, but at least the booze can talk. Me, not the G. I. Joe that people see, but the real me, lots of times he can't think of anything to say, so he lets the booze talk for him."

That's how it went. My father's attempt at formal speech fell apart and he just rambled on, and I sometimes missed half of what he said because I was distracted. The beer made me see the cabin in a different way. Why was there no door to the tiny bedroom? I wondered which of my dad's Army buddies got the big bed that took up almost the entire room? Was it acceptable for two men to share a bed?

My father grabbed my arm, "Are you listening to me?"

"Yes," I said. "I was wondering who sleeps where during your fall hunt with your buddies."

"What a fairy question. I sleep on the couch, the others on cots."

"The ones in the barn from the Army Navy store?"

"Yeah, we just haul 'em over."

"What about the bed in the bedroom?"

My father didn't answer my question. He just shook his head, a smile on his face as if I'd unintentionally said something stupid-funny.

"Can I have another beer?" I asked.

"No, one is plenty for the first time. When you get older, you'll want to add a shot of Seagram 7, better yet CC or VO, to give the beer some respectability, but for now, go easy."

My father opened another Schaefer for himself. He was about to say something, stopped, drank, stopped again. With his voice a little shaky he said, "I know you wanted to work with me, learn to cut wood, tap maple trees, hunt, fish."

"And trap."

"Yes, and you're wondering why I have not encouraged you."

I nodded, but he was looking at me only through the corner of his eye. He was somewhere else in his head, and his words seemed to come out of a different person.

"It's because I want you to do something better with your life than your disheveled, beaten-all-to-hell old man and . . ."

I must have given him a defiant look, because in a split second his demeanor changed again, and he interrupted himself.

"You can get away with that smarty-pants look with your mother, but don't try it with me. If truth be told, I don't think you're constitutionally suited to be an outdoorsman. Simple as that."

"You think I'm a momma's boy."

He ignored me and talked on and on, about the Army and the rats in the trenches along the 38th parallel that Harry Cromwell shot and that Pass Landrieu drew with stubby pencils, and the crabs, and the cold, the bitter cold of Korea, and how on patrol when it was snowing you couldn't tell friend from foe, but snow was great at keeping a machine gun barrel cool and operational, and how coming home he was thinking about the spring of the following year when he and Grandpa Norman would cut hay—the smell of cut hay—and how in Lawton, Oklahoma, in September of 1953 when he was getting out of the Army he met a girl named Sarah Boyd from Tahoka, Texas.

"Tall girl, taller than myself. Like the taller the tree the greater the timberrr! when you cut it down. Tallness was the come-on. Met her in . . . a laundromat? Can't remember, and through it all there was the idea of working with my dad to cut hay, that first sweet cut, the smell, strong in the cold of Korea thinking about it, and, finally discharged, taking the bus home from Fort Sill . . . cut hay, the smell of hay . . . at a bus station in Memphis where I had a half-hour layover to switch buses, I felt this wave, a tidal wave of homesickness, so on impulse I phoned the farm collect. That's how I got the news. And you know what happened."

"I do," I said. "Grandpa Norman had a heart attack and died."

"No, that's what happened to him. What happened to this G.I. Joe was the war. Every man has his war, a private war that he fights over and over again. That's what they say and it's true. It goes on and on until everybody dies. See, in war it's more than the official casualties. In war everybody dies, or it ain't a war. You don't mind if I say ain't, do you? You fucking sissy."

In retrospect, I think he read the hurt on my face, because he stopped suddenly before resuming in a conciliatory tone.

"Look, I'm sorry, Junie, I'm so sorry. I didn't mean to say that—it just slipped out. I never wanted you to... like when my dad died, forlorn, lost, me back in the war of my mind all over again but no hope . . . things happened, you can't imagine . . . so what that I couldn't love you the way I loved dad and he loved me, loved the farm . . . I loved Sadie, how could anybody not love Sadie . . . signed on to the nuptials . . . to . . . to protect you. Listen, this is not the booze talking; this is the real G.I. Joe."

My father was crying now, crying hard, a drinker's temporary insanity or maybe sanity in the insane world. Whatever he was doing I couldn't follow.

I didn't know what he was talking about. All I knew was that he called me a fucking sissy and I was not going to break down in front of him.

"I'm not like you," I said, "I'm not a cry baby, crying, babbling cry baby."

"It's good that you hate me," he said. "Well-deserved, son, well-deserved." And he cried and cried.

A lot of what happened the rest of that day I don't remember very clearly, but one thing I do remember is that what I hated about my father was that he cried. I promised myself that something like that would never happen to me. I would never cry. No matter what, this fucking sissy would never ever shed a tear.

Ambush of the Heart

MAURICE TEXTED US. "Good morning, Trinity, good morning, Junie. Harry Cromwell is dead. I'm the last of our cadre. I think it's time I told our story."

The news snapped Trinity out of his Stephen Boone persona. Before leaving for Trinidad, Trinity shape-shifted herself back to female to match her grandparents preferred image of her.

"I sensed early on that they were more comfortable with me when I was a girl—you, too, right?" she said.

"True enough," I said. "I wonder if other people's ideas of you matter to you."

"You think that if I, or you, or anybody, fabricates an identity so that other people relate to you based on that fabrication that as far as your world is considered, that identity is you. But if in your heart, it isn't—then what?"

I had no answer for Trinity, either then or today as I type these words trying to make sense of it all. I don't believe Trinity has an answer either.

Her clothes were casual garb as any young woman traveler of some means might wear—designer blue jeans, white blouse with an abstract design in cross-stitching, hair long and black and swirled over one shoulder, a simple outfit except for the green and gold earrings of streamer flies of my own design.

"You're walking differently now," I said. "Back straight, kind of slow."

"It's how the people of Trinidad walk, a dignified saunter, which makes us North Americans look like scurrying crabs."

It's a long flight from New England to Trinidad, but not a particularly taxing one, because there's only an hour difference in time zone going toward the dawn. Fly from Boston to Miami, then after a two-hour layover, to Port of Spain, the capitol city of the two-island country. While Trinity was in transit, I sat on my porch in Shinbone Shack and went over my notes on Maurice Landrieu.

From the time that he was a child, Maurice wanted to be a fine arts painter. Some of his early oils on his website showed a tremendous talent and sensibility. The work was in the tradition of creole art from New Orleans— colorful, confident, free-flowing, Caribbean, Southern American, African,

Roman Catholic, with an emphasis on masked faces. Art inspired by the Carnival tradition. One reviewer wrote: "These images inhabit the interstices between realism and abstraction, as one might conjure in a morning dream just before waking."

All that work was done as a youth before Landrieu was drafted into the Army. Though he continued after the war to paint and study and immerse himself in the art world of New York, his paintings did not come close to reaching the excellence of his teen years. In his own reckoning, his life had been a failure, because he never fulfilled his potential as a fine arts painter. The only recognized work from the war years were his pencil drawings of trench rats.

In the early years of his career Landrieu was far from a successful artist, and he and Olivia got by on her income designing masks for Fat Tuesday parades in New Orleans and the Caribbean islands. The pressures of impending fatherhood gave him an insight that changed his fortunes. Here's what he told a staff writer for a well-known art magazine after he'd become a rich man:

"I noticed that nearly all my painter and sculptor friends had a storage problem. What do you do with works that nobody is buying? Meanwhile, when I looked at the art world from the perspective of a nouveau riche art lover, the problem I saw was that buying art placed a psychological burden on the owner. Eventually, the stuff on your walls gets too familiar. You want to replace most of it, but no art lover can bring himself to throw away art. It's an ache to sell it and a pain to store it. The result was that many people didn't bother to collect original works, even though they wanted to. Instead, they made do with prints that could be discarded without conflicted feelings.

"My idea was to act as a broker between art buyers and art creators. In my company, you lease art from me with an option to buy. The creators solve a storage problem, gain exposure, and make money on the rentals while they continue to own their art. The art lovers get to hang interesting work on their walls until they decide to exercise their option to buy, renew, or turn it in for other artwork at the end of the lease period. My company gets a fee."

Within ten years, Interstices by Maurice had offices in major cities all over the world. Maurice Landrieu, this self-described failure, who as a young, traumatized GI had been hospitalized with what was then called a nervous breakdown, was now a millionaire many times over. The Landrieus kept residences in New York, New Orleans, and Tunapuna, Trinidad, where Olivia Johnston held forth on the history of Carnival masks as a frequent guest lecturer at the University of West Indies.

≈

A car was waiting for Trinity when she stepped off the plane at Piarco International Airport in Port of Spain to drive her to the Landrieu compound. Here, only seven degrees from the equator, the sun rose rapidly in the morning and fell equally rapidly in the evening. It was dark.

"Hi, Royden," Trinity said to the driver. "Don't take the priority highway, take the Main Road. I want to get the feeling."

There were three roads that ran more or less parallel at the heavily populated north end of the island. One was a four-lane highway designed like a United States freeway. Another road was the "priority highway" for cabs, police, government vehicles, and specially licensed vehicles. No speed limit on the Priority Highway. The Eastern Main Road was an old two-lane commercial road—slow traffic, many people, stores, groceries, open air markets, boarding houses, small businesses, movie theaters, bars, tattoo parlors—in a word, life.

Suddenly, Trinity said, "Pull over and zip the windows down."

They stayed on the roadside for about a minute. At first, I didn't know why Trinity wanted to stop, and then I heard the sounds of a steel band rehearsing. Somebody was singing a Trinidad classic, "Black Bottom in the Middle of the Road" about an East Indian man in love with an African woman.

Upon arrival at the compound, after going through a gate with a uniformed guard, the car stopped in front of a formal garden in the tight-sphincter French topiary style where twenty or more people had gathered for a welcome home party.

Trinity was greeted with applause from the group that included family friends and relatives and with hugs from her grandparents. Everyone was happy to see Trinity, but as time went on it became clear to me that she wasn't an insider in Trinidad, more like a family celebrity figure living on the outside, admired perhaps but not loved.

That evening and all the next day Trinity, family members, and friends celebrated with rum concoctions, food platters that made me hungry, and spirited conversations about local politics and issues of the world. There was no talk between grandfather and granddaughter about the terrible Korean War and its terrible aftermath. That talk was all to come.

I enjoyed a voyeur's tour of the compound from Trinity's body cam. I could make out a tall, concrete wall that surrounded the stuccoed buildings of the Landrieu place—lawns, gardens, paths, labyrinths, black iron gates and fences, urns bursting with flora. The Landrieu compound could have been a villa on the Mediterranean.

Several related families in multi-generations lived on the estate, the skin color of the people in varying shades of brown. The grounds included a cricket court where I watched young people play. I never figured out the game. My only knowledge, acquired from Trinity, was that a cricket ball is so hard that it's dangerous in its state as s flying missile, so that Grandfather Landrieu decreed that tennis balls be substituted when children under fourteen were playing. I thought: Fourteen, that is a transitional age, is it not?

The passion of Maurice Landrieu's old age was on display everywhere on his grounds, a world-class orchid collection, many of which were in bloom. They were in the house in hanging pots, outside on the grounds, in ornamental trees, in formal gardens, along the walls, windowsills, and doorways. The more delicate blossoms resided in a climate-controlled greenhouse, presided over by a full-time gardener.

Maurice was a handsome specimen as octogenarians go—medium height but still square-shoulders with nearly a full head of white hair and a trimmed white beard.

Finally, on the third day of Trinity's arrival, grandfather and granddaughter got into the back seat of Landrieu's town car.

Royden, the driver, followed the priority highway traveling at speeds of a hundred miles an hour or more along the flat lands. The road narrowed, the car slowed, and turned on a winding black top that snaked up into a heavily forested mountain with little human habitation.

The road ended at a building that looked surprisingly like an updated version of a traditional New England cow barn, in fact like a grander version of the barn G.I. Joe built but never used for its stated purpose to house cows. Maurice and Trinity had arrived at a bird sanctuary and nature center open to the public. They were greeted by a staff member. I could tell by the casual but efficient way Maurice and Trinity moved through the building that they had been here before.

They walked to a deep porch with lounge chairs set up around tables. Landrieu carried a businessman's briefcase. A woman server brought tall drinks. The building was set into the side of a wooded hill. Below the porch, feeding stations laden with fruit attracted exotic birds, especially humming-birds for the viewing pleasure of visitors. I listened to a backdrop of bird songs. Meanwhile, Maurice Landrieu began to talk to his granddaughter.

"When your father was killed it left an empty space in our hearts. You have filled it, Trinity. Olivia and I feel so lucky to have you in our lives."

"Thank you, grandpa."

"Junie, can you hear me?" All the time he spoke, Maurice Laudrieu watched the birds.

Trinity handed an ear bud to Maurice who plugged it into his ear.

"Yes, I hear you just fine," I said.

"Where are you anyway?"

"I'm on the porch of Shinbone Shack looking out at Grace Pond."

"I know you're a man of sixty-something now, but in my mind, you'll always be that shy fourteen-year-old boy on the day your dad died. It wasn't until my own son died a violent death in a foreign land that I understood that some griefs never end. What do you want to know?"

"Can we begin with Korea?" I asked, "Something in that war that you and dad and Pete and Harry experienced, something you shared that made you brothers?"

"Yes, and that changed us. I got off easiest. All I had was a breakdown and permanent loss of creativity. Pete lost faith in his God and belief in himself. Harry learned to love killing, and Joe went into a deep depression that he could get out of only one way."

"Only one way? What do you mean?" I asked.

"I think deep down you know."

"No, I don't know. My guess is that Dad's death was not an accident. He was murdered, probably by a former lieutenant in the Army."

"You're close to the truth and yet far, far away. Your father was deliberately targeted, yes. But for a reason that he orchestrated."

It took a moment for those words to sink in. "A suicide! G.I. Joe wanted to die?"

"Yes, that's exactly it: Your father wanted to die. It's not unusual for a person to want to die. It happens every day. Suicide is built into some people's DNA. It often gets triggered by an event. Joe didn't want the stigma of suicide, and he wanted as much as possible to provide for his family to spare you and Sadie as much anguish as he could. Sadie couldn't have collected that skimpy insurance money if it was known that Joe killed himself. Also, Joe wanted to die on the family property on Grace Pond, and in his own crazy way he wanted a firing squad. He settled for a firing squad of one, and he chose Rock Ridge as the scene."

"Harry! Harry was the shooter, wasn't he? He had no qualms about killing."

"Harry would have been the logical choice, but we didn't do things that way. Golden Rule 3: draw straws. Even Joe drew a straw. If he had drawn the short one, he would have been obliged to shoot himself. But he didn't draw the short straw, nor did Pete, nor Harry."

"You? You shot my father?"

"I drew the short straw. He wanted me to shoot him in the heart."

"'It's all about the heart'—that was one of Dad's sayings."

"He faced me, so I had the perfect angle. For years I told myself that I flinched. I have finally come to terms with the truth. I didn't flinch. I never flinched. Joe moved suddenly a split second before I pulled the trigger, and that's why the bullet hit him in the head instead of the heart. For all I know he tried to duck. At the last second, he didn't want to die. Olivia believes that's what happened, so he's in heaven today."

Maurice Landrieu opened the briefcase and pulled out a small, exquisite jewelry box. He opened the box and removed a squashed piece of metal. I thought it looked like a 3D Rorschach test.

"This is the bullet from the Winchester Model 94 that killed your father, Junie. Pete found it when he pulled Joe out of the stream."

I think I made a gurgling sound, or maybe I said something. I'm not sure because there's a blank spot in my memory, like after you've been socked in the jaw. I came back to the moment with the sound of a tropical bird song, then Maurice Landrieu's voice.

"I hurt you, didn't I?" he said. "It was like an ambush, wasn't it? I know ambushes. We were the best. The four of us were renown in the trenches of the front lines along the 38th parallel, feared by the Chinese and North Koreans, hailed by our ROK brothers and fellow G.I.'s. Joe, Pete, Harry and I had only one thing in common—we could all shoot straight."

At that point Trinity joined the conversation, "Grandpa, you said an 'event' triggered Joseph Blaise's depression. That same event swept over the four of you, bonded you, and messed up your respective heads. What was it, grandpa?"

"I knew coming out here today that I was going to confess my part in Joe's death. I was eager to do it, to selfishly unburden myself. But the event, I don't know if I'm ready to talk about it. I don't know if I can relive that horror."

"Grandpa, you must bring it out into the sunlight, and I will start you off," Trinity said. "I've researched the Korean War at the Stanton Library, reading letters, diary entries, and documents from court martials. Here's what I've concluded. You tell me where I'm right and wrong."

"OK."

"Lieutenant Gerard Stanton was a brave, ambitious, and daring young officer but also arrogant and overconfident," Trinity said. "I don't know the reason, but Lieutenant Stanton personally took command of a patrol and brought them into an area of the Jane Russell hills that went against orders from his superiors. By the time they arrived at their destination, it was night. Clouds had closed the sky and it had begun to snow. Visibility was limited. Somebody said something that led to a brief firefight. I bet it was over in less than a minute."

There was a long pause. Landrieu took a moment to watch the humming-birds feeding. Finally, he spoke.

"Yes, that's close enough, Trinity. You knew it all along, didn't you?"

"No, only after my recent trip to the Stanton Library," Trinity said.

"We were set up on a little knoll with a nice field of fire. Junie, your father had his B.A.R. on a tripod. It did most of the damage, though Pete and Harry and I each went through a couple clips on our M1's.

"We walked down into the killing field. These young men, these boys, were not as we believed the sons of China or North Korea. These were the sons of America. We had ambushed our own people.

"Quicker than you can say Brooklyn Dodgers, one of the victims, who'd been faking death, got up and started to run away. Harry—Harry being Harry—raised his rifle to shoot, but we pulled him off. We watched him disappear in a veil of snow. We never got a look at his face."

"That had to be Stanton," Trinity said.

"We went through the carnage, hoping to find somebody we could save. They were all dead or bleeding out. One guy held my hand and said, 'Tell my mother I'm sorry. I didn't mean to.' I never did find out what his transgression was. His voice faded and he died in my arms.

"I collected the dog tags of the soldiers with the intention of turning them in to the brass, but we never did. We voted to wait for our superiors to call us in for court martial. Never happened. We were never found out, never held accountable."

"From what I gathered from the information I compiled from the library, the enemy were in the area shortly after," Trinity said. "They must have discovered those bodies and moved them."

"Where?" Maurice asked.

"No data," Trinity said.

Maurice Landrieu reached into his briefcase and produced a handful of dog tags, which he dumped on the wide porch ledge.

Trinity stood and I got a glimpse through the body cam of the hummingbirds feeding on fruit hung on poles.

Grace Pond in Winter

THE ICE WAS TEN INCHES THICK. I kept three active holes open for ice fishing and water gathering. A couple times a day I would scan the pond with binoculars to check the flags on my tip-ups. I caught enough to keep a nice fish stew going throughout the cold season. The only hard times for this fisherman were when the ice was unsafe to walk on or there was not enough open water for the boat. But I got by, casting from shore.

Last weekend there was an event at the pond that only occurs once a decade or so. We had a thaw that softened most of the snow on the pond and that ended with a day of heavy rain followed by a quick hard freeze-up with temperatures well below zero degrees Fahrenheit. I woke in the morning, and it was as if Frank Zamboni himself had personally smoothed the pond ice.

Trinity and I put in three hours work on our laptops, but broke off to go onto the ice, I with my brown-white hockey skates and carrying an iron pike that resembled a peasant's weapon in medieval battle but that in our day and age was perfect for chipping open an ice fishing hole. Trinity wore men's figure skates. He had a perfect body for figure skating, and it showed on the ice.

"Where did you learn to do those spins and jumps?" I asked.

"On the rink at Rockefeller Center in New York back in the day at my grandparents Sutton Place apartment," Trinity said.

"A little more room to work with here."

"Yes, and I plan to take advantage of it."

I reopened my fishing holes and set my tip-ups. I used a hand pump to move the water from the pond to five-gallon water jugs on my sled.

I watched Trinity put on a show. He looked as if he was auditioning for the Olympics.

After I finished my work, I lay down my pike for later pickup and Trinity skated over.

"Want to build a campfire at the pagoda site?" I asked.

"No, I want to stay on the ice," and he skated off.

A minute later, I heard the doink! on my phone to alert me. "They're here,"

I shouted, but Trinity was already looking at the shore. He'd gotten the text message, too.

"They" were half a dozen members of an iceboat club from upstate New York. The club had a motto: Follow the Ice. Checking and evaluating the weather in the Midwest, Northeast US, and lower Canada for the club's unique needs was an art form for the members. On this particular weekend, they were certain they would find the right kind of ice for their boats on Grace Pond.

It had been almost two decades since I'd last seen some of these members.

We watched as the boats zipped around the pond at speeds of sixty plus miles an hour. They would glide along at wind speed with their backs to the wind, but when they close-hauled their sheets, the sails stiffened, one runner would dig into the ice, the other would lift high and the craft would rocket forward with such force and acceleration that the sailors would tell you that they could feel the G-forces. It was that feeling that justified the expense of the boats, the hassle of finding ice to sail them, and the long drives hauling boat trailers. It was quite exciting to watch them, but the boats made an awful racket, and I was soon annoyed at the disturbance of the normal sounds of winter.

Late in the day the wind had died down, and the ice boaters returned to the land. These people had traveled many miles for a few hours of fun. I admired them very much.

Trinity removed his skates, put on his boots, and helped me haul the water cans from the sled to the cistern in the barn. We went inside Shinbone Shack for Geek Chorus Amber and popcorn sprinkled with Sage Farm goat cheese.

It was nice to get a break. It had been an extremely busy and stressful five months for Trinity and me, but especially for Maurice Landrieu. When he displayed those dog tags at the bird sanctuary back in Trinidad last August, he asked us to track down the next of kin of those ten dead American soldiers. I guess you'd say he was our first official client, because he paid us for our work and when it was completed, encouraged us to continue our partnership.

Maurice wouldn't come out and say it, but I think he would have preferred to surrender himself to the authorities early on, but he was outvoted by his buddies. (Golden Rule 2: WST, We Stick Together).

Maurice Landrieu created a successful business, had a successful marriage, many friends, and the esteem of his contemporaries. He lived a moral, stand-up life. But it wasn't enough.

It seemed to me that among the four friendly-fire shooters, Harry handled his war trauma in a way best for him, if not for his victims.

Back in September when Maurice gave us our assignment, Trinity and I had a long discussion about it over tea in Trinity's ad infinitum cabin of stone and mirrors.

"What's this project about?" I asked. "Peace of mind for an old man who made a great big mistake in his youth? Or is it something greater and more abstract, like justice?"

"I don't think anything we find will bring grandpa peace of mind," Trinity said, "Too much time has gone by, too many participants have died, so there will never be any justice. It's just that stories need an airing, an ending, and somebody's adjudication, or else they haunt us with that elusive mystery word."

"The Uncanny, capital U," I said.

"The Uncanny never quite goes away, because real life stories never have an ending. In real life, stories peter out and are replaced by new stories. All that remains of the old stories is the haunting."

"Like my own story," I said. "I learned that my dad arranged his own death . . . But . . ." I clammed up, because I couldn't think of anything else to say.

"But you sense there's something missing, some last piece of information, Harry's secret reason for shooting Gerard Stanton."

"Yes, how did you know?"

"I'm a fucking genius, or haven't you figured that out yet?" Trinity said, accompanied by his mocking laugh.

"That laugh of yours is real close to G.I. Joe's Woody Woodpecker laugh."

"Me and Woody—ha-ha. I've never actually seen a Woody Woodpecker cartoon."

I think part of me knew then that Trinity actually possessed that last bit of missing information and that he withheld it to spare me the knowledge. But at the time I didn't question him.

Instead, I said, "Let's get back on topic. The dog tags."

"Yes, the dog tags. Let me remind you of Chief Seattle's line and our motto: 'The dead are not altogether powerless.' Those dog tags are asking us to complete the story."

So now it was winter, and our work was winding down.

Trinity and I had spent five months finding the few remaining loved ones of the soldiers killed in the friendly fire incident in 1953 in the Jane Russell Hills. It was an arduous, often disheartening, but sometimes rewarding, journey. Trinity returned to the identity of the blonde female hiker with the East European sensibility. She worked on those paper files with Pauline Alvar at the Stanton Library in Bellevue, Washington. And of course, she resumed her relationship with Pauline.

I researched online. A couple of those soldiers had no loved ones we could find, but some had left behind somebody who cared about them and who needed to know what happened to them. I have hundreds of pages of journal and research notes on our attempts to discover what happened to the remains. It's an interesting and very detailed story, especially how it affected the man who set it in motion, Maurice Landrieu. But it's a story outside the purview of this book.

Meanwhile, Trinity announced that he was taking some time off to head West. He was gone the next day.

A week went by. I got used to being alone, but I didn't like it. Weather forecast: Snow.

It was bedtime, and I stood on my porch for a moment and watched snowflakes collect on the screens. Behind, no stars, no moon. Just blackness. I could hear and feel the wind kicking up. It was going to be a nasty storm, blizzard conditions. Good! I loved being cozy in Shinbone Shack while winter raged outside.

My phone doinked. Text message from Trinity.

"It's about your mother," the message read. "She's gravely ill. I don't think she has much time."

"She never told me," I texted back.

"She wanted to spare you the anxiety of leaving Grace Pond."

"You knew this all the time and you wouldn't tell me?"

"I promised her, but now that she's fading I'm breaking that promise. She needs you, Uncle Cyclops, and you need her, so get over your ridiculous agoraphobia and go to her. Right now!"

Demon Panic and the Hitchhiker

I TRIED TO BOOK A FLIGHT, but planes were grounded because of the storm. Busses not running. Trains delayed. I dressed, grabbed some things in a plastic bag, unhitched the plow on my pickup, stuck it in four-wheel drive and headed out in half a foot of fresh snow. It wasn't until I pulled onto the unplowed blacktop that my familiar demon instigated a conversation between us.

What does this particular panic attack feel like, Junie?

Like what I imagine to be that moment just before they push you out of the helicopter.

Your freak-out-ness is a sign of your weakness, you fucking sissy.

I'm a snowflake, falling.

You won't hit earth ground. You'll land in hell.

I hadn't gone half a mile when I was shocked to see a figure alongside the highway with his thumb out. Nobody in our area hitchhiked anymore and certainly not on a country road in the middle of the night in a snowstorm. My first thought was that a motorist had broken down, but when I pulled over, I realized it was not the machine that had broken down, it was the man.

After he shook the snow off, he removed a backwards baseball cap from his mostly bald head, stuffed the cap into his greasy parka, and stumbled into the passenger seat of the pickup. He was about my age—bent back, scabs, moles, and old-age brown spots on the balding head, a beard thick and snarled, and wearing polarized sunglasses, as if he were at the beach. I got a whiff of competing stinks—body odor, marijuana, piss, and maybe garlic breath.

I put the pickup in gear, and we lurched forward. "What are you doing in a blizzard on a road like this?" I asked.

"I dunno."

"You don't know how you ended on this road?"

"It'll come to me."

"Where do you want me to drop you?"

"South."

"How about an answer with a little more detail?"

"Take me as far south as you are going."

"I'm headed for Peru."

"Wherever it's at, I always wanted to go there."

"Actually, New Orleans."

"I'll take it. I know a bridge to stay the night under in that town."

Last time I heard a New England hill accent as thick as the hitchhiker's was at the Tunbridge World's Fair in Vermont when they had girlie shows. The accent, so familiar, and yet so rare these days, charged me with nostalgia that pushed a little of the panic out of the way.

"Do you drive?" I asked.

"Course I drive. Wanna see my license?"

"Yes, I do."

He reached somewhere into the terra incognita under the parka, produced a worn wallet, and showed me a Mississippi driver's license, the plastic milky with age. It was hard to read and watch the road, but I managed. The name said Kenneth Jordan.

"You don't talk like a Southerner," I said.

"I was born in a manger in Darby. Who are you?"

"My name is Joseph Jourdain Blaise. People call me Junie."

"We're probably related," Kenneth said.

"You might be right. My Dad and grandmother never talked about the Jourdain side of the family, except they did mention a family feud that went back to Canada. But you've been living in Mississippi?"

"No, I've been living all over."

"I need more information, Ken. Is it okay to call you Ken?"

"No, call me Kenneth."

"I apologize, Kenneth. Now how about some personal history." I wiggled my fingers into a come-hither gesture.

"After the farm in Darby Depot went down in the days when I was young and good looking, I hitchhiked south. My attitude was poor Darby, you can't live here no more, the flatlanders have taken over. Ended up in Flatland. Actually, Biloxi. Bounced around, got a job on a shrimp boat out of Cut Off, Louisiana. Made a living wage until Katrina sank the boat and killed the Captain. Wasn't the storm done him in, 'twas the broken heart. Me? Out of a job. Nobody hire you if you got no education and you're over fifty-five. Been bummin' the roads ever since."

"What brought you back to these parts in the dead of winter?"

"Funeral. My sister."

"So you still have family in the area."

"Many cousins, but none to give me succor, because I'm not one to surrender his ascendancy. She was the last one to go of my people. We don't live long but we eat well and we drink well."

"You forgot to mention you inhale marijuana well. I can smell it."

"You prejudice against weedski? You can drop me off here if you want. I don't mind a little snow."

"What *do* you mind?" I asked.

"Stinging jelly fish," Kenneth said. "Old barns with slumped roofs. Sunk boats. Vermin in the hairs of armpits."

"Do you have a place to call home?"

"Sure do. Own a plot in Center Darby Cemetery. Inherited it from my sister. She had two plots because she had a husband once, but he walked out on her. Can't say I blame him. She had an awful disposition. Come summer I'll be back at Center Darby Cemetery to set up my tent on that plot. No doubt somebody will call the cops. Nobody likes us homeless—we make civilians uncomfortable. When the cops come and get me, I'll show them my deed to my cemetery plot. As close to family as we Jordans without clan-succor will ever get, because none of us actually enjoyed each other's company and went our own way. Those years on the Gulf, I liked the salt smell, but I missed— you know what I missed?"

"Maple syrup?" I asked.

"That sicky sweet 'S-H-I-T'? Phttt! No, I missed the smell of lilacs in the spring, which is why I'll be coming back after the snows melt and shed a tear for my kin."

"You have fond memories of your sister?"

"She wasn't as mean when she was a youngster. She probably got mean, because her baby drowned, and her ex was a boozer. Actually, there's another ex, but I never met him, and don't knows he's got any claim to my cemetery plot."

There was a long pause. The wind and snow had let up a little bit, which had the effect of giving my panic a little more room to dissipate. I concentrated on slowing down my breathing while Kenneth resumed his monologue.

"Where am I now? Oh, yeah, after the funeral I said to myself, 'Self, head south but don't go too far because it'll get cold again.' They say the Southern cold at the bottom is worse than the Northern cold at the top. Why would they name a place with all that ice after ants?"

"Ants? You lost me, Kenneth."

"I can't imagine there's a whole lot of ants in Ant-arctica. Ha-ha." Kenneth's joke reminded me of G.I. Joe and his corny sense of humor. I couldn't conjure a pleasant surge of nostalgia or resentment. Nothing. It was just a thought.

"After the funeral, you left to hitchhike south?" I said.

"That's right, but I got turned around, so I was hitching in the wrong direction. This fella picked me up and dropped me off on your road. Something about me he didn't like. Imagine that. His last words to me were, 'Get a job.' He practically pushed me into the roadside. I started walking. No rides. I noticed, hey, it's snowing to beat the band. Kept walking. Walking. Enjoying the snow. And here I am with you."

"Kenneth, how would you like to help me drive to New Orleans—straight through. We stop only for gas, toilet, and food, which I pay for."

"Sounds like a plan. You know I recognize and admire plans in other people, but I never had one. Would that be a failing or a character flaw?"

"Probably a little bit of both, Kenneth."

I drove all night while my companion slept. I had flashes of anxiety, but my panic attacks subsided. My defense was to repeat a jingle in my head from my boyhood, "Schaefer, the one beer to have when you're having more than one." Over and over again. My prayer. It's the fear of a panic attack coming on that creates the anxiety, but anxiety itself is not the same as panic. I'll take anxiety any time. It's more manageable, more normal. Panic feels like what the ancients called demon possession.

Soon, I realized that the truck had become a mini Shinbone Shack. As long as I was in the truck, I was relatively whole and functioning, but when I got out to pump gas or go to the bathroom a wave of terror would wash over me.

It was an exhausting night, but by the time we reached Maryland the snow had changed to rain and I-81 was in decent shape. At dawn I got suddenly very dopey (well, more dopey than usual), and Kenneth took over the wheel while I slept.

I woke around 2 p.m. We were making good time. Kenneth must have driven like a cab driver on the Trinidad priority highway. I figured we'd arrive in New Orleans a little after midnight. I emailed my mother:

"Hi, Mom, I know that you often follow-up late when I email you, so I'll give you a call as soon as I send off this message. Guess what! I expect to arrive in NOLA late tonight. Let me know a good time to visit with you tomorrow morning. Love, Junie."

My follow-up phone call was met with a standard robot recording, and there was no response to my text message. I kept checking my email throughout the day and into the night but did not receive a response.

We arrived in New Orleans around 1 a.m. the next day. Earlier, I had made a reservation at Olde Town Inn, that little hotel where Lynn hid from Sig Howl.

I offered to rent a room for Kenneth, but he declined. He asked me to drop him on Claiborne Avenue under the I-10 overpass where some homeless people had set up a tent city. I held out a couple of twenties and he snatched them out of my hand and shoved them into a pocket. Then he surprised me. He removed the polarized sunglasses and handed them to me.

"You're not fit to look at with that sewed up eye socket. Put these on. They'll save your soul, if you've got one."

Before I could respond, he jumped out of the car, moving with surprising agility and took off without a goodbye. I realized he didn't have a homeless man's backpack, nothing, just the backwards cap and the greasy parka, which he no longer needed to keep warm.

I looked out at the tent city. At this time of night there weren't many people up and around but there was plenty of street lighting, so I should have been able to spot Kenneth Jordan, but he had vanished.

Maybe he was never there, suggested my demon.

I put the glasses on for no better reason than to convince myself that the hitchhiker had been real. I wondered if he had been in the Vietnam War. He had that shattered-veteran look.

The doink! on my phone told me I had a text message. It was from Trinity, "Sadie is staying at the home of her boyfriend on 927 Desire Street."

My dying mother still had a boyfriend after all these years?

I experienced the chest-crush of resentment. But I don't think I was unique with that reaction. Children, even after they grow up, tend to think about their parents in relation to themselves. It's always a bit of a jolt to realize that one's parents have many experiences strictly on their own and completely outside of their relationships to their children.

I drove to the little hotel, parked on the street, checked in, went to bed, and fell asleep immediately.

The Day of the Frog

I WOKE A COUPLE HOURS LATER in a half dream, half memory of the day I hated my mother.

After dad died, I didn't feel normal grief for the loss of a loved one. What I felt was unresolved hatred that built up in me. It reached a boiling point when Sadie announced that she was now the man in the house. It was as if she had captured dad's energy, energy that rightfully belonged to me, and now I was denied it. Makes no sense but that's what I felt, and the feeling played itself out as an urge to kill, to kill my mother, to kill everybody, to kill myself. I do not use that common phrase "urge to kill" metaphorically. If this had been a later era, post Columbine, I might have devised plans for a mass murder. But it was 1969 in my rural state and the scenarios in my head for violence by a teenager were limited.

I unlocked the gun cabinet, grabbed my father's heirloom .22 bolt-action Remington rifle and a box of .22 long rifle rounds. I put my nose against the breech so I could smell the gun oil. The feel of the weapon in my hands made me cold-hearted and powerful. My destination was the shallow cove of Grace Pond where I knew I'd find lily pads and frogs. My plan was to murder frogs. Birds if they came in range. With luck a beaver or a woodchuck, even a damn skunk. Ha-ha. Let the world in on the stink. Whatever critter I could find in my sights, I would kill.

In the time period I write these words, a teenage boy hitchhiking with a rifle case at his side would attract the attention of local police and he would be unlikely to catch a ride soon, but not in 1969 in our country setting.

Two rides later I found myself dropped at the long driveway leading to Shinbone Shack. Carrying the .22, I walked along the shore until I reached the shallow cove where the lily pads covered the surface. The sunshine beat down on white blossoms that sucked in the light. I saw a dragonfly hover. I raised the rifle to my shoulder, but the dragonfly dashed away before I could pull the trigger. I scanned the pond in search of frogs.

Just beyond the lily pads was a beaver lodge and almost as if I'd summoned it, I saw a beaver surface from under the lodge and swim toward the far shore. The beaver would soon be out of range, so I knew I had to get it quick. I raised the rifle to my shoulder. I wondered whether it was a male or female, and how did beavers tell each other apart? Smell probably. I took aim. The rifle was remarkably steady in my hands. Instead of squeezing the trigger I watched the beaver through the sights, and that action pulled me away from the material world. None of what I was experiencing seemed real. It was as if I was in a movie. Then the beaver was gone, and a second later I heard the slapping sound as the tail hit the water, like a gunshot, and the beaver dove into the depths.

When the beaver surfaced it was farther out in the pond and out of range. I dropped the rifle across my lap and watched the beaver until it disappeared in a shimmer of sunlight.

For the next fifteen minutes or so I walked up and down the shore looking for something alive to kill. Finally, a frog cooperated. It was a small one, barely out of the tadpole stage parked on a lily pad close to a flower only about ten feet away. I lined it up in my sights, but the flower distracted me.

I put the flower in my sights. Flower, frog. Get out of the way, frog. Somebody wants you dead. The frog would not move. Frog. Flower. Get out of the way, flower. Somehow shooting a flower struck me as an abomination. I tried to consider my mood as funny. Ha-ha. Flower. Frog. Abomination. What was the lifespan of a frog? What was the lifespan of an abomination?

I tried to find some information in my head derived from reading *Fur, Fish, and Game*. I remembered you could eat the legs of frogs. How many frogs would you have to kill to make a meal?

This one in your sights is too small.

I looked around for another frog to shoot. If you recognized an abomination and you shot it would it stay shot? Did the state establish a season for the hunting of abominations?

That was the nature of my thinking until finally I started to shoot. I'd almost finished with the fifty rounds in the box when I sensed a presence behind me, and I whirled around. It was my mother. I should have known that somebody in our circle of acquaintances had spotted me hitchhiking with a gun and called Sadie. She knew exactly where I would be.

My voice cracked as I spoke. "Mom, I came out to kill frogs, but I couldn't do it. I couldn't shoot the beaver, either. I couldn't even shoot the lilies. All I could shoot were the lily pads. Mom, I'm not a hunter, I'm not a soldier, I can't kill anything."

"I know, my darling son, I know." She put her hand on my shoulder, and I experienced Sadie's powers of touch.

I dropped the rifle. Mother and son flew into each other's arms, and for the first time since the death of G.I. Joe, the momma's boy and new man of the house, wept long and hard.

After that episode, Sadie moved us out of our apartment in Keene and into Shinbone Shack. I painted the johnboat green and gold, the colors of Grace Pond frogs, my colors.

The Seventh Death

I WAS UP AT 7 A.M. I grabbed my phone and checked my email. I was relieved to see a message from Sadie.

"Trinity said she let the cat out of the bag. Meow! I probably should have told you that I've been ill. Come between 10 a.m. and noon." The note was signed, "With all my love, your Voodoo Hoodoo Oodoo Mom."

"I'll be at your place between ten and ten-thirty," I wrote. From the upbeat tone and diction of Sadie's note I couldn't believe she was actually in danger of dying any time soon. I found myself oddly upbeat.

My mood went down a peg when I happened to see myself in the bathroom mirror. A startling sight. It was as if that shaggy homeless hitchhiker had left parts of himself on my face. I showered and shaved and looked again in the mirror. The sewed eye socket seemed to wink at me. "Kenneth," I said aloud, "you were right. Nobody wants to look at this face." I put on the polarized glasses.

"Cool dude," I said to the mirror.

Get a haircut, the mirror replied.

Online I found Factotum Barber + Supply on 902 Piety Street, a block away from my destination on Desire Street.

I made an appointment and headed out for breakfast at a cafe in the same locale, billed in a review as "hipster-friendly." Soon as I left the hotel lobby and stepped into a celestial Vitamin D machine, a wave of panic hit me, but it was different from the usual. I waited for condemnation from my demon, but it remained silent, and the panic subsided.

It was about a mile walk to the cafe, just right to build an appetite. The streets gave me a good feeling because I associated the neighborhood with Lynn and our daughters. Most of the houses appeared to be small, because they were narrow and only one or two stories high at the street, no front lawns, but many of the houses ranged far back and sprawled upward in the rear into, as the local lingo would have it, "camel backs."

Homeowners had no qualms about announcing their personalities and sometimes their politics with their plantings, wild paint jobs, iron gates, "No Parking" and "Beware of Dog" signs, porches with decorated pillars, overweight lounging cats, eccentric window treatments, and crazy-design doorways. The streets and sidewalks were cracked and full of potholes, no doubt from sinking, shifting Mississippi River alluvial soil under foot. It was like walking on an ongoing, never-ending mini earthquake. Stimulating.

For breakfast I ordered a BLT with avocado wedges and coffee. Trinity would have fit in nicely with this crowd—young, energetic, rappelling down the edges of their handhelds. I was much older than most of the customers, and they didn't pay any attention to me except with an occasional nod or the whisper of a smile.

My usual effect on people was aversion. Now that I had covered my sewed-up eye with Kenneth's sunglasses, people treated me as normal, taking an extra second or two to turn away or nod.

Why had I spent all those years presenting myself as a pariah?

At Factotum Barbershop, Hannah, my barber, offered me a drink of whiskey and I accepted. I sat in the barber chair and sipped Four Roses while Hannah went to work. In a corner, close to the barber chair, sat Hannah's very small dog, looking content. The dog's demeanor of quiet acceptance of its fate helped support my mood.

Lynn used to cut my hair and did a passable job. After she died, I didn't pay attention to my hair until it grew out to the point that it became a nuisance, and I would cut it back myself. Now as Hannah worked, I could feel something on the nerve-endings of my hair follicles that neither Lynn nor I could provide—skilled barber hands. I shut my eyes and thought: For $28, Hannah was my god for half an hour.

With my haircut and sunglasses, I had some added confidence, though a wee bit of anxiety, as I walked a block to Desire Street and the meeting with my mother.

When I arrived, I found a high wooden fence that blocked the view of any structures behind it. The fence seemed solid enough, though it was rotting at the bases.

A sign read, "WARNING! Moving Gate Can Cause Serious Injury or Death."

To one side was a security box. I didn't have to fiddle with it, because a male voice that I did not recognize seemed to issue from the box, "Come in, Joseph." A section of the gate swung open.

I stepped through and found myself in a lush garden. I removed the glasses, put them in my breast pocket, and followed a winding path to a brick-front building covered with vines. There was an arched window and doorway like you'd find in a church. I didn't have to knock, because the door opened just as I approached it. In the doorway stood Trinity Landrieu. She was dressed in flea market chic, tattoos on bare arms, a piercing through a nostril, hair streaked with the colors of Mardi Gras—purple (justice), gold (power), green (faith). Hipster woman.

"How long have you been in town?" I asked.

"Just got in last night."

"You were watching me from the window."

"I was watching you from the window on my phone. Come in."

I looked around the room. It reminded me of a lurid drawing from a romance novel cover. The formal French furnishings from the 18th century, and the varnished oil paintings, European landscapes from earlier centuries, did not represent the tastes that I associated with my mother.

"Sadie would not stand for this," I said.

"Correct. This is her boyfriend's place. He's a retired judge."

At about the moment that Trinity spoke, a slightly undersized old man with wispy white hair and dressed in a business suit appeared from the next arched doorway. He came right over to me and shook my hand. He exuded the confidence and poise of a man who is respected by his community. I wanted to punch him.

"I've heard a lot about you, Joseph," he said in a refined NOLA accent. I am Bartholomew Spring, the executor of Sadie's will, her former law partner, and her dear, dear friend."

I didn't like that extra "dear" he threw in. "Call me Junie," I said. "How is she?"

"She's a trooper," he said and accompanied his words with a noncommittal gesture that sent an unaccountable surge of rage through me.

What was it about this guy that I didn't like? With the formulation of the question in my mind came the answer: his seemingly overweening confidence reminded me of Uncle Oggie. My irrational anger suddenly morphed into an irrational admiration for Harry Cromwell and his marksmanship. My next thought was to tell my dying mother that she had terrible taste in men.

"Can I see her now?" I said.

"Yes, yes, of course. Please," Judge Spring said. "Let me check with her, to see if . . ." He didn't finish his thought, just left the room.

"I was fine coming here—no panic—" I whispered to Trinity, "but all of a sudden, I'm a little confused and anxious. I had a crazy notion to harm the judge."

Trinity gave me a muffled version of her mocking laugh.

"That's only human nature—you're in love with the same woman. Love him and you'll feel better about yourself."

"Impossible."

"Then fake it. Insincerity, if you do it with zeal, is almost as good as the real thing."

Judge Spring returned. "She wants to see you alone. Please," he said and led me into a small parlor and up some stairs of dark, varnished wood. Sadie's bedroom door was open. I went in. Sadie was sitting up in bed. She pointed at the door and I shut it. We were alone.

Beside her on the bedside table was a glass of something or other with a bent hospital straw, and an envelope with my name in typescript on it.

I was surprised to see that Sadie was wearing makeup, her hair permed, and though she was in bed she was fully dressed, at least from the blanket edge up.

"You look fabulous," I said.

"You know how when the body dies the funeral people spruce it up, well, that's me—I'm jumping the gun."

I sat on a chair beside the bed. She held out her hand and I took it in both of mine. The hand was icy cold. That cold went right into me. During our conversation I could feel the chill, and it was all I could do to refrain from demanding that the heat be turned up in the room. I think she sensed my discomfort, because she pulled her hand back and laid it on the bed cover.

"The doctor gave me something to make me alert enough to talk to you, said it might kill me, and I said, 'Perfect.'"

"I should have kept closer tabs on you, Mom. I've been selfish."

"True enough, but aren't we all?"

"At breakfast this morning, I was thinking that when I was a boy and we were living in the apartment in Keene I would pick flowers from that raggedy lawn and give them to you."

"Yes, violets and dandelions. I wanted so much to put them in a vase on the windowsill."

"But you never did."

"You picked them with the stems too short."

"You should have told me," I said.

"I didn't have the heart."

We talked some more, and then very quickly she began to fade. Her breathing came in short gasps. Her eyes rolled and I could see moisture seeping through her makeup.

"The envelope," she said.

"Yes."

"There's information in it for you."

"What information?"

Sadie smiled a little. "I don't know exactly, and I don't want to know. It's something that Trinity cooked up."

The cold in me deepened.

There was a long pause in which Sadie closed her eyes and didn't breathe, so that I thought I was going to lose her.

But she took a breath, opened her eyes, and said, "I don't remember what happened to me that day. It wasn't until later that I began to suspect."

"What day? Suspect what?"

"The day you were made. I can't be sure."

"Can't be sure of what?"

"I think Potato Head got to me after Joseph did. Potato Head's ex-wives both called him a 'wham-bam without the thank-you-ma'am' kind of guy. I think, I think . . . I don't know what I think. You might want the truth, Junie, but I'd rather not."

"Harry!" I said. A mixed feeling of horror and excitement gripped me with the realization that I now understood why Harry sneaked me money when I was a kid and his secret reason for killing Uncle Oggie. He was trying to save me from following an asshole to Jonestown. Harry believed I was his son.

There was another pause, and then Sadie spoke again, "I didn't want to tell you this, but you have to know. Joseph never believed that you were his. It's why he couldn't love you. All these years, isn't that the shadow that hung over you?"

"Yes, of course. I never recognized it. He truly did not love me. I thought I was unworthy."

"Please don't hate him. He tried to love you, but he couldn't do it. I've been lucky in love. It's always come easy for me. I feel bad for people, like so many of my clients, who try but can't seem to love."

She reached out her cold, cold hand, and I enveloped it in both my hands. She shut her eyes. Then the magic: a surge—like the power of the sea—roiled her. She made a sound like I'd never heard before or since, like wind-blown snow on ice. In the next instant there was silence, and her body went completely still.

It was a moment that one might anticipate at the deathbed of a loved one. But it was the next moment that surprised and took hold of me. A flow of warmth poured into me through her hand. Sadie was giving me her strength and equanimity and maybe just a little bit of her wisdom. It was a state of mind—or maybe of grace—that has stayed with me ever since. I am today a stronger, better person for that flow of warmth.

Sadie's eyes closed.

I left the room with the envelope in my hand. There was someone waiting for me outside Sadie's door, but it wasn't Judge Spring, it was Trinity Landrieu. Sadie's gift to me must have raised my IQ, because I had an insight.

"You, you were Kenneth Jordan, the hitchhiker."

"Yeah, that was me. I was afraid that, left on your own, you'd fuck it up." The mocking laugh.

"And the envelope, you know what's in it and what it means."

"Yup and nope. It's an interpretive DNA report—yours, Harry's, and G.I. Joe's DNA, which I got from tissue samples from the medical school that Sadie donated the body to. I can't tell you the results, though, because I didn't look. That's your prerogative, not mine. Gotta go—catch my flight to Sea-Tac."

≈

Sadie's funeral was attended by hundreds of people. I learned that I wasn't the first person to be consecrated by Sadie's touch. Several of her former clients told me how Sadie had imparted her powers to them. Sadie had touched—literally touched—many lives in her work as a family-practice attorney and partner in the law firm of Fulton, Chambers, Canal, Spring, and Boyd-Blaise. I was in awe. She had made something of herself far away from Grace Pond, G.I. Joe, and me. The knowledge left me a little disconcerted.

When I drove out of New Orleans, I placed the envelope with the DNA results on the passenger seat beside me and headed back to the North Country. Certainly, I was very curious about who my father was. There were even practical matters involving future possible medical conditions that supported the idea of my knowing my biological roots. Later, lying on the motel room bed, I stared at the envelope on the nightstand, but I did not open it. I was waiting for a sign.

Whirlybird Directive

I STILL HADN'T OPENED THE ENVELOPE when I arrived back at Grace Pond. I stuck it in the sleeve of my iPad and there it stayed through winter, spring, and summer. If Sadie and G.I. Joe had one thing in common that they taught me, it was that when one is uncertain about making a momentous decision, it's best to wait for a sign. So, I waited.

During that period, Trinity and I set up a business through the office of the New Hampshire Secretary of State. Though we never advertised, we did appear on LinkedIn under, "Consulting Inquirers: Trinity Landrieu, Shape-Shifter, and Junie Blaise, Scribe. Coding and language skill sets in Java, C, Ruby, Java Script, PHP, Object C, Swift, and American English. Words we live by: 'The dead are not altogether powerless.' —Chief Seattle."

Though technically I'm a partner, in reality Consulting Inquirers is Trinity's business. She does all the investigating and any work involving coding. I research, write reports in great detail, answer emails, deal with clients, and act as the business manager. I'm Trinity's man Friday or maybe only Tuesday.

Trinity and Pauline Alvar maintain their romance, in their own way. Trinity hasn't cut back entirely on her Internet liaisons with strangers, and it's still not clear whether Pauline is an agent for the Kremlin or not. Since Trinity and Pauline rarely meet in person, I want to say their relationship is shaky, but really, I don't know.

Anybody who has read this narrative will wonder why the author has not made clear whether Trinity is a man, a woman, or perhaps an intersexed person. The reason is simple. I don't know Trinity's gender, and she doesn't do anything to clarify the situation. Rather, quite the opposite. She chose to designate herself a shape-shifter to obscure references to gender. When I'm not certain which pronoun to use I go with "she," because it's Trinity's female mode I'm most comfortable with. Does Trinity's gender matter? Of course it matters, but not to me. It's none of my beeswax. Right, Sadie?

One early fall day after a rain I went down to my rickety dock to bail out water from my johnboat. On the surface of the pond was a whirlybird. There were plenty of sugar maples in the local forests, but their whirlybirds were different from the great maple of Whirlybird Island whose whirlybirds had smaller, lighter seed hulls and longer and wider wings to allow them to sail further on the wind. This whirlybird came from the island.

The voice in my head spoke: That's your sign, Junie.

I waited another couple weeks until the leaves on the maple trees were in full color—orange, yellow, red, and remnant green—before I rowed to the island with the still sealed DNA envelope in my pocket.

I thought about Joseph Jourdain Blaise, the only father I'd known. Decades ago, Uncle Oggie suggested that G.I. Joe was likely having an affair when he'd leave our family for days, sometimes weeks on end. Now, knowing of G.I. Joe's depression, I was sure that he spent those dark hours alone. His affair was with his own soul.

It wasn't Joe or Harry or any particular old soldier who was my father. I was the offspring of four traumatized Army veterans. I was the offspring of their friendly fire victims and the survivor who stalked the shooters. I was the offspring of shell shock, of battle fatigue, of post-traumatic stress syndrome, of PTSD, or whatever it was going to be called in future generations.

I was not unique.

There probably wasn't a human being on the planet who was not in some way infused with evil from wars they had nothing to do with. We are all the offspring of war. As G.I. Joe once said to me, "In war everybody dies." The cold I had felt in my mother's room that morning she died did not come from the room, nor from her, nor even from me, it came from history. It's the Sadie's of this world who save us with their warmth and touch.

≈

I pulled the boat up on the granite and walked over to the ancient forever-dying great maple. "Well, tree, are you happy now that you have brought us into your bosom? Maybe if we all suffocate together, like ancient Pharaohs entombed with their mummified baboons and servile attendants, will that satisfy you?"

The returning answer came not from the maple, but from wind blowing out the whirlybirds from their tree launchpads, blowing, blowing to carry steamy stem cells dispatched to conquer the world.

I could feel it now, my duty to the juvenile frogs on the lily pads, creatures clueless as human kids watching human kid shows on Saturday morning TV, wondering, wondering . . . what? What am I doing here? Somebody out there, some entity, some emissary from the Past, some specter from the Future, forget your assignments, and instead of the prepared and packaged despair give us hope.

I piled rocks high enough to allow me to drop the envelope into the sullied defile of the tree.

Acknowledgments

I'M GRATEFUL TO SO MANY PEOPLE for helping me see my way through the writing of Whirlybird Island that I know I will leave some of you out. Here are a few who come to mind: my dear wife Medora and daughters Lael and Nicole; the members of Fubar, my writing group; my talk-pals: Tom Washer, Terry Pindell, Jack Hitchner, and George Osol for the intangibles of friendship that keep one stimulated.

I would like to recognize a few individuals who had a direct effect upon me and upon the writing of this novel. It starts with Mary Baglione, a phrase in her conversation with me about growing up an only child with alcoholic parents—"It was sometimes lonely in that house"—sent me off in 2017 on a three-year writing project.

I'll be forever indebted to Andrew Lohse who read, critiqued, and supported this project at the vulnerable early stages. Later, Michael Lowenthal helped me organize the book with a few choice comments, especially a suggested change to the beginning. John Christie inspired me with his memoir and introduced me to his publisher George Geers, the force behind Plaidswede Publishing. I'll always be grateful to George not only for publishing Whirlybird Island but for connecting me to Linda Chestney, a great editor whose patience, prodding, and thoroughness helped shape the final product.